WRITE TO DIE

WRITE TO DIE

SUSAN C. RICHARDS

TORONTO • NEW YORK • LONDON
AMSTERDAM • PARIS • SYDNEY • HAMBURG
STOCKHOLM • ATHENS • TOKYO • MILAN
MADRID • WARSAW • BUDAPEST • AUCKLAND

For Jack
The first one, of course, is for you.

WORLDWIDE™

Recycling programs
for this product may
not exist in your area.

ISBN-13: 978-1-335-58915-6

Write to Die

First published in 2020 by Camel Press, an imprint of Epicenter Press, Inc. This edition published in 2022 with revised text.

Copyright © 2020 by Susan C. Richards
Copyright © 2022 by Susan C. Richards, revised text edition

For questions and comments about the quality of this book, please contact us at CustomerService@Harlequin.com.

Harlequin Enterprises ULC
22 Adelaide St. West, 41st Floor
Toronto, Ontario M5H 4E3, Canada
www.ReaderService.com

Printed in U.S.A.

ACKNOWLEDGMENTS

The excitement of seeing my first book published is only surpassed by the gratitude I have for all the people who helped to get me here.

Many thanks to the following people for their assistance, knowledge, direction and support: Dave King of Dave King Edits, for teaching me things every author needs to know; my agent Dawn Dowdle of Blue Ridge Literary Agency, for helping me to take this book to the next level; my editor, Jennifer McCord of Coffeetown-Camel Press, for guiding me through this process; Tim Goulet and Rod Richards of Echo Creative for web guidance and hand-holding; Phyllis Lindberg for invaluable research assistance; as always, to my family and friends for love, support and encouragement—you are all rock stars in my book.

ONE

"ARE YOU DOING this deliberately?" Hank Amundson—tall, blond, borderline good-looking under the damage done by worry, alcohol and not enough time at the gym—was standing behind his desk, across which was spread Sunday's edition of the *Omaha Tribune*, right next to his computer.

I was sitting primly in his visitor's chair, my hands folded in my lap. But reading upside down was a handy skill for an investigative reporter to have, so I was able to tell the "Lifestyles" section was open to the book review he'd asked me to write.

"I told the truth, Hank," I said.

He picked up the paper. "'If you're just meeting Ethan Miller's work for the first time, you will find the character development in *Another Midnight* engaging and delightful.'"

"Hank, this is just one review. I saw he got raves in the *Chicago*—"

"'If you're a casual reader of his work, though, you'll find the latest hauntingly familiar. And if you're a fan of the story, you'll realize this latest is essentially *Mystic* run through global search and replace.'"

"You asked me to review a book. That's what I did."

"I asked you to review *this* book. I thought it was something you could do without stirring up controversy."

"The book sucked. I said the book sucked. Where's the controversy?"

His fist hit the desk, and his face turned crimson. "Ethan Miller is one of the finest writers in this country—probably one of the finest writers of the twenty-first century. He's been a best-selling author for four decades."

"And now he's phoning it in."

"I thought you were a fan of his."

"I am a fan of his. Why do you think I was so disappointed? Ethan Miller wrote some truly great books twenty years ago, and since then he's just been rewriting them under different titles. Why applaud a book that isn't worth the paper it's printed on just because it's got his name on it?"

"Because he's got money and clout, dammit. Because I can't sell this dying paper for two cents. Ethan was the one who—" He stopped short.

We stared at each other for a full fifteen seconds and then the lightbulb went on over my head.

"I see," I said quietly. "I was supposed to coddle Ethan Miller? Give him rave reviews so he'd pull your fat out of the fire? I wish you'd told me that when you gave me this assignment. I could have handed in my resignation then and there."

"It's not too late." I swear, there was almost a look of glee on his face when he said, "You're fired. Go clean out your desk."

Twenty minutes later I was in my cubicle, packing the boxes I'd filched from the storage closet. Even after eight years my roots hadn't gone very deep. There were a few pictures, some personal research files, books and a pair of comfortable shoes.

My editor, Bob Elliot, came in, coffee cup in hand, and stood for a minute watching me. He nodded his head toward the boxes. "I'm guessing it didn't go well."

"See, this is why you could have been an investigative journalist."

"You seem to be taking it well."

"It was just a matter of time. We both knew it was coming." I sat down behind the desk. "How'd you find out so quickly? Did Hank call you to gloat?"

"Actually, Glenda called me with a terse, business-like message that I needed to find a replacement for the Sunday edition."

Glenda, a mousy woman in her late forties, was Hank's secretary/personal assistant. She'd been at the *Trib* less than a year and I'd yet to determine what she brought to the game. Her office skills were questionable and her personality all but nonexistent.

I sat staring at the boxes that held the anemic remnants of my eight-year career. "The body isn't even cold yet."

Bob walked over to the small opening in the wall that passed for a window. Raindrops dribbled down the glass. He shook his head. "What a miserable day."

I wasn't sure if he was referring to the weather or my current state of employment. But, in all honesty, they were both pretty damn miserable.

Something nagged at me through the gloom. "Bob, why would Hank go ballistic over this book review?"

A smile tugged at the corner of his mouth. "Because you hit him where he lives, Jess. He hates this paper. The last thing he ever wanted was to actually have to work to keep it going—and I use the term *work* loosely. Better papers than us are going under all over the country. If he could, he'd dump this rag faster than you can blink and be on the next plane headed for the Caribbean. The trouble is, he couldn't give it away if he tried."

"Okay. Where do I fit into this dynamic?"

Bob moved over to the chair across from me and dropped his large frame into it. "You panned the great Ethan Miller."

"Who has power and influence, I get that part. Hank made that very clear to me."

"So, you didn't know that the great one might be putting in a bid to buy the paper?"

"What? No. I just assumed Hank was sucking up. Why would Ethan want a newspaper?"

"Have you ever met Ethan?"

"I saw him at Eric's funeral, but I never got a chance to talk to him."

"Ethan and Eric were best friends for more than forty years, so maybe nostalgia or a favor to an old friend. Even if he doesn't buy the paper, Ethan's got money and notoriety. He might be willing to put in some financial backing or maybe even grant an exclusive interview. Either one would boost the paper enough to make it attractive enough to unload. Hank's been wining and dining him for months."

"Ethan Miller hasn't given an interview in over a decade."

"Hank's a desperate man. He's been playing on Ethan's sympathies with everything he's got, even implying that Ethan owes something to the memory of his dear departed friend, Eric."

"And was Ethan falling for this emotional blackmail?"

"Hank thought so, until your book review. Ethan's

publicist called Hank this morning and threatened to cut off all negotiations. It really put the fear of God into Hank."

"And I'm his sacrificial lamb. How do you know all of this?"

"I have my sources. Did you know that Hank just happens to be Ethan Miller's godson?"

"No, but it does shed some light on Hank's reaction."

"Ironic isn't it that your downfall should be the great Ethan Miller?" It was the second time he'd called him the *great Ethan Miller* and I wondered if I detected a hint of sarcasm in his voice.

"It really was a bad book."

"I know. I've read it."

"Hank will never understand how difficult that review was for me to write, it actually made me sad. Ethan Miller was an incredible writer." I ran my hand over the cover of Ethan's book. "I was thirteen the first time I read one of his books. I couldn't put it down. There were days when I felt overwhelmed by all that was going on around me, but I could always get lost in one of Ethan's novels, they took me places that felt safe. I think I fell in love with him the first time I saw him on a talk show. God, he was so handsome…"

Bob was watching my face as I rambled on but didn't interrupt. He knew this wasn't an easy topic for me to discuss.

"After my father died, Ethan's books were just about the only common thread between my mother and me. When we could think of nothing civil to say, we could always talk about his latest novel."

"Was it that bad?" Bob asked.

"Yes. At times. She was never willing to admit it

was the stress from his job and the, uh, situation that brought on his heart attack. Her thinking was that he should have left well enough alone."

I stopped. What else was there to say? A cop turning against his fellow officers, even if they were as dirty as sin, wasn't acceptable in their world. The silence that followed hung in the air like the dark clouds that hovered over the city.

I picked up Ethan Miller's latest book, the one that had cost me my job, and turned it over to look at his picture on the back of the dust jacket. "He was my idol."

"I thought *I* was your idol."

I narrowed my eyes at him. "You, sir, have been my nemesis. You could have saved me from this. Why didn't you stop me? You knew what Hank's reaction would be."

"I should have told you to turn your review into a puff piece? Like that would have worked?"

"No, I guess not. Not that it didn't cross my mind. I wanted so much to like this book, I wanted even more for people to see Ethan Miller the way I once did."

For all I knew, Ethan Miller was the reason I'd become a writer. I don't know why I'd never realized that before. My career had taken a different path than his, but the reality was his influence on my life had been significant. Through him I'd learned that, for better or worse, the power of words could change someone's life. Maybe that's what made me so sad, I thought he'd lost his power.

"You know, Jess, Hank actually did you a favor."

"Really? Right now it just feels like I don't have a job."

"I've told you before you're too young and talented

to be wasting your time on this dying rag. Now, if Eric was still alive…"

Eric Amundson. Hank's late father and the man who turned the *Trib* into the paper it once was. His integrity was one of the things that had made me the kind of journalist his son was prone to fire. If Eric was still alive, Bob would stay at the *Trib* until his dying day. Now he was merely counting the hours until his retirement. Eric had been like a surrogate father to me, since I started at the paper. His death had left a huge hole in my life. I missed him. And right now, I needed him.

"What now?" Bob finally asked.

I shrugged. "I haven't thought that far ahead."

"Don't worry. You'll figure something out."

"I'll tell my landlord you said so."

Bob put his coffee cup down and reached for the book I still held. "You know, I was just thinking…"

"I was thinking the same thing."

We looked at each other then Bob picked up the phone and punched in a few numbers.

"Anna," he said, "get me Ethan Miller's phone number and address, it's on my Rolodex." A few seconds later he scribbled something on a piece of paper. "Thanks." He hung up and handed me the paper. "There you go, kid. Your future's in your hands."

"What? You want *me* to call? I'm the upstart who just trashed his book."

He raised his eyebrows. "You're also one of the best reporters I've ever worked with. If you can't get to Ethan Miller, no one can." He stood and stretched. "Look, Jess, it's up to you. You know as well as I do that if you got an interview with Ethan, every newspaper and magazine in the country would be falling all over themselves to buy it."

Then he laughed. "Also, Hank will pee his pants if you get an exclusive with Ethan Miller. Let me know how far you get. I still have a few favors I can call in if I need to."

He turned and walked out. That was the most support I'd get from Bob.

After he left, I sat staring at the paper in my hand for a full ten minutes, trying to decide if it was worth the effort. Finally, I picked up the phone and dialed.

Somewhere in southern Missouri the Miller phone rang seven times before a male voice said, "Hello?"

"Ethan Miller, please," I said.

"Mr. Miller isn't taking any calls. Perhaps I could help you. I'm Dan Ketner, his assistant."

"Well, maybe. I'm a journalist and I'd like to interview Mr. Miller. I was wondering if I could make an appointment to see him."

"I'm afraid that isn't possible," Ketner said. "Mr. Miller doesn't give interviews anymore, Miss..."

"Kallan," I said. "Jessica Kallan."

There was a long pause. "*Omaha Tribune* Jessica Kallan?"

"Um... I'm afraid so."

"We read your recent hatchet job, Miss Kallan. Ethan certainly doesn't need your kind of press." He slammed the phone in my ear.

Okay, I should have seen that one coming. But stubbornness was an occupational requirement for reporters. I'd just have to try a different tack. Like begging, for instance.

I picked up the receiver and dialed again then

drummed my fingers on the desk. This time we were up to ten before someone picked up the receiver.

"Hello," said a voice I immediately recognized as Ethan Miller's. My mouth suddenly went dry, as all of my adolescent fantasies raced through my head.

"Hello?" Ethan said again. "Is anyone there?"

"Mr. Miller, this is Jessica Kallan—"

He let out a whoop of laughter. "You're the girl from the *Trib* who chewed me up royally in your book review, aren't you?"

"Well...kind of...yes."

"I read your stuff all the time. You're a damn fine writer. Don't know how you can stand to work for that horse's ass, Hank. What can I do for you, Jessica?"

"Mr. Miller—"

"Ethan," he interrupted. "Call me Ethan."

Okay, the last thing I expected was for my adolescent fantasies to start coming true. "All right, Ethan, I was hoping to get a chance to interview you."

"Interview? With you? I haven't done that in years, but it might be just what I need right now. Does anyone call you Jessie?"

"Mostly Jess, though sometimes—"

"Jessie, I like the idea. I like it a lot. Why don't you come down here? Plan on staying for as long as you need. We've got plenty of room."

Before I knew what was happening, I had arranged to show up at Ethan's house that Friday. He gave me directions, called Hank a few more choice names and hung up.

As I carried the boxes out to my car, I could barely contain my excitement. I was going to get a chance to interview my childhood idol. I had a twinge of guilt about the review I'd written, but Ethan hadn't sounded too upset about it, so I let some of the guilt slide away. Maybe I could even ask him what was happening with his writing, why he hadn't been up to his old form. Maybe I could even help.

I wished at that moment that I could see Hank's face when he found out Ethan Miller was going to be interviewed for the first time in years and *I* was going to be the one to do it.

But the thought that kept chasing around in my head was, "Be careful what you wish for."

TWO

By Friday morning I was ready to go, giving little thought to what exactly I might be getting myself into. The car was packed, mail stopped, rent and bills paid up for the month and my savings seriously depleted. I made one last call to my mother before I headed for the freeway. She'd been so excited earlier in the week when she found out I was going to interview Ethan Miller. The fact that I'd been fired was a minor detail once she found out it had led me straight to Ethan's house. I promised to call with frequent updates.

The day was threatening any minute to let loose with yet another early spring shower. I-29 led me south toward the Kansas/Missouri border and, with each passing mile, the accumulated stress of the past several months drained away. This, despite the fact I was jobless, without any idea when I would next see a paycheck and traveling alone to an unfamiliar area to stay with people I'd never met, for an indeterminate period of time. Maybe it was a sign of how far my work at the *Trib* had deteriorated that all of this made me feel like things were looking up. Of course, the great Ethan Miller had seemed surprisingly eager to break a silence he'd held for over a decade to be interviewed by the likes of me.

Bob was right. Every newspaper and magazine in the country would be clamoring to buy an exclusive with Ethan Miller. I hoped it would put me in a position to pick and choose my next job. Thumbing my nose at Hank in the process was just one of the perks.

About noon I passed through the Kansas Cities and stopped for lunch at a small cafe on the outskirts of the Missouri side. The waitress brought me iced tea, and as I waited for my meal to arrive, I looked over my route. If I drove straight through, I should be able to reach Ethan's house by mid to late afternoon, according to Google.

I wolfed down a cheeseburger and fries and went to pay my bill.

The waitress took my money. "Everything okay, hon?"

"Just fine."

While she was counting out my change, I looked at the magazine rack behind her. On the front cover of one of the tabloids was a picture of Ethan Miller in a tuxedo emerging from a limousine with a beautiful blonde in tow.

After a little hesitation, I bought the paper. After all, no one I knew would ever know.

Outside in the car, I read the brief article on Ethan Miller and *his lady friend* (that's what the paper called her), who had graced the premier opening of the new civic center in St. Louis.

Without a doubt, Ethan Miller was an imposing presence. The handsome middle-aged face I'd fallen in love with so many years ago had aged wonderfully in that maddening way men did. Deep lines and creases only added to the definition of character. The once jet-black hair was replaced with a thick, wavy silvery gray.

Lady friend was almost Barbie-doll perfect from her bleached blonde hair to her pouty pink lips. At least a quarter of a century younger than her escort, she was a well-chosen accessory.

I looked more closely and realized I hadn't picked up the paper through sheer prurience. The photo was meant to look spontaneous, but the lighting was too clean, the composition too good. It was posed, or at least Ethan and lady friend knew the photographer was there. I scanned the two graphs of copy again. It was breathless and gossipy, but with a professional edge. This wasn't a story. It was a press release.

So, Ethan's career had reached this point. The man who had once been on the cover of everything from *GQ* to *Rolling Stone* was now courting publicity with the checkout-counter rags. That, more than anything, left me feeling sad.

The inside of the car was suddenly stuffy. I started the engine and flipped on the air conditioner.

Ethan had never had to try to drum up interest in his love life before. Married and divorced three times, he had two grown sons—from marriages one and three—and two previous live-in *companions*. The woman with whom he was now involved, Jolene Pitner, he'd met at a cocktail party in Hollywood a little more than a year ago. Beyond that, the woman was an enigma. I'd been unable to find out much about her, other than she was an aspiring starlet. It was almost as if she'd materialized, on the spot, at the party where she met Ethan Miller. It was just as well. From her few acting credits in B movies, Ethan was about as close to fame as she'd ever get.

Ethan, himself, was no stranger to being center-stage in the midst of bad press. In the late sixties, he'd been actively involved in anti-war protests. Over the years, he'd been arrested in a few drunken brawls and sued for plagiarism in a case that was later dropped, and twenty years earlier a young woman had been found murdered on his estate. Although the murder was solved and his involvement seemed nonexistent, it had marred his popularity for a brief period of time. But, as always, he rebounded.

Now he was planting stories about himself in tabloids? And he was probably expecting this interview to be another puff piece, despite the way I'd panned his book. But it was looking more and more as if he needed someone to ask him some tough questions. It remained to be seen how far I would get.

I tossed the paper in the backseat, put the car in gear and headed back toward the highway. It was late afternoon by the time I reached the town of Sedgewick. There was a single stoplight in the center of town and a wide main street that took me straight through the business district, such as it was, and back into the countryside.

Three miles out of Sedgewick I made a left turn off the county highway onto Lentil Road, where I followed a wide dirt track up the hill past three small farmhouses and over a wooden bridge and a rushing stream. The road came to a dead end two miles later at a wide turnaround and a wrought iron gate. I slowed for a moment, feeling a rush of adrenaline, not sure if it was fear or excitement.

The large double gate stood open, and I swung the car onto the roughly paved driveway, half hidden with overgrown bushes and trees badly in need of pruning. For almost a half a mile I traversed the path as it wove and curved its way through the thick green foliage, before it released me into a clearing where I saw Ethan's house for the first time.

It was huge. And gorgeous. The front was pillared with large white gothic columns, the sides spread out in both directions with numerous additions that had accumulated over the past century and a half. Surrounding it were grounds that had been cleared and were as immaculately manicured as a golf green.

My little blue Toyota seemed obviously out of place parked in front of this mansion. I pushed open the door and ambled over to the brick walkway that ran down the middle of the front yard, where I could get a better view of the monstrous structure. Tulip gardens on both sides of me were in full bloom, their colors vivid against the green lawn. Cupolas and bay windows returned my gaze as I looked back at the house. A large portico overhung the drive that ran along the right wing.

I didn't hear the deep low bark off to my left until it was too late. I turned just in time to see two big black paws and a long pink tongue come flying through the air straight at me. The next thing I knew, I was flat on my back in the tulips, being enthusiastically greeted by the biggest, and heaviest, black Lab I'd ever seen. He had me pinned by all fours, while his big wet tongue licked my face. I squirmed and pushed, trying to free myself, but I was outmatched.

"That isn't good for the tulips, you know."

I turned my head to see two grimy work boots and the frayed bottom of a pair of jeans. "If you're so worried about the stupid tulips, then get this beast off of me."

With one snap of his fingers, the dog was at his side.

I struggled to my feet and brushed the dirt off the seat of my pants.

His gaze traveled from my head to my toes and back again. I looked at him and smiled. He raised his eyebrows in question, as if smiling were an unfamiliar custom from another land. His thick wavy hair was as black as the dog's, except for a few telltale strands of gray that fluttered in the breeze.

"What are you doing here?" he finally asked, as I pulled the leaves out of my hair.

"I'm Jessica Kallan. I'm here to see Ethan Miller."

The last part elicited a grunt from deep in his throat.

"Do you work for Mr. Miller?" I asked.

"I'm Matt Wheaton." He didn't bother to extend a hand. "I mostly take care of the grounds around here." Which explained the denim work shirt and the incredibly muscular arms.

"And you've already met Satan."

"Satan?"

I glanced at the dog, who sat watching us, his tongue still hanging out. His tail thumped twice when he saw me looking at him.

"He's our pathetic imitation of a watch dog."

I patted Satan on the head and his tail beat rhythmically in a welcome that was by far friendlier than the one I'd received from his master.

"If you're a guest of Ethan's," Matt said, "then they're probably expecting you at the house."

With that he turned, snapped his fingers again and sauntered off with Satan bobbing along beside him. I watched his retreating back as he crossed the lawn.

I turned to face the house then, as my brain finally

kicked into gear, swung back around toward the two walking away from me. "Matt Wheaton!"

He turned. "What?"

"You're Ethan Miller's son—"

"Yes, I know." He headed off again across the lawn.

Well, that was stupid—and embarrassing.

Matt Wheaton was Ethan's oldest son from his first marriage. He'd been raised by his mother and stepfather, just a few miles from the Miller estate, but his mother had chosen early on to give him his stepfather's name to keep him out of the limelight.

I turned back to look at the house. I wasn't off to a great start and had to muster my courage once again before I crossed the driveway and mounted the few long steps that led to the front door. I reached out to ring the bell then stopped.

Somewhere inside the house, voices were raised in argument. I put my ear to the door, but the muffled shouts were too indistinct to catch more than a single word here or there. All too aware I would fall flat on my face if the door was yanked open and, given my luck so far, it probably would be. I straightened up and rang the bell. At the sound of the melodic gong, the voices ceased, and a few seconds later the door swung open.

A pallid, moon-faced man in his late fifties stood there squinting at me through narrowed eyes and Harry Potter glasses. "Yes?"

"I'm Jessica Kallan. I'm here to see Ethan Miller."

He actually said, "Humph."

I took a not-so-wild guess. "And you must be Dan Ketner."

This time he grunted something that might have been "Uh-huh." Then, after a moment, "Well, I guess you might as well come in." He stepped away from the door as if I might contaminate him.

I hadn't been accused of having cooties since the fourth grade.

The long hallway was dark and cool. Ketner was halfway down it when he said, "Close the door."

I did and followed him into the lion's den. If everyone was as unenthusiastic about my arrival as the two men I'd just met, it was going to be a very long couple of weeks.

The voices I'd heard from outside had resumed. And now I was close enough to hear what they were saying.

"Get over it, Ethan," one said. "It's not that big a deal. I have a *right* to have a little fun."

Something thudded loudly—a fist on a table perhaps—and then Ethan's voice sounded angrily, the voice I would recognize anywhere. "Dammit, John! I will not continue to clean up your messes! The next time you get thrown in jail, you can just sit there until you figure out how to get yourself out!"

"Oh, come on, Ethan. You and I both know you would never do that. You'd have too much to lose, wouldn't you?"

"Get out!" There was such finality in the statement that the ensuing silence wasn't surprising.

Earlier, I'd merely been eavesdropping out of professional curiosity. Dan Ketner's face was alight with undisclosed interest. He turned as if to say something to me, when the first door on the right opened and out stepped one of the most gorgeous men I'd ever seen.

He was tall, lean and tanned, with thick blond hair, dressed in white Dockers and a cotton shirt. When he turned and saw me, he did a quick double take then smiled, and the handsome went into overdrive.

"Hi," he said, his voice warm and friendly. "I didn't know anyone was here."

I smiled back. I couldn't help it. "I'm Jessica Kallan."

His gaze traveled appreciatively over my body. To be perfectly honest, that look just blew me away. "So, you're Jessica."

"Jessie?" came Ethan's booming voice from the room beyond. "Is Jessie here?"

The unknown man, John, I had to assume, nodded, still smiling at me. And then, Ethan Miller was in the doorway, elbowing the other man aside, a broad smile on his big rugged face. His gray eyes looked straight into mine and I felt as if I were thirteen again, totally captivated by this man I had never met.

This was why I was here. Ethan Miller. An American legend. This charismatic man, full of life and wit and humor—a master of his craft. Or at least a past master of his craft. One I might be able to help.

"Jessie!" he said, in that commanding voice of his. "I'm glad you finally showed up."

In three long strides, he was in front of me, furiously pumping my hand. Never in my life had anyone who didn't have paws seem so thoroughly glad to see me. But then, I guessed, that was probably part of his charisma. The questions started, with my hand still clasped in his. How was the drive? Did I have any trouble? Was I hungry, tired, thirsty? How long could I stay? My answers consisted mostly of nods and monosyllables.

When he finally stopped his rapid-fire questions, he turned his attention to the other two men. "Have you met everyone?" He didn't wait for a reply. "This is Dan Ketner, my assistant, publicist, agent and manager."

I nodded grimly at Dan and he nodded grimly back at me.

Ethan must have noticed the exchange. "Dan's got a lot more talents than he does personality."

Ketner mumbled something and slunk away into the depths of the house.

"And this is my son, John." Ethan turned toward the remaining man.

John took my hand away from his father, who was still clutching it. "It's nice to officially meet you, Jessica. Ethan's been babbling about you all week."

"Call me Jess, please."

"That's right, John." Ethan reclaimed my hand. "Jessie's going to be around for a while. We don't need to be so formal."

The two men, father and son, stood looking at each other eye to eye, almost nose to nose. I had the feeling my perfectly innocent hand had become the prize in some stupid male competition, although I really didn't understand the game.

While Ethan was still in possession of my hand, Jolene Pitner, a.k.a. Lady friend, sidled up to him. Her hand went around his waist in a markedly territorial manner. "Who's your friend, Ethan?" There was a smile on her lips that never quite made it to her eyes.

Ethan gave her a quick glance. "Jolene, this is Jessie Kallan. She's the writer I told you about who's going to interview me. Although, I doubt if you remember my saying it."

If that was intended as a put-down she seemed unaffected.

"Jessie, this is Jolene Pitner, my…friend."

I nodded. There was more than *friend* implied in the way Jolene guarded Ethan.

"Well, enough of this," Ethan said. "Jessie's probably tired. Jolene, why don't you take her upstairs and show her to her room. John, take care of her bags. We have cocktails at six, Jessie, and dinner at six thirty. I'll see you then."

Ethan looked around and bellowed, "Where the hell is Chatman?" He did a complete three sixty and was back facing me when a young woman appeared from the hallway that led to what I assumed was the back of the house. She reminded me of Velma from *Scooby-Doo*, with that nerdy look going for her. Or not going for her.

"I'm here, Mr. Miller," she said in a breathy voice. Not so much sexy as timid. "And it's Chatsworth."

"What? Oh, right. Come along. We have work to do, Chapman."

She opened her mouth, shrugged and closed her mouth again.

Ethan returned to the room behind him with Chatman-Chatsworth-Chapman close on his heels and closed the door.

John warmed to his task more willingly than Jolene did. He smiled, took my car keys and headed out the front door. With no audience left to play for, Jolene lost her affected smile and eyed me critically. Without a word, she turned and headed for the wide central staircase, with me trailing along behind her.

The stairs led to a large carpeted landing with French doors that opened onto a small balcony. Cement flowerpots filled with begonias and marigolds decorated the wide concrete railings, and beyond, a massive lawn stretched out behind the house. To one side was one of those wrought iron table and chair sets that always looked to me like medieval torture devices.

At the landing, we turned and climbed the few remaining stairs to the second floor, Jolene always a few steps above me. She had a very fetching wiggle in her practiced walk and a "very fine caboose," as my grandfather would have said. Her blonde hair was expertly dyed, so as not to be obvious. She was maybe five-seven, about an inch taller than me, and her figure was trim, her skin a light golden tan. I got the impression Jolene spent a lot of time taking care of Jolene.

The hallway at the top was wider than most of the type and held as much furniture as my living room... little half-tables with flowers and delicate Queen Anne chairs. The art on the walls was mostly hunting scenes with an occasional landscape. I couldn't tell if it was original or not. All these things I noted in passing, for Jolene kept a steady pace. I had to almost trot along, fearful I might get lost in the cavernous house, never to be seen again.

She paused at the third door we came to. "This is your room." She opened the door onto a front bedroom, walked in and sat down on the edge of the four-poster bed, crossing her long legs. It was the first time she'd looked at me since we'd been downstairs.

"So? What's your story?"

I stood, looking around the room, which, at first glance, was somewhere between country manor house and upscale hotel.

"Story?" I looked her in the eyes.

They were a shade of blue that could only be achieved

with tinted contacts. "You know. What is it you want to get out of Ethan?"

"An interview."

She laughed. "Yeah right, honey." She watched as I made my way around the room. When she must have realized I had nothing of interest to say, she stood. "Well, I've got things to do. Drinks in the front parlor at six."

She left before I even had a chance to ask where the front parlor was.

THE ROOM WAS EXQUISITE, the color scheme a muted rose, the furniture provincial. At one end was a door that opened into a large walk-in closet, the other end held a door that led to a ceramic-tiled private bath.

While I was exploring the bathroom, which was as big as the bedroom in my apartment, John poked his head through the doorway and found me playing with the whirlpool jets in the sunken tub.

"I brought your luggage up, but I can see you're busy." There was a smile on his face.

"I was just trying to figure out how these work." I followed him back into the bedroom. "You know, I don't think Jolene believes I'm here to interview your father."

He placed a suitcase on the luggage rack at the end of the bed. "No, I suppose not. She probably thinks you're a gold digger too. Takes one to know one."

"I...um...overheard the end of your conversation with Ethan."

"Would have been hard to avoid. So, I guess you know he's a tad miffed at me." He smiled again.

"Sounded like more than a 'tad.'"

"Well, if you're around here long enough, you'll probably hear about it anyway. I got picked up last night.

Had a little cash-flow problem with a bar tab, and they called the cops on me. I wasn't about to hang around and wait for them, so I left."

"Just left?"

"Well, at high speed, with a couple of cruisers on my tail. That didn't go over too well. Live and learn, huh?" John noticed my cell phone lying on the bed next to my purse. "Good luck with that. It's a dead zone around here for a five-mile radius."

"Wow. What do you do for internet?"

"Would you believe dial-up?"

"You're kidding, right?"

"Nope. 'Fraid not."

"So, who is the Chatsworth girl? Ethan didn't bother to introduce us."

"Her name's Trisha, I think. She's an intern or something from the U at Columbia. She's been working with Ethan on some mysterious research project for the past six weeks. I guess she's nice. I don't know her that well." He moved toward the door. "I'll let you unpack and see you at dinner."

I had about an hour before I was to make my appearance downstairs and I spent that time unpacking and soaking my weary body in the deep, wide tub. When the skin on my fingers and toes started to resemble small prunes, I reluctantly climbed out of the tub and wrapped a towel around me then went to search for something suitable, and slightly less wrinkled than my appendages, to wear to dinner.

I was searching through my clothes when there was a knock on the door.

"Just a minute," I yelled, pulling the towel tighter

around my body. I opened the door a crack and stuck my head out.

Trisha Chatsworth was standing there, looking all timid.

"Yes?" I asked.

"I'm sorry to bother you, Ms. Kallan, but I just wanted to meet you. You know, because you're a reporter and all." She looked up and down the hall. "Do you mind if I come in?"

"Well, it's not really a good time right now. I just got out of the tub—"

"Oh, I don't mind." She pushed open the door and walked in.

All of a sudden, the extra-large bath towel didn't seem large enough.

Chatman-Chatsworth-Chapman sat down on the bed and pushed her glasses up the bridge of her nose. I waited for some sort of dialogue to start. Nothing.

"Was there something you wanted to talk to me about?"

"I want to be a reporter too," she said in that breathy voice. "It's been great working with Mr. Miller and all, but it's not really what I want to do with my life. I mean, it's been good experience helping him with his research, but really investigating a story on my own, wow, that would be exciting, I'm just an intern here right now and I graduate in June, so, how hard is it to get a job as a real reporter?"

The words came out in one long sentence and I realized why Chatsworth always sounded breathy. It was all exhale.

"Maybe we could talk about this at dinner—or, you know—after I get dressed."

"Oh, I don't mind. I can wait."

Well, great. I sat down in one of the Queen Anne chairs, careful not to cross my legs. "What is it that you and Ethan have been working on?"

"His next book, I guess. I'm not really sure. It's been all hush-hush. Well, not between the two of us—I mean, Mr. Miller and me—not me and you—I've had to do some of my own research and that was fun, but it's about some girl that got murdered here, like a bazillion years ago. I don't think people are really interested in that sort of thing, do you?"

My head was starting to throb. "I'd have to know more about it. Maybe we could talk about this at dinner—or, you know—after I got dressed." Great. Now I was starting to talk like her.

She must have finally caught on that I really wanted to get dressed. She stood and backed her way toward the door. "Oh sure. No problem, but I really, really do want to talk to you later, okay?"

"Absolutely." I closed the door on her.

Okay, well, that was weird.

I fumbled through the closet and found a pair of beige cotton slacks that had survived the last several hours pretty well, along with a pink V-neck sweater that showed just a smidgen of cleavage. I added gold earrings, a gold chain at my throat and a matching bracelet. Then I reapplied my makeup, ran a brush through my hair, took a couple of deep breaths to calm my nerves and headed out in search of the unknown parlor.

At the bottom of the stairs, two large sliding doors, off to my right, stood open, spilling light and the sound of voices into the hallway. I had apparently found the unknown parlor, but I still didn't feel ready to make my appearance. So, I rounded the bottom of the stairs, heading down the long, tiled hallway that pointed toward the back of the house.

The third door on the right held a large screen TV and one wall filled with DVDs and videotapes. Ethan Miller must have been a mystery buff. Looking at the titles, I counted at least four different Miss Marples on the Agatha Christie shelf. There was an overstuffed red leather couch in the middle of the room, with matching club chairs flanking it on each end. A wet bar was on the wall opposite the TV.

I made my way back into the hall and opened a door on my left, groping along the wall until I found a light switch and flipped it on. A veritable sports shrine came to life. An oak cabinet held high school trophies Matt Wheaton had won for various sprints and dashes and relays. Rifles and pistols polished to a high-shine covered an entire wall. I walked past them to the framed photographs that filled another wall.

Ethan was center stage in many of them. Ethan shooting skeet and Ethan driving a racecar. And Ethan standing next to his racecar surrounded by a much younger Dan Ketner and youthful versions of Matt and John. All were dressed in jumpsuits, holding crash helmets to their chests. There was a photograph of Ethan actually sitting in his car with the hood up, his sons and Dan acting as his pit crew.

"Ethan's a sports nut, in case you hadn't guessed," said a voice behind me.

I turned. Jolene stood in the doorway wearing a sequined jumpsuit that fit her like a second skin and revealed more cleavage than I possessed. And, I might add, I'm not particularly lacking in that department.

"He's quite accomplished." I waved my hand at all the awards cluttering the walls.

"Yeah, he thinks so too."

I walked over to the gun wall. "Does he hunt?"

"No. Just target practice. Skeet shooting, you know." She looked me up and down and I wasn't sure I passed inspection. "My father was a sharpshooter."

"Was? Is he still alive?"

She shrugged. "Who knows. Ethan sent me to find you. He wondered if you got lost."

"No, not lost. Just exploring." I walked out into the hall and waited for Jolene to lead the way back to the parlor.

I stepped hesitantly through the doorway and surveyed the assemblage. Matt was standing off to the side, one shoulder leaned up against the wall, a near-empty glass in his hand. He was dressed in clean jeans, a light blue shirt, a buff corduroy jacket and cowboy boots. His free hand was stuck deep in the pocket of his jeans. His gray eyes studied me for a moment before he nodded in my direction. I returned his nod. Trisha was standing next to Matt and I tried not to make eye contact.

John sat on the couch and Jolene made her way directly to him, where she sat down so close their knees touched. She placed a hand on his thigh, as if to get his attention, but it was obvious she already had it.

In front of the mammoth stone fireplace, Dan stood talking animatedly with a tall man and a frail-looking woman, both of whom had their backs to me. You know how you sometimes spot someone familiar in a new context—you meet your hairdresser in the grocery store—and it takes a moment for recognition to hit? It was like this for me, now.

Ethan called me over to the drink cart. "What will it be, Jessie?"

"Scotch. Neat. Lots."

He poured a generous amount into a tall glass, came out from around the cart and laid claim to my arm with his big warm hand. "You look great."

"Thanks." I grabbed the glass and took a sizable sip.

He started to steer me toward Dan's group by the fireplace. "I want you to greet our other guests."

"I'm not sure I want to."

"Come on. It'll be fun."

I did not say, *for whom?* but let him lead me over to the group by the fireplace.

"Take a break, Dan," he said, and Ketner stopped mid-sentence.

"I think you both know my girl, here," he said to the backs of the two people in front of us.

They turned around.

"And, Jessie, I think you already know Ms. Burke and my godson, Hank."

Glenda gasped when she saw my face and Hank's mouth actually dropped open.

Ethan, I could tell, was enjoying this immensely. So, fun for him.

"Hello, Glenda. Nice to see you again, Hank," I said.

"Ethan, what on earth is she doing here?"

"She's going to interview me, Hank. You've been telling me for months it's just what I need to boost my next book."

"But, good God, Ethan, not by *her*!"

I was saved from further humiliation when an older, pleasant-looking woman appeared in the doorway to announce dinner was ready. As Ethan escorted me to the dining room, Hank and Glenda followed close behind us, whispering.

I sat at Ethan's right at the head of the long oak dining table, with Jolene at his left. John was at the opposite end, and his eyes shone with amusement as he looked at the two women flanking his father. Matt was seated next to me, with Dan on the other side of him and Trisha Chatsworth on Dan's right. Hank was next to Jolene and Glenda was between Hank and John. Was it merely an accident that the least attractive woman in the room was seated next to John? I was beginning to see that Ethan had reached the endpoint of the rich and powerful and was playing games with people, including me.

John looked at Glenda and smiled and her face lit up like I'd never seen it before. He had her engaged in conversation and completely captivated before she knew what was happening. It was a remarkable transformation. Glenda was in her late forties and had only been Hank's secretary for about a year. In the entire time I'd known her, she'd never looked as alive as she did with John.

We dined on soup, roast chicken, new potatoes, fresh peas and homemade biscuits. Between the soup and the main course, I said to Ethan, "What *is* Hank doing here?"

He smiled wickedly. "I'm sorry about that. I guess I should have told you they were coming, but I couldn't resist seeing everyone's reactions."

I thought I should draw some lines right at the beginning. "People make good toys?"

"Oh, it's not that. Hank's been coming down here almost every weekend for the past three months. He's been trying to get me interested in buying the *Trib*, or writing a series of articles for it, or just about anything, so he can use my name or money."

"And?"

"I'm not interested in any of it. But I let him keep coming. He's been very amusing to have around. I haven't had the heart to tell him that newspapers are a dying industry."

"And Glenda?"

He shrugged. "I have no idea why he brings her. Maybe they're lovers."

I tried to squelch the visual that popped into my head, but it was too late.

"Hank really panicked last week when you wrote that book review about me," he said.

"Yeah. I'm well aware of that."

"Dan was mad enough to spit nails when he read it and he called Hank and told him all negotiations were off. Not that we were seriously negotiating anything to begin with."

Had it only been a week since I wrote that review? It seemed like longer than that. "You do know Hank fired me, don't you?"

"I heard about your job, Jessie. I'm sorry. I can get it back for you with one word to Hank."

"Actually, I'm not sure I want it back."

"Good."

"Ethan," I said, "I'm sorry if that book review hurt you. I'd wanted to do a better job than that, but…"

I didn't quite know how to explain that the problem with the book review was the book. How could I tell my idol he'd been skating on his reputation for too long? That his great literary talent was being wasted writing formulaic serial novels? How could I tell Ethan Miller that his books had gotten me through the worst days of my life and he needed to get back to that place—to be the writer he was meant to be. Sitting next to him, I was at a loss. I couldn't begin to articulate those feelings to him or to myself.

For the first time since I'd met him, his face was entirely serious. "There's nothing to be sorry about. What you said was absolutely true. When *The Last Man Standing* was published and I realized how much people loved the characters, I couldn't resist a sequel. Then it just got easier and easier to keep those running characters, and that limited the situations and techniques I could use. It got so I could crank those things out in my sleep, which is pretty much what I did. I've been coasting and I know it."

If I was going to do a serious interview, I had to get used to asking tough questions, and he had to get used to hearing them from me. "Do you know why? What happened?"

He raised his shoulders as if in surrender to fate. "It's just that I've had other things on my mind. And it was easier to keep the momentum going than to have to really be creative again."

I didn't know what to say. It was a painfully honest self-revelation. I realized that I might learn something from this interview too about a creative life.

I wanted to pursue the matter further, but apparently, Jolene was becoming bored with Hank and jealous of me. She took hold of Ethan's arm and leaned over, exposing her impressive cleavage, and Ethan's attention went with it.

I turned my attention to Matt. "Have you ever thought about writing?"

"No."

"But you're working for Ethan now?"

"Yes."

"How long have you been working for him?" I thought that would require at least a two-word response.

"On and off, over the years. Mostly summers."

He went back to his dinner, and I did the same. I smiled at John a few times when he caught my eye and wished that he were sitting beside me.

When we'd made it through the ample meal, the plates were removed and a remarkable chocolate mousse was served. Ethan picked up his spoon and clinked his glass soundly, to get everyone's attention.

When all eyes were on him, he smiled, "I have an announcement to make. I'm going to be starting on a new book, and I thought you might be interested in the subject."

He paused for effect. Given his new hobby of toying with people, I wasn't sure I liked what the effect would be.

Finally, John said, "Well?"

"Chapman—"

Trisha raised her hand. "Chatsworth."

"What? Oh right, Chatman has been helping me these past weeks with the research. I'm going to be writing about the Rawlings trial."

There was dead silence for almost half a minute.

Matt leaned back and folded his arms across his chest; his jaw muscles tightened. John raised his eyebrows, and Hank's face turned as white as the tablecloth. Jolene and Trisha were the only ones who seemed unaffected.

I don't recall who spoke first. It was more a general explosion. "Ethan, you can't."

"You shouldn't."

"Why now?"

"You're out of your mind."

I'd come across the Rawlings case in my research, but I hadn't gone into it very far. Bonita Rawlings was the young woman who'd been murdered on Ethan's estate twenty years ago. The case had been solved when a local man was arrested for the crime. I wondered about the timeliness of this endeavor and why this piece of old news would cause such consternation.

When the furor finally died down, Ethan dropped another bomb. This time, I was as flabbergasted as everyone else was.

"And since Chapsworth will be heading back to school shortly, I've decided I'm going to hire Jessie to be my researcher."

My face must have shown my feelings, for Ethan looked at me and laughed.

"Don't look so scared," he said. "We'll be great together. It'll be fun."

"Ethan, this is ridiculous." Dan stomped out of the room.

"I can tell you from personal experience," Hank said, "you'll live to regret this. That woman is impossible to work with." He stood, looked pointedly at Glenda and left in a huff.

Glenda rose and followed in his wake. I took that as a compliment.

Matt threw his napkin on the table, knocking over his water glass. "Ethan, this is the stupidest thing you've ever done, and you've had more than your share of stupid." He stormed into the parlor.

John was the only one besides Jolene who seemed more or less unaffected. "Good luck, Jess. I hope this works out for you. Ethan can be a bear to work with, just ask Trisha. Now, if you'll excuse me, I have a few phone calls to make."

Trisha watched John's retreating back then turned toward Ethan. "I don't have to go back to school yet, Mr. Miller. I can finish out the semester here if you need me."

"Now, now, Chatsworthy," he said, "you don't want to neglect your studies."

"But…" Her face turned red as Ethan stared her down. She stood, pushed in her chair and headed for the parlor.

Jolene returned her attention to dessert. "You certainly know how to clear a room, hon." She finished and pushed her chair back. She smiled at me. "Don't get any ideas," she said with a drawl.

I was going to say that I was a professional when it occurred to me that, in her own way, so was she. I let it go, and she glided out of the room.

When she was gone, I was alone with Ethan. "So… we're not doing that interview?"

"I could really use your help on this. You're a damn fine writer and I know you know how to research a story. Eric trained you well."

"And it saves you the trouble of talking about yourself, doesn't it?"

"Jessie, I know you think I'm just a spoiled rich man who enjoys toying with the people around him—"

"You certainly sent this crowd down like ninepins."

"I know. But this isn't the game you think it is. There are probably a lot of skeletons in this closet that no one wants to look at. But maybe it's time."

Now that I thought about it, I was curious why the reopening of a long-settled case should get everyone so upset. Whatever Ethan's motives, there was a story here. I asked the first, obvious question. "Why does Hank care so much about this? What does it have to do with him?"

"He used to spend a lot of time here when he was growing up. He and John went to prep school together in St. Louis and Hank came home with John for holidays and summer vacations. He was here the summer it happened."

Hank and John as friends was a picture I just couldn't conjure up.

"Let's talk about this tomorrow," Ethan said. "I want to show you my terrace by moonlight." He reached for my hand and, I have to admit, my heart was fluttering just a bit.

The French doors led us onto a stone terrace, and we strolled to the low wall at the far end. The air was thick with the sweet smell of spring and the night was clear, the sky littered with stars.

We stood for a moment, side by side, looking out over the steps that led to the fountain on the lower terrace and the lawn spreading beyond. It was a scene straight out of my most intense adolescent fantasies.

Ethan pointed off to our left. "There's a small lake over that ridge and some hot springs and some caves beyond that. I'll take you there sometime."

As distracting as the setting was, though, I couldn't let go of the conversation at the dinner table. I pushed my adolescence aside. "How long have you been hatching this scheme of me working for you?"

"Most of the week. I've been thinking about it ever since I knew you were coming down here."

"What about Trisha?"

"She's good, but she's not a trained professional, like you are."

I turned to look at him.

Trisha Chatsworth moved out from the French doors. "Ms. Kallan, I was hoping to get a chance to talk to you tonight. I thought maybe since you're going to be taking over my research, I could, you know, bring you up to date on what I've found."

She started to make her way across the terrace, and then, in one of those awful, mind-numbing, slow motion moments, a cement vase came hurtling off the balcony above us, straight for Trisha's head.

I think I screamed. Ethan pushed me and as I hit the ground, I heard the loud vibrating crash behind me, as fragments of concrete showered my head.

THREE

THE STILLNESS THAT followed was almost as deafening as the crash. Seconds ticked by as I lay on the terrace with my face pressed hard against the cold stones, listening. No sounds from Ethan or Trisha. Only silence.

Then the sound of feet pounding through the dining room. Doors banging. Voices shouting. Two strong hands grasped my shoulders and turned me over, and I was looking up into Matt's face.

"Are you all right?" he asked.

"I think so." I touched my cheek with my hand and stared at the blood that appeared on my fingers. "Well, maybe not…"

"I think it's just a scrape."

"Oh my God!" someone said. "Oh my God!"

The shock was passing. I pulled away from Matt. "Ethan? Trisha? Are they okay?"

Matt glanced over at the group of people gathered on the terrace. His breath escaped in a long low sigh.

Ethan was getting to his feet, a deep cut on his forehead, the blood glistening in the moonlight. Large shards of concrete from the vase lay on the ground around Trisha. She wasn't moving. Dan and John hovered over the girl's body.

The large cement vase that had been resting on the railing of the balcony above was shattered into pieces.

Ethan made his way over to Dan. "Is she…"

Dan looked at him and nodded. There was a halo of blood fanning out around the girl's dark hair.

Even in the moonlight, I saw the color drain from Ethan's face. I pushed myself up off the ground, barely noticing the throbbing in my knee and the scratches on my hands. "Has anyone called an ambulance?"

Everyone looked at me.

"It's, uh, too late," Dan said.

Again, that unnerving silence.

"Then we need to call the sheriff," I said.

Everyone looked at me again. "Why?" Jolene's eyes bored into mine.

"There's a dead body lying right there. The authorities need to be notified. And…"

"And what?" Jolene took a step toward me.

"It might not have been an accident."

"What exactly is that supposed to mean?" Jolene took another step toward me until her face was only inches from mine. "Do you think someone did this? On purpose? Just who do you think you are to come waltzing in here accusing us of—murder?"

For a moment, I thought she was going to pop me one. Right on the jaw. The same thought must have crossed Ethan's mind. He took her by the arm and pulled her away.

"She's not accusing anyone of anything." He spoke as if soothing a child. "Something horrible has just happened, Jolene, and none of us are thinking too clearly right now."

"Well, she better not be saying that because I won't tolerate it!" Her voice was too loud for the quiet that surrounded us and it made my ears hurt. "And why? Why would anyone want to hurt Tracy—or Tina—or that girl?"

It was obvious Trisha Chatsworth was just a nobody in their lives and that made me sad.

"I'll call the sheriff." Matt walked into the dining room.

The adrenaline rush finally kicked in and I started to tremble.

Ethan looked at me. "Are you all right?"

I nodded, but I wasn't sure he believed me. I wanted to walk it off, but there were too many people now on the terrace and then there was Trisha...

John was kneeling near the body, examining the point of impact. "What in blazes happened out here, Ethan?"

"One of the stone vases fell from the second-floor balcony."

"Holy crap," John said. "How did that happen?"

Ethan shook his head, a blank look in his eyes. "I can't even imagine. Dan?"

Dan knelt next to John to examine the remains of the vase. He picked up a few pieces and sifted them through his fingers then raised his eyes to the balcony above.

I finally moved over to look at Trisha Chatsworth's body. She was so young and now she was gone. Why? Yes, it could have been an accident. I knew that. But everything about it was so freakish, it defied the odds. The vase just happened to fall when she happened to be standing below it?

An idea popped into my head and I blurted it out before my internal censors had a chance to pass judgment and silence me. "Ethan, could this have something to do with the book you talked about writing?"

He looked confused. "What? No." He shook his head. "No, that's not possible."

Jolene was ready to pounce again.

Ethan grabbed her arm. "Why don't you wait inside. I'm sure the sheriff will want to talk to each of us."

She looked at him then at me and turned and went into the house.

I felt like I should say something, but I had no idea what. My circuits were a bit overloaded at the moment.

John took my arm. "Why don't we go inside and get you cleaned up?"

It felt surreal and so disrespectful to leave Trisha lying there, but I didn't know what else to do. We went through the French doors of the dining room, and into the large, spotless kitchen, complete with stainless steel sinks, a large butcher block island in the center of the room and glistening pots and pans hanging from hooks on the walls.

John pulled a stool out from under a counter and I sat down on it.

Matt came in through the swinging door. "Sheriff's on his way." He opened a cabinet door and pulled out a first aid kit.

Dan busied himself making coffee. Ethan dropped onto the stool next to me. Somewhere between the terrace and the kitchen, Glenda had disappeared, but Hank had followed us and stood by the doorway, watching.

Matt ministered to my wounds while John took to doctoring his father.

Neither of us was hurt very badly. There was a deep gash on Ethan's forehead and the middle of his right forearm was swollen and discolored, where he said he hit it on the railing after he pushed me out of the way.

John wrapped his father's arm and applied a neat butterfly bandage to his forehead and Ethan ended up looking like a gallant war hero.

My own wounds were minor. They hurt like crazy,

but when I thought about Trisha, I knew how lucky I was just to be alive. Matt poured peroxide on my scraped hands and cleaned the cut on my cheek. Finally, he rolled up my pant leg to look at my knee, which was already puffy and as red as a beet. He wrapped it tightly in an Ace bandage.

When Matt was finished with me, he turned to Ethan. "What are we going to do about this?"

"There's nothing to do about it." Ethan's voice sounded weary. "It's all over. All we can do is to make sure the other vases are secure enough that something like this never happens again—and wait for the sheriff."

Matt shook his head. "Hundred-pound vases don't just fall, Ethan."

"What do you want me to say, Matt? This is an old house. Things are falling apart faster than we can keep up with them. There's no way we could have known what would happen to, uh, that girl."

The fact that Trisha had been a part of their lives for almost two months and she wasn't even worthy of a name bothered me almost as much as her death.

Hank had been watching the exchange between Matt and Ethan with some interest. When he saw me looking at him, he turned and went out through the swinging door.

Dan handed me a cup of steaming coffee and put another one in Ethan's hand then left to see if the sheriff had arrived.

Ethan took a few sips from his cup then put it on the counter behind him. He stood and looked at me. "Are you okay, Jessie?"

I shrugged. "I guess so."

"We should probably wait in the parlor for the sheriff."

I followed Ethan into the front parlor just as Dan was ushering in the sheriff.

Sheriff Stevenson looked more than a little annoyed to be called to the Miller place so late in the evening.

He sat on the couch and looked at Ethan. "So, what's the story?"

Ethan gave him his account and I gave him mine. The sheriff didn't even bother taking notes. When I was finished, he stood and Dan took him out to the terrace to look at the girl's body.

When he came back in, he nodded to Ethan. "Darn shame, Mr. Miller. She doesn't look very old. Who is she?"

The look on Ethan's face told me the girl's name eluded him still.

"Trisha Chatsworth," I said. "She was an intern from the University of Missouri at Columbia, helping Ethan with some research for a book."

"Well, it's a darn shame. Terrible accident. I'll send the coroner out here to collect the body. Do you want to contact the girl's parents or do you want me to?"

I stood up. "How do you know it was an accident?"

"What else would it be, miss? Did she have any mortal enemies that wanted to get rid of her? Maybe she was in the Witness Protection Program and the mob tracked her down to Sedgewick, Missouri?" He laughed.

I wanted to punch him in the face. "Or, more likely, she was working on some sensitive research involving a twenty-year-old murder case and someone thought she may have discovered information they didn't want anyone to know."

He laughed again and moved toward the door. "Maybe, but I doubt it." He took his smug attitude and left.

Ethan was watching me. He nodded his head at the retreating sheriff. "He's right, you know. It was a terrible accident. Nothing more. Don't make yourself crazy trying to find a reason for something that none of us could foresee."

I felt like everyone was dismissing me. And, who knows, maybe I was wrong, although my instincts told me otherwise—it could have easily been me under that vase. But, maybe I was right, and no one was going to bother finding out.

"Okay," I said to Ethan.

"Good. Why don't you try to get some sleep? And, I'm sorry, Jessie. This isn't much of a welcome for you." Ethan headed for the front hallway.

Matt headed him off before he reached the door. "We need to talk."

Ethan sighed. "All right. Come to my office."

When they'd left the room, John and I were alone.

"I'm not so sure you're okay. I think I know what you need." He sat me down on the couch, proceeded to the liquor cart and came back with a double brandy for each of us. "This should help." He handed one to me.

I took a sip and the warmth traveled through me as I closed my eyes and leaned my head against the back of the couch, but all I could see behind my closed eyelids were images of Trisha lying on the terrace. I opened my eyes to look at John. "Do you really think what happened was an accident?"

He shrugged. "I can't see that it could be anything else. An old house like this takes a lot of money to keep in habitable condition. There's always something that needs to be repaired or replaced."

He was sitting at the other end of the couch, watching me in a way that made me uncomfortable. It wasn't long before his glass was empty. When he got up to go for a refill, I moved off the couch and settled myself in an armchair a safe distance away.

"Did you grow up here?" I asked when he was seated on the couch again, a look of amusement in his eyes.

He nodded. "When I wasn't away at school or spending a vacation with my mother, I was here."

"Ethan said Hank used to come here with you. It's funny, but I can't picture you and Hank as pals."

"We weren't," John said. "Ethan and Eric were best friends and they tried to manufacture a relationship between Hank and me. We went to school together in St. Louis, and Hank came here a lot, but it wasn't my choice. It probably wasn't his either." He took a long drink from his glass. "It's not like we hated each other, but there was never anything that clicked between us. Hank was convenient, at times, when there was no one else to hang around with. But, a lot of the time he was just a pest, following me around everywhere I went."

"That I could picture. Hank always struck me as the kind of kid nobody played with unless their parents made them."

John laughed, but it was more politeness than humor. I think the brandy, on top of whatever else he had drunk that evening, was having its effect.

He crossed the room in easy strides and bent down, his face inches from mine. Too close.

"Why don't we go out for a while," he said his voice

husky. "Just the two of us. I think I could find a way to entertain you for a couple of hours."

Seriously? A girl had just died and he was moving in on me? "I'm exhausted. And, well, Trisha…"

He looked me in the eyes for several long seconds. "Sure. I get it." He stood up. "I'll see you in the morning, Jess."

I barely had a chance to say good night, before he was out of the parlor. Moments later, the front door closed soundly.

I didn't realize how tense he'd made me until he was gone. What was that all about? And the timing was just too inappropriate.

I got up slowly, a stiffness seeping throughout my body from the hard landing on the concrete terrace. The house was quiet and I made my way out of the parlor and into the dimly lit front hallway. The door to Ethan's office was closed, but muffled voices carried through. The words weren't loud but were deliberate and emphatic. I paused in the hall to listen and heard Matt's voice.

"Dammit, Ethan!" he said. "Haven't you taken this far enough? Look what happened. Someone is dead. And still you're going through with this? What could you possibly hope to accomplish?"

"Justice, truth, honor."

"Nice words, Dad. Why don't you tell that to Trisha's family?"

Something moved in the hallway and I looked up as Dan moved out of the shadow of the staircase and came toward me.

His look was chilling. "Why don't you go to bed, Ms. Kallan. There's nothing down here that concerns you."

I nodded and made an effort to move past him, but apparently, he wasn't finished.

"I think it might be wise for you to make other arrangements in the morning. There's a small motel in town or maybe you should think of going home."

"I'll leave when I've finished what I came for." I moved toward the stairs and had my foot on the first step.

"All right. But after what happened here tonight, you should be careful. It could have been you."

I turned. "I know and is that a threat?"

He shook his head. "Not at all, just a warning." And he opened the door to Ethan's office and went in.

I stood staring after him for several seconds then turned and hurried up the stairs to my room, as fast as my injured leg would allow.

With the bedroom door closed behind me, I swore under my breath. Dan Ketner had not been at all happy to see me there. I shouldn't let him get to me. Normally, I wouldn't, but after what had happened to Trisha, I didn't know if it really wasn't a threat or not.

I went into the bathroom and carefully washed my face. I spent a few minutes brushing flecks of cement from my hair. Back in the bedroom, I pulled my nightshirt from the drawer, climbed out of my clothes, got ready for bed and crawled in. I unwound the bandage from my throbbing knee, to see that it was still red and puffy and sore to the touch. I wrapped it tightly again and propped a couple of pillows under it then switched off the light, leaned my head back and closed my eyes.

I lay there in the darkness, picturing Trisha lying on the terrace and Dan's words ringing in my ears.

After ten minutes or so, I sat up and flipped on the

light, hunted for my slippers and grabbed my robe then opened the door as quietly as possible. I wasn't going to sleep until I assessed what had really happened.

The hallway was lit by a few delicate wall sconces. I looked up and down and listened before I ventured forth. The house was completely still. I made my way to the carpeted stairs and the landing below. I had expected the French doors leading to the balcony to be locked for the night, but I tested the handle and found that they weren't.

I clicked the door closed behind me and crossed to the railing. There wasn't much light, and I wasn't even sure what I was looking for.

Judging from the gap in the row, the cement vase had been third from the corner that afternoon. I felt my way carefully along the railing. There was a hollow feeling in the pit of my stomach as I looked down to the terrace below and saw the cracks in the pavement radiating out from the point of impact, right where Trisha had been standing, the crimson halo of her blood still evident. I was relieved not to have to see her lying there.

I was just about to turn away when something stopped me. I'd had this feeling before, the feeling I was being watched. I turned and screamed when I saw him in the shadows on the balcony, leaning up against the house.

"Shh." He moved forward. "Do you want to wake the whole house?"

"Matt! You scared me to freaking death. What are you doing here?"

"Same thing you are, I suspect. Did you find anything?"

"I can't see a thing and I don't know what I'm looking for if I could."

He produced a flashlight, which he switched on and aimed at the spot where the vase had been. "Look."

I did. There was a circle of dirt in the middle of the light's beam—an outline of where the vase had sat on top of the concrete railing for many years. And a line of scratch marks leading along the top of the railing for a couple of feet, almost where Ethan and I had been standing and bullseye where Trisha had been.

I had the sickest feeling in my stomach, not the fearful hollowness from before, but a cramping, nauseating feeling that made me sick all over. That vase hadn't just slipped or fallen. It had been pushed. By someone.

"Trisha was standing right below us," I whispered. "Someone killed that girl."

"You were standing right there too, weren't you? How do you know that wasn't meant for you? Or Ethan?"

I looked at him. "What are you talking about?"

"I don't know. It's just too much of a coincidence." He hesitated. "I don't like the way this looks, Jess. Maybe you should think about leaving."

"What is it with you people? You're the second person who's made that suggestion tonight."

"Let me guess—Dan?"

"Yes, Dan. Why am I such a threat to have around?"

"You're not to me. Maybe you're not to anyone. But something's going on around here and until we know what really happened, we shouldn't take any chances."

"I'm going back to bed." I turned away.

"I'll walk you back."

We walked back down the hallway. "Thanks," I said and he left me at my door.

Once in my room, I locked the bedroom door and fell asleep with the light on.

FOUR

WHEN I AWOKE the next morning at nine, there was a shaft of sunlight wedging its way through the slit in the curtains.

I was very stiff in some places, but my knee felt better. The reflection in the bathroom mirror showed the skin under my right eye was dark and bruised.

As I stood in the warm shower, letting it work its magic on my aching muscles, I wondered if Matt had told Ethan about the evidence he'd found on the balcony the night before and if anyone had called the sheriff back. I tried to convince myself there must be other reasonable explanations for the falling vase. I just couldn't come up with any. Was Ethan's new book really such a threat to someone they would consider an action so drastic? And was the life of an innocent young woman the price to be paid for their protection? None of it made sense to me. I needed to know more about the twenty-year-old murder to find out whether what happened to Trisha was related. I needed to talk to Ethan.

I wrapped my knee, slipped on a pair of jeans and a tan sweater, applied some camouflaging makeup under my eye and headed for the dining room.

John and Jolene were lingering over coffee. She was laughing at something he'd said.

"Morning, Jess." John smiled over his cup. He looked none the worse for the night before.

They both seemed in good spirits, and I wondered if Trisha's death would even put a hiccup in the lives of these people.

Jolene watched me as I took a seat across from John.

"There's coffee here, and Millie's been keeping your breakfast warm for you." He lifted a little silver bell and rang it.

Millie, the short plump woman who had announced dinner last night, came scurrying from the kitchen.

"Jess is ready for her breakfast, Millie," John told her.

"Of course." She smiled at me before she hurried away.

"Where's Ethan?" I asked.

"He ate hours ago," John told me. "I think he's in his office with Dan."

"What about Matt?"

"My, aren't we the nosy one," Jolene said.

"Matt's probably out doing battle with the dandelions," John said.

Millie was back in seconds and put my plate before me then reached over and filled a cup with hot black coffee. "Just let me know if you need anything else, dear."

I looked at the heaping plate, piled high with scrambled eggs, several strips of bacon, toast and an orange slice and wondered how much she thought I ate. "This is fine. Thanks, Millie."

She patted my shoulder and left me to attack my breakfast.

I was polishing off the last of the eggs and finishing my second cup of coffee when I tried to bring up the subject of last night. The reporter in me was ready to begin questions.

I reached for the coffeepot. "This is a big house. I'm surprised any of you heard what happened last night on the terrace. Where exactly were you when the vase fell?"

John glanced at the table for a second, but Jolene narrowed her eyes at me. For all her outward glitz and apparent shallowness, she wasn't a stupid woman. She knew a demand for an alibi when she heard one.

"I was in my room, talking on the phone. My room is in the back wing." John pointed to the long wing of the house, part of which was visible through the French doors. "My windows open onto the terrace side of the house. I heard you scream and dropped the phone. I heard the crash before I was even out of my room. Sounds really carry around here, especially on a still night."

"I was in my room, too." Jolene's jaw was tight. "It's down the hall from yours."

That was a long distance for sound to carry on a spring evening, when the house had probably been shut up for the night.

"I know what you're thinking," Jolene said, "and I don't have to put up with this. I had no reason to want to hurt Trisha. No one does."

She glared at me for several seconds then huffed out of the room.

Oh, yes, Jolene wasn't a stupid woman. She was a force to be reckoned with. I looked up.

John was studying me. "I understand your questions, but let's keep this in perspective. There was a terrible accident last night. That's all it was—a terrible accident. If you're going to start looking for monsters, you're just going to make yourself crazy and make everyone else mad as hell. Besides, Jolene is a bearcat. I'd hate to see you tangle with her."

Millie popped her head through the doorway to tell John he had a phone call.

He stood and winked at me. "Let's go out sometime. I've got plans for tonight, but let's do it soon. I really think you'd have a good time. Think about it, okay?"

I nodded noncommittally and he left me alone. What a weird, uncomfortable situation this was turning out to be. And, again, in their eyes, Trisha was a nobody.

Millie came through the doorway to clear away my breakfast dishes. She was old enough to be matronly, but she had a smooth healthy complexion and thick blonde-graying hair, cut short and softly framing the outline of her face. She began stacking dishes. "Can I get you anything else, dear?"

"No thanks. Do you know where Ethan is?"

"He's in his office with Dan. They had breakfast in there. I think they were having a conference call with Ethan's publisher."

"Do you take care of this house all by yourself?"

"I've always had a couple of girls from town come out a few mornings a week to do the heavy cleaning. Back when the boys were young and Ethan had company almost every week, I usually had someone full-time to help."

"Millie, did you hear about what happened last night?"

Her eyes started to well up. "Oh, yes, that was dreadful, just dreadful. That poor, sweet girl." Well, at least someone in the house had the decency to acknowledge Trisha's passing appropriately.

I waited as she took a tissue from her pocket and

dabbed at her eyes. "Did you know Trisha had been helping Ethan on a book he's writing about the Rawlings murder?"

"No, I hadn't heard that. Why would he want to write about that?"

I didn't really have an answer. "I suppose he thinks it's important."

Tears came to her eyes again. "That was a terrible time. My husband, Paul, was the groundskeeper back then. I don't think he ever got over it. I don't think any of us were ever the same."

She shook her head. "It's a mistake to go dredging up the past. You only end up hurting people." She gathered up the dishes and retreated to the kitchen.

I APPROACHED ETHAN'S office and knocked.

"Come in!" he bellowed.

Sunlight blinded my first look into his sanctuary as I pushed open the door. Through squinted eyes, I could make him out behind a massive, ornate mahogany desk.

"Come on in and take a seat," he said. "Dan and I were just getting caught up on some work."

My sight cleared enough that I finally noticed Dan sitting in a chair off to one side.

Ethan still bore the Band-Aid covering the cut on his forehead and the Ace bandage wrapped around his arm. He studied my face. "How are you feeling this morning?"

"Okay, my knee is better and I'm a bit stiff." I took a seat across from him, ignoring Dan, which wasn't that hard.

I looked around the room. The walls were paneled in dark oak and large windows looked out across the front lawn. French doors to one side opened onto a small garden that led to the portico in the driveway. The office held big comfortable furniture—a number of over-stuffed chairs that matched the mahogany desk in bulk. A monitor and keyboard sat on Ethan's desk. Behind it was a bookcase filled with awards—probably from back when Ethan could still call himself a writer. The wall on his left was covered with photographs of Ethan hobnobbing with various beautiful people.

"This is where I work," he said as if it were no big deal.

"It's a wonderful room." I met his gaze.

"Yes?"

"I was wondering if I could talk to you about last night. I want to call a story into the *Trib*."

"Already been done," he said.

"What? When?"

"Dan issued a news release late last night."

Something didn't feel right. I looked at Dan. "Is he a journalist now too?"

Dan snorted and Ethan leveled a glance in his direction. "I've told Dan to mind his manners. Why don't you give Jessie and me a few minutes? I'll call you when I need you."

Dan got up but, instead of heading toward the door, he moved toward one corner of the room. His hand slipped inside a bookcase, and the wall in front of him swung open. He disappeared into a chamber and the wall closed behind him.

I looked back at Ethan. "Secret passages? Really"

"This house was once part of the Underground Railroad. Slaves could be hidden back there, for days at a time. Then when the coast was clear, they would sneak off into the hills at night and continue their journey north. There's a circular stairway back there that leads up about half a flight—it's a floor built halfway between the first and second stories. In fact, your office will be up those stairs next to Dan's. There's a small bathroom up there now and a window. They weren't part of the original structure."

He watched me for a minute. "So, how are you really?"

"Concerned. Very concerned. Did you talk to Matt about what he found on the balcony last night?"

"Yes. And I'm not happy about the fact he got you all worked up about it."

"There was some very real evidence there."

"Jessie, if I thought there was any real danger here, don't you think I would have called the sheriff back here immediately?"

"Those scratch marks on the railing didn't appear by themselves. Someone was out there last night and pushed that vase off the side of the balcony. Look what happened to Trisha. Someone is dead and a few feet more and it could have been us." I was trying to keep my voice under control. I didn't want Ethan to think I was some hysterical female. But hysteria was feeling a bit justified at the moment.

"I looked at the scratch marks last night and again this morning. Look at them again in good light. They're weathered. They've been there for years. Matt just discovered them last night."

"Then how did the vase fall?"

"The railing tilts. There's a slight downward slope to it. No one ever noticed it before because we had no need to look. Unfortunately, uh, the girl was in the wrong place at the wrong time. It was just one of those sad, weird, unpredictable accidents. You hear about them all the time and you don't really believe it until it happens to you."

Ethan was trying very hard to convince me. It was all very logical—and pat, as if he'd been prepared for my questions. Even though it made perfect sense, somewhere deep inside I didn't believe a word he said. Which opened the question, why was he trying to convince me?

"I'd still like to call in an article to the *Trib*."

He cocked his head to one side. "It's all been taken care of. Dan's very good at his job."

He watched my face for a while, as if trying to see whether he had worked his magic. Finally, he reached into the bottom desk drawer and produced a fat red folder. "Maybe you need something to get your mind off of what happened. Are you ready to get to work?"

We were switching gears. "Is that about the Rawlings case?"

"Yes. Trisha had been gathering preliminary information. It's as much as we had so far."

Finally—the girl had a name. "Tell me about the murder."

He rubbed a big hand across his forehead. "Bonnie Rawlings lived about three miles from here. Nice kid, a little boy-crazy maybe, but nice. She'd just graduated from high school two months earlier. She and Matt were engaged to be married."

"Really?" That put a new spin on things. And went a long way toward explaining the reactions at the dinner table the night before. Especially Matt's.

"Yes, I'm not sure exactly when that happened, though, to tell the truth. It was August when she was killed. Matt was home from college that month, but it was the first he'd been here since spring break."

"He didn't come home often?"

"He had a job at the university and stayed on after the end of the spring semester to get in as many hours as he could until summer school started. He was trying to graduate early and took summer classes too."

I picked up the folder and thumbed through old newspaper clippings. Trisha had been busy. "So, you hadn't seen Bonnie since Easter?"

"Oh no. She used to come up here all the time, even when Matt was gone. I don't think she had much of a home life. Just her mother and an older sister." Ethan walked over to the French doors, his back to me. He was silent for quite a while.

"Are you okay with this, Ethan?" I finally asked. "It's going to bring back a lot of unpleasant memories. Are you sure you want to pursue it?"

He shrugged, still looking off into the hills. "I don't see that I have much choice," he said, but I didn't think he was talking to me.

Had Trisha's death resurrected memories he'd never dealt with? I tried to pull him back to the facts, hoping some objectivity might help his mood. "Go on."

"What?"

"The day Bonnie was killed. Your version."

"Oh, yes. She'd been up here most of that morning then left for a couple of hours. I think she had to run some errands for her mother or something. Anyway, she came back sometime after lunch." He turned away from the window and was back with me again. "I got the impression she and Matt had had a fight. They weren't talking, and John and Hank went for a walk with Bonnie. I don't know where Matt was at the time."

"Were John and Bonnie close?"

"I'm not really sure. Knowing John, he could have been spending time with Bonnie just to get a rise out of his brother. I wouldn't put it past him."

"Did you ever find out what the fight was about?"

He looked confused for a moment.

"Between Bonnie and Matt."

"No, I never did."

"What happened next?"

"I wish I knew. The next thing I knew the sheriff's deputies came tearing up the driveway with their lights flashing and sirens blaring."

"Who called the sheriff?"

"I have no idea. Whoever it was didn't give his name."

"Go on."

"I went out to meet them. By the time I got to the guesthouse, they were hauling Tommy Markowski out from behind the cottage in handcuffs. Bonnie was inside, half naked, and dead." He let out a long breath, as if it been an exertion to tell it.

"Tommy Markowski was the young man arrested for the murder?"

"That's right." Ethan made his way over to his desk and sat down again. "But there was a lot of controversy surrounding the case. Some people in town thought Tommy was just a scapegoat."

"Was he? Do you have anyone else in mind?"

He didn't answer.

"Ethan?"

"I know you and Eric were close," he finally said. "He thought very highly of you."

Eric Amundson, Hank's father, owner and publisher of the *Omaha Tribune*, had been so much more than my boss. "Eric was like a second father to me," I said. "He gave me a job straight out of college and taught me everything I know about investigative reporting. But what does Eric have to do with this case?"

"Eric was my closest friend for most of my adult life. He knew me when I was struggling to get my first book published. Over the years, he saw me through everything from my divorces to bad press and lawsuits, even a few run-ins with the law. He was a true friend to me when I needed one. Always."

"Ethan, I don't see what this has to do—"

He held up his hand. "Eric was here when Bonnie Rawlings was murdered. He used to come down every August and December and spend a month at a time. John and Hank were home from school. Matt, as I told you, was here that month too."

He paused and I waited for him to go on, though I wasn't sure I liked the direction this was heading.

"There were so many questions surrounding the murder that were never answered. But, Eric and I…well, we never wanted to pursue the truth. We just didn't want to know what really happened here that day. We were afraid—"

"Afraid of what?" Then it hit me. "You were afraid one of the boys was guilty of murder. Matt, John, Hank."

"Yes. We did everything we could to protect them. What father wouldn't? We hustled John and Hank off to school as soon as we thought we could, without drawing suspicion. But, people were watching every move we made up here. In retrospect, it wasn't a wise move."

I took a deep breath. "Okay. I think I understand the situation better. But why, after all these years, did you finally decide to write a book about it?"

He removed a key from his pocket and opened the middle drawer of the desk, extracting an envelope from it.

"Shortly before Eric died, he made me promise to find the truth. We both knew we'd put it off too long. He wrote me this letter, soon after he found out his cancer was terminal." Ethan reached across the desk to hand the letter to me.

I took it and held it in my hands. I really didn't want to read a letter from Eric Amundson at that point in my life. I missed him too. My own loss throbbed all too often when I least expected it. I especially didn't want to read a letter written to Ethan Miller telling him that perhaps one of their sons was a murderer. And after last night—well, I was still shaken.

"Ethan," I said. "I hope you know what you're doing. It's one thing to set the record straight. It's quite another to publish it for the world to see. From what you're saying, Matt or John could be the guilty one."

He looked very old and very tired. "I know."

"Then you do realize what you'd be doing to them? Your book will be a bestseller just because of who you are. They'd be offered up for public crucifixion, and so would you, for hiding the truth for so long."

"That's pretty much what Dan said. But I have to do it. I promised Eric and it's time the truth was told."

"I hope you know what you're doing," I said again.

"So do I."

THE SPIRAL STAIRCASE ended in Dan's office. Given that it was hidden away in an odd corner of the house, it was a fair-sized room, with large windows on the east side and a small bathroom directly opposite the windows. I imagined the rooms as they must have been years ago and concluded their very concealment must have made the people hiding there feel safe for a while.

Dan was seated at his desk but didn't look up as I made my way through to the connecting office. It was smaller than Dan's, but cozier. It also had windows facing the east side of the house and the morning sun poured through.

Built-in bookshelves covered three walls. There was a small desk with a padded chair and a laptop on a separate stand beside the desk.

I sat down and opened the folder, feeling the warmth of the sun on my back. Trisha had made a good start in gathering research. The news clippings were yellowed with age but intact and sorted by date. A sadness settled over me, thinking of Trisha and realizing she would never have a shot at being the journalist she'd dreamed of becoming. I tried to push those thoughts away and started reading from the beginning.

As I read the newspaper articles, editorials and a few police reports, I began to understand Ethan's and Eric's reservations about the ultimate outcome of the case.

I booted up the laptop and started taking notes.

It was mid-August when Bonita Rawlings was found dead in the guesthouse on Ethan's estate. An unidentified man had called the sheriff's office at two fifteen p.m. to report the crime. The sheriff and deputies arrived shortly after two thirty.

Bonita had a cut on her forehead and some bruising

on her wrists and temple. Some of the furniture had been overturned in the room where the partially clad body was found. An autopsy discovered the presence of semen and that she died of strangulation.

Tommy Markowski, a twenty-eight-year-old man described as mentally challenged, was hiding behind the guesthouse, almost hysterical, when the police found him. His fingerprints were on some of the objects in the cottage.

The case seemed straightforward enough on the surface. Almost no legal defense was offered for Tommy. Initially he denied raping and killing the girl, but a later confession emerged, one that some thought was coerced. All the occupants of Ethan's house were questioned.

The editorials were typical in their reaction to such a brutal crime, demanding blood for blood, but wondering if the police were doing their utmost to solve the case or merely using Tommy as a defenseless scapegoat.

With no documented request for change of venue, Tommy was convicted at the county courthouse in Sedgewick. Due to his limitations, he was sentenced to five years at a state institution for the criminally insane, with the possibility of being paroled after that time to a residential facility for the developmentally delayed, based on his behavior. Given the apparent brutality of the crime, I got the impression the judge didn't quite believe in the conviction either.

Trisha had created a spreadsheet, naming all the people who had been in residence that day or on the estate. Next to each name was a column with the person's relationship to the murdered girl, and where each person was now. Empty cells and question marks filled the page. Still, it was a good start and I was impressed.

I leaned back, stretching the kinks out of my shoulders, postponing the inevitable. Eric's letter lay on the desk in front of me. The last thing I wanted to do was to read that letter.

In the past week, I'd thought of Eric and my father so many times I felt as if I'd picked the scab right off the raw tender skin of my emotions. The two men who'd made me what I was were gone, and I felt I needed them. That, perhaps, I always would.

I stood and looked out the window at the remarkable view, catching a glimpse of the small white cottage burrowed in the valley. The guesthouse. My view was partially blocked by the overhang of the portico, and I made my way into Dan's office. Dan was gone, but his windows offered a better view, the cottage totally visible from where I stood.

I went downstairs and entered Ethan's empty office through the paneled wall. The main hall was deserted as I walked through to the front door and out into the bright sunlight. It was one of those spring days that held a promise of things to come.

I found the flagstone path that led to the guesthouse, most of the stones half-hidden by encroaching grass.

The structure itself was sturdy, but time and neglect had left their mark. The white paint was peeling and the shutters and trim that had once been a bright Kelly green were now faded and sun-bleached. Barren flower beds surrounded the house. After Trisha's accident and reading about Bonnie's murder, Ethan's estate didn't seem like a very safe place for young women.

I jiggled the doorknob on the front door. Locked.

Stepping into the weedy flower bed, I put my face up against the dust-streaked window.

The curtains once had a floral pattern but were now faded nearly white. There were two love seats facing each other across an oval coffee table, a blue armchair and a wooden rocking chair. A stone fireplace was on the outside wall to my right.

"Millie has the keys if you want to look inside. Or do you prefer peeking into windows?"

I jumped at the familiar voice. "Probably not as much as you enjoy sneaking up on people." I turned to face Matt.

He was dressed in his work clothes, jeans and a denim shirt.

Satan came sniffing around the side of the cottage and, at the sight of me, bounded forward, wagging his tail. I braced myself against the building as his front paws landed on my shoulders and he covered my face with slobbery kisses. I laughed and began to rub his ears.

Matt snapped his fingers and Satan obediently sat at my feet, a look of utter adoration in his big brown eyes.

"Good boy." I crouched down to his eye level and slipped my arm around his shoulders. He leaned into me, resting his heavy head against my shoulder, his tail thumping in the dirt. Doggie hugs. He was a bright spot in an otherwise maudlin morning.

Matt shook his head. "He's hopeless."

Satan looked up at Matt, oblivious to the criticism, then sank his head back into my shoulder. It was all I could do to keep my balance.

Eventually, I pushed him away and struggled to my feet. "Where did you two come from?"

"We were up in the greenhouse." He gestured off to his left. "I was working and saw you heading down here."

Up in the direction Matt was pointing and over another rise was the top half of a large, commercial-looking greenhouse.

"Do you want to see it?" he asked.

"Sure."

We moved up the hill, with Satan prancing along at my side.

"How do you feel this morning?" Matt finally asked.

"Not too badly, I guess, a little stiff and my knee isn't as bad as I thought it would be. I just can't believe how the death of a young woman seems to have so little effect on everyone here. Ethan was eager to dismiss the evidence you showed him last night."

"I expected that." He didn't elaborate.

We reached the door to the greenhouse and stepped through the doorway into a glass world that simply breathed life. The humidity in the enclosed building was at least eighty percent. The air smelled green and rich, new-mown lawn after a rainstorm rich. I noticed the plants were all cash crops—corn, tomatoes, green beans and peas—and that they all rested in long, narrow troughs of water.

"Hydroponics?" I asked.

"Yes. It's for some research I'm doing for the Department of Agriculture, although Ethan is currently bankrolling everything."

"The Department of Agriculture? As in the federal government?"

"Yeah, that one. I teach at the University of Missouri at Columbia, but my first love is research—biotechnology. I have my doctorate in Biochemistry and Plant Pathology.

Ethan talked me into taking a year's sabbatical here so I could work on some of my projects."

I already knew all of that, but Matt didn't need to know how thoroughly I'd researched his family during my week of unemployment.

He went on to explain his research in great detail, with an enthusiasm I couldn't have imagined coming from Matt Wheaton. It involved hydroponics and hybrid plants and gene splicing and things too technical to understand in a few minutes' time.

"This is designed to give the farmer more control over his produce. He won't be as dependent on the whims of the weather, and it will result in more efficient land usage. Ultimately, it will be good for the consumer too. It will provide more nutritious produce at a lower price."

While Matt was talking, Satan wandered up and down the long rows, sniffing here and there, occasionally pouncing on a ray of sunlight that moved as it filtered through a tree outside.

Matt looked down as Satan sidled up to us. "It's probably about time for lunch. Why don't you go ahead, I have a few things to finish up."

I was reluctant to leave, although I wasn't sure why. Maybe I felt safe in the cocoon of glass or cleansed by the healthy growing plants who knew nothing of murders or rapes or mysterious accidents.

Satan followed me to the door and stood for a moment when he looked back and realized Matt wasn't coming. He looked back and forth between us then left me to follow Matt.

The air outside felt chilling as it cooled the humidity on my skin. I was halfway to the house when John intercepted me.

"Millie sent me to find you. Where have you been?"

"The greenhouse."

"Oh. Brother Matt was showing off his science project again. I hope he didn't bore you."

"No. It was really quite impressive. You don't think much of your half-brother, do you?"

"On the contrary. I think he's intelligent and quite capable of anything." He glanced at me then we walked the rest of the way in silence.

FIVE

It wasn't until the middle of the afternoon as I was going over the file again in my office, that it dawned on me I hadn't seen Hank or Glenda all day.

The small office was so hidden in the depths of the house, that once the noon sun had reached its zenith, the room got very little natural light. A few clouds were forming in the sky and I switched on a desk lamp to keep reading. If nothing else, Bonnie Rawlings was keeping my mind off of Trisha Chatsworth.

According to the police report, everyone in the house had been questioned. Ethan, Matt and John; Hank and Eric Amundson; Millie and her husband, Paul Gunderson, the former groundskeeper, were all interrogated. The police got nothing. No one admitted to finding the body or calling the police. But with Tommy Markowski already in custody, the officer in charge didn't press matters. Nor did he bother with alibis.

The autopsy revealed Bonita was two months pregnant.

Putting the folder back on the desk, I picked up the envelope that held Eric's letter, turning it over in my hands.

"You shouldn't have left me," I said out loud, feeling again the overwhelming betrayal of loss.

I slid my finger under the flap and extracted a single piece of white paper. Eric's cramped, erratic handwriting covered the page. I took a deep breath.

Ethan, what we've pretended these past months wouldn't happen to me—finally has. I'm dying. The doctor says three months, but I'm not sure I'll make it that long.

I've tried to clean up all the loose ends of my business affairs and personal life, but you and I both know that with time running out for me, we need to take care of the past.

Help me with this, old friend. I've never asked you for anything before, but I am now.

I won't be here long enough to see this thing through. You're going to have to carry the burden alone and I'm sorry for that.

But it has to be done. Now. We both know it. We've let this go on too long. Promise me you'll make things right.

—Eric.

I tucked the letter away in its envelope and secured it under the corner flap of my desk blotter, determined not to cry.

I glanced at the envelope. I could hear Eric saying those words out loud. I could almost hear him saying them to me. I got up and headed into the bathroom, letting cold water from the faucet overflow into my cupped hands. I splashed some on my face and reached for an embroidered hand towel hanging from a stainless-steel rack on the wall. There would be nothing easy about what lay ahead.

But Eric was right. It had to be done. I knew beyond a doubt that this was where Ethan had faltered. That what happened twenty years ago had taken its toll on his writing, and his life. And somewhere inside of me,

I knew Trisha's research had made someone very nervous, no matter what Ethan said. And I couldn't let that girl's death be pushed to the side.

I wanted so much to be the person who finally found the truth about what happened to Bonnie Rawlings. Part of me knew the reporter in me was itching to find the answers—to investigate this story in a way it obviously hadn't been looked at before. But I also knew there was something deeper igniting those feelings. Trisha and Bonnie deserved justice. And if Tommy Markowski had indeed been a scapegoat, then someone needed to speak for him.

I wanted to do this for Ethan too, hoping to help him get his life and his writing back on track. And I wanted to do it for Eric, to prove to him that all the faith he'd had in me, was not unfounded. He'd taught me well, and I wanted, somehow, to show him.

When I emerged from the bathroom, Jolene was just coming out of my office.

"I've been looking for you. Ethan wants you downstairs right away."

"Okay."

She followed me back into the office and watched while I switched off the lamp. For some reason, it felt like a violation to have her there. I headed for the doorway, hoping she would get the hint and follow.

She did. "How can you stand it up here?" she asked, as we moved into Dan's office.

"It's quiet and out of the way." I stepped back to let her go ahead of me down the narrow stairs.

"What are you so dressed up for?" I asked Jolene. "Are you going out?"

"We're on our way to a dinner party. There's not much nightlife around here, so you have to grab the action when you can. God! I've always hated this place. I've been trying to talk Ethan into buying a place in Malibu. I think I almost have him convinced."

She stopped at the bottom of the stairs and turned to look at me, her tinted blue eyes examining my face for a response. Like she was sizing me up. For someone so apparently intelligent, she didn't seem to realize I was merely a temporary fixture. She had nothing to worry about from me.

Jolene was a beautiful woman. Her perfectly sculpted features were striking. I looked closely for telltale signs of a surgeon's touch. No one was born with that much perfection. I suspected Ethan wouldn't mind that the beauty came with a price.

Ethan was sitting in the front parlor with a middle-aged man and woman. I knew immediately they were Trisha's parents, the woman an older version of her daughter, even wearing the same dark-rimmed glasses that slid down her nose.

Ethan, clearly uncomfortable, stood when I entered the room. "Jessie, these are…"

I could tell he was searching, once again, for her name.

"Trisha's parents." I moved forward to shake their hands. "I'm so very sorry for your loss. I only just met your daughter, but she was a lovely girl and was ambitious about her writing."

I shook her father's strong calloused hand. "Thank you," he said in a low voice. "I'm Greg and this is my wife, Rhonda."

I took Rhonda's hand. Understandably, she was having a difficult time holding back her tears.

"I'm so sorry," I said again.

"Thank you." She pressed a tissue to her mouth.

Ethan looked at me. "I was just going to take Greg up to get, uh, his daughter's things. Millie has them all packed up. Maybe you could stay here with Rhonda, while we go upstairs."

Interesting that the job of grief counselor was given to me and not Jolene, as Ethan must have known Jolene wouldn't be of much comfort to a distraught parent.

"Of course."

He looked relieved then turned to Jolene. "We need to leave soon. I hope you're ready to go."

Rhonda and I were alone in the room. I sat next to her on the couch. "This must be so incredibly difficult for you."

She nodded.

"Did Trisha tell you what she and Ethan had been working on?"

Rhonda nodded again and cleared her throat. "She said she was helping Mr. Miller with some research for a book he was writing about an old murder case. At first, she was thrilled, working with a best-selling author, but she started to get bored after a while, which is pretty much what Trisha did about most things." A very small smile appeared on her lips.

"That's understandable. An old murder case might not be of much interest to a girl her age."

Rhonda's gaze darted around the room. I'm not sure what or who she was looking for, but when she was satisfied that we were alone, she leaned in closely. "I think there was more going on than Trisha realized."

"I don't understand."

She scanned the room again, leaned over and took hold of my hand. "Trisha kept me up to date on what she was doing for Mr. Miller—about the book and all.

I was trying to encourage her to keep going," Rhonda said, "because it would be, you know, good experience and everything."

"Uh-huh." I wasn't sure where this was headed, but it was important for her to say.

"Anyway, it really wasn't very interesting, but when she told me someone had gone through her files, that got my attention."

"Maybe it was Ethan."

"No. She asked him. And one of the things she had in her files was a receipt that she thought was connected to the murder somehow, and all of a sudden it was missing."

"What kind of receipt?"

"I'm not sure, but she thought it meant something. And then, all this weird stuff started happening." Her hand tightened its grip on mine.

I wasn't sure what to make of her, the investigative reporter in me kicked in and I wanted to hear this story. "What sort of weird stuff are we talking about?"

"She went into town a couple of times and thought she was being followed. When she called me from the house phone, I was sure I heard breathing on the line."

I couldn't tell if this was real or not, but after what happened to her daughter, I was willing to give her the benefit of the doubt. "I can understand those things would be concerning."

She moved in closer. "I think my daughter was murdered, Jessica."

The little hairs on the back of my neck stood up. Finally. Someone was sensing what I thought too.

"Maybe you should talk to the sheriff."

She rolled her eyes. "We already did."

"When?"

"I made Greg stop there before we came up here. Sheriff Stevenson is an ass. He wouldn't listen to a word I said. Told me Trisha's death had already been ruled an accident."

"What does your husband think?"

"He thinks I'm hysterical."

We heard Ethan and Greg moving down the stairs.

Her grip tightened, cutting off what little blood flow there was to the tips of my fingers. "Please, Jessica," she whispered. "If someone murdered my daughter, I want that person to pay for it."

Her desperation struck a chord. And, yes, Sheriff Stevenson was an ass.

"Please," she said again.

"I'll do what I can." I answered.

Ethan and Greg walked into the room.

"We'd best be going," Greg said to his wife then turned to Ethan and shook his hand. "Thank you, Ethan."

Ethan was at a loss.

I jumped in. For some reason, this had become my role. "When is the funeral?"

Greg looked at his shoes, blinking back tears. "Tuesday."

After they'd gone, Ethan walked into the front hall, bellowing for Jolene.

"Are you ready to go yet? It's an hour's drive, you know," he said when she appeared.

"I know, I know! Do you mind if I get my purse and jacket?"

"Well, hurry up," he said to her retreating back then turned to me. "Sorry to be leaving you alone tonight, but we made these plans weeks ago. I hope you can find

something to do. I think John's going out, but Hank
and Glenda and Dan will be here. Matt too, probably."

Oh goody. "I'll be fine. Have a good time. Don't
worry about me."

The smile he gave me slid right off his face as Jolene
returned, her three-inch heels clicking across the tiled
floor.

"Good night, Jessie," he said over his shoulder as
he followed Jolene outside. Whatever he snapped at
her was indistinguishable as the door slammed shut
behind him.

I made it to the parlor in time for cocktails and found
Hank and Glenda already there. Each held a drink and
occupied a chair at opposite corners of the long room.
I almost fled.

The two of them were barely tolerable on a good day.
If they were both as moody as they seemed, I'd be ready
for the booby hatch before dessert arrived.

I poured myself a stiff drink, looked at my glass,
glanced at the other two people in the room and made
it a double. Glenda watched me behind hooded eyes as
I seated myself on the couch by the front window and
forced a smile at Hank.

"What have you two been up to today?" I said in my
best attempt at polite conversation.

"Why do you want to know?" Glenda asked.

Okay… I shrugged. "No reason."

Hank snorted; an innocent grin overtook his features. "We've been up to no good," he said and I knew
exactly what he'd been doing for the past hour. Getting drunk. And doing it well, from the looks of things.

"What do you mean by *no good*, Hank?" I asked,
more to see Glenda's reaction than anything.

She shot him a warning glare, but he didn't seem to be paying any attention to her.

"That's for me to know and you to find out." He giggled—it wasn't a pretty sight—and downed his drink.

At this rate, I didn't think I'd even make it to dessert. Matt's arrival would actually be a relief.

As if on cue, Matt sauntered in, looked around and poured himself a drink. He took a chair in a far corner and surveyed the room with a slight smile in his eyes. Then Dan made his appearance and almost bolted when he saw what a convivial group we were.

Matt chuckled when Dan turned and realized the only available seating accommodation was on the couch next to me.

He sat down primly, crossing his legs and straightening the crease in his pants, then looked hopefully at Hank, unaware that Hank was in his own happy place.

"Gee, this is fun," Matt said.

"You'll never find out, you'll never find out. Ha, ha, ha, ha, ha, ha," Hank sung to himself, although I couldn't quite make out the tune, then he grinned at me. Oh yeah, good times.

Dan watched Hank in horrified fascination then turned helplessly toward me.

"It's some big secret what he did today," I explained. "Apparently, I'll *never find out*."

"Oh, shut up, Hank!" Glenda snapped.

"Glenda doesn't like you," Hank said to me. "She says you're bad."

It finally occurred to me this social purgatory was actually an opportunity. Always ask your questions when their guard is down. "Why am I bad, Hank?"

Hank looked into his glass, as if the answer was written there. "Oh, you've done many, many bad things."

"Like what, for instance?"

In the months I'd known Glenda, I'd been very aware I wasn't one of her favorite people, but I had no idea she'd formed such an opinion of me.

The silly grin was replaced by a childish pout. "She says you never ever liked me and you didn't want me to have my newspaper or any money. And… Glenda says you're going to make Ethan write bad things about us."

Things were looking up. "What kind of things could I make Ethan write, Hank? He just wants to tell the truth."

"But he doesn't know the truth. Nobody does. Well, almost nobody."

I willed my face straight. This was the money question. "Do you know the truth, Hank?"

A sloppy smile spread across his face and he put his finger to his lips. "I'll never tell," he whispered and laughed maniacally.

Millie popped her head through the doorway to tell us dinner was ready and Hank lumbered unsteadily to his feet and headed for the dining room. And there went my opportunity for further questioning.

Matt managed the wine at dinner, pouring sparing amounts into Hank's glass and when Hank wasn't looking, filling it the rest of the way with water. We ate in silence for a while, everyone doing their best to ignore Hank, who was becoming increasingly boisterous as he swung between wild euphoria and deep melancholy. I found it telling—there was something deeply wrong here, and the alcohol was just bringing it out. It made for an awkward meal.

The strain of avoiding interaction with Hank finally grew so great Dan turned to me for an attempt at conversation. "Did you have a chance to go over Trisha's file?" He placed one hand over the top of his wineglass to protect it from the ripe olives Hank was lobbing at it.

"I started. She did a good job, but there's a lot of information to cover. The newspaper articles were helpful, but there are other reports and records I want to get copies of. I'll probably have to go into town on Monday. And there are people I would like to talk to."

"There are a few questions I'd like to ask." Hank rose to his feet. He tried to grasp invisible coat lapels, in a pathetic imitation of Spencer Tracy's Clarence Darrow in *Inherit the Wind*. Since he wasn't wearing a jacket, he settled for his shirtfront that was open several buttons at the neck. His hands pulled the shirt open wider, revealing an appallingly white, hairless chest.

Glenda grabbed for his arm. "Hank, you're making a fool of yourself."

He sidestepped her and Matt jumped up to catch him before he went crashing to the floor.

He righted himself and stepped away from the table. "As I was saying, I have a few questions of my own. Matt, just exactly how close were you to the lovely Miss Bonnie?"

"Sit down, Hank," Matt said. "This isn't the time or the place."

Hank turned toward Dan. "Mr. Ketner…may I call you Mr. Ketner? Just exactly where were you when the lovely Miss Bonnie lost her life on the day in question? And, for that matter, where was I?"

This produced another laughing fit from Hank, who collapsed into his chair with a thud, guffawing hysterically. Matt grabbed the chair before it went over backward.

"Dan, a little help?" Matt took Hank by an arm. Dan went around the table and grasped the other one. Between the two of them, they got Hank to his feet.

"Hey, where're we going?" he asked as they turned him around.

We could hear Hank protesting all the way out into the hall.

Glenda and I were alone.

"Hank sure makes things interesting," I said.

"He drinks too much and makes a fool of himself." She stood up. "I'm tired. I think I'll go to bed now."

It was only eight. What was I supposed to do for the rest of the night?

Millie smiled at me as she came through the door and started clearing the table. "Have you had enough, dear?"

"Yes, thanks." I'd had three helpings of lasagna, a salad and garlic bread. Just how much would I have to eat before she'd be satisfied? "You sure put in long hours, don't you?"

"Oh, I don't mind. Everyone here is like my family. I enjoy taking care of them."

"Do you have any children?"

"No. I guess that's why being around those boys when they were growing up was a joy for both Paul and me."

"I'll bet you have some great stories. What were they like growing up?"

"Matt lived with his mother most of the time. But he spent a lot of time here in the summers, following Paul around everywhere, asking a million questions, doing everything Paul did. I think Paul was as proud as

Ethan was when Matt graduated from college and went on to get his doctorate. I've never seen a boy work so hard. When he was at the university, he went to summer school every year—just coming home for semester breaks."

I started helping her pile plates onto the butler's cart. "And John?"

"Now, that one was a rascal, always playing tricks and just being all boy."

"All boy" was one way to put it. "Do you enjoy working for Ethan?"

"Oh, yes, and Paul did too. There isn't anything Paul wouldn't have done for him. These last ten years, since I've been alone, Ethan's been so good to me. He takes care of his own, Ethan does."

"If you want to hear the virtues of the Millers, just ask Millie," Matt said from the doorway. He was leaning up against the doorframe, his hands stuck deep in his pockets. The teasing grin could not hide the genuine affection in his eyes as he watched Millie.

"Oh, go on with you," she said. "I should have told her the truth that you were a horrid little boy who used to steal my cherry pies."

"Once I stole a pie, only once. And Ethan let me have it good, after you told on me."

"That pie was for company," she said as if he were still twelve.

"Millie, you have a very selective memory. You think that we were just mischievous little boys and nothing bad ever happened here."

The light went out of her eyes. "That's the way I like to remember it. And who's to say it's not the truth?" She turned and wheeled the cart into the kitchen.

Matt took the chair at the end of the table and sat, stretching his long legs out in front of him.

"Millie's special." His voice was surprisingly wistful. "She only sees the good in people, even us."

"It's nice to have someone like that on your side."

"I guess. It'd be nicer to deserve it. What are your plans for tomorrow?"

"I haven't any."

"Sundays around here are usually casual. If you'd like to go exploring, there's a whole group of caves about two miles from here. There are legends that they're all connected by hidden passageways and the original owner of the estate was so eccentric that he hid his fortune out there somewhere. When we were kids, we explored every inch of them. That we could find."

He told me about the trail and how beautiful it was in the spring, and I told him I would like to see them. Anything was better than spending the day with Hank and Glenda, or sitting around wondering what really happened to Trisha Chatsworth.

Millie agreed to pack us a picnic lunch, and I wondered if either of us would be strong enough to carry all the food Millie would think we'd need. Matt told me to meet him at his place at ten the next morning, then he said good night and left me alone.

I wandered into the parlor though the room was depressingly somber and all I could think of was the night before and Trisha lying on the terrace, so I made my way to bed.

AT TEN MINUTES TO TEN the next morning, Millie had me loaded down like a packhorse. I was dressed in jeans, a denim shirt and hiking boots. Millie made me go back to my room for a sweater ("you never know"), loaned me a hat ("to protect your pretty complexion from the sun") and helped me into a backpack that weighed about ten pounds ("I hope I packed enough food"). Then she pointed me in the direction of Matt's cabin and hustled me out the door so I wouldn't be late.

The sun was out in an inspiringly clear sky, and a warm gentle breeze was ruffling the lawn. I went out the front door and followed the path past the greenhouse. Matt's place wasn't far from the main house but secluded enough to offer some privacy. It was a one-story, made of cedar logs, with a huge picture window and a deck that ran the entire perimeter of the house. Window boxes and planters were overflowing with growing things, and the view from the front was fantastic. I climbed the three steps to the deck and knocked on the door.

"Come on in," he yelled from the other side.

I shouldn't have been surprised at the welcome I got as the door swung open. I got a brief glimpse of Matt seated in a recliner lacing his boots before Satan had me pressed against the door, licking my face.

"Oh, yes, you're a good boy," I said. "Now get down."

He obeyed instantly.

I began scratching his left ear, and he leaned into my hand, closed his eyes, and made small grunting noises. "I don't know why he gets so excited every time he sees me."

"Neither do I."

I looked up in time to see the smile on Matt's face.

He grabbed a jacket off the hook by the front door and patted the pack on my back. "Millie's done it again. Do you want me to take that thing?"

I was about to enter into some asinine feminist oration about my capabilities but realized my shoulders were already starting to go numb. I slipped it off and helped him readjust the straps and put it on his back.

He snapped his fingers and Satan bobbed out the door. Matt closed it behind us and led the way to the trail.

The dirt track wound its way over hill and dale, up and down and up again, but mostly up it seemed. I was huffing and puffing, trying to keep pace with Matt's long strides. I had no complaints that he'd relieved me of the backpack.

He knew every plant that grew in the area, pointing out goldenrod, milkweed, sweet William, columbine and verbena. The sun was strong enough that I took off Millie's "you never know" sweater and tied the arms around my waist. Satan ran ahead of us on the trail then back again, covering three times the distance we did.

Eventually, the path grew only wide enough to walk single file, with dark close-growing brush on either side. I kept a constant eye out for anything that might decide to spring at me from amongst the wild flowers and weeds. We were in snake country, and I was utterly phobic about them. I wished my hiking boots covered about six more inches of leg.

A grasshopper took it upon himself to jump in the trail in front of me and then fly in my face.

I let out a strangled scream and was immediately embarrassed when Matt turned around to see me prying the insect off of my nose. There was a glint of amusement in his eyes, but he restrained from comment.

"Maybe you'd like to rest for a while," he said.

"How much farther is it?"

"About ten minutes."

"No. Let's keep going."

We were there in almost no time. I'd spent so much time looking at the ground that I was oblivious to the mountains of stone ahead until they were almost upon me, huge rock formations jutting out of the hillside. The gaping hole of the entrance showed nothing but darkness.

"Is this safe?" I asked.

"Safe as houses. Come on."

He took my hand and led me inside. As we passed beyond the fringe of foliage that rimmed the entrance, the outside insect noise died away. The stillness was disorienting. Switching on the flashlight, we looked around. The floor near the opening was covered with something foul.

"Guano," Matt said. "Bat droppings."

Great. Bats and snakes. I was ready to turn back, but he gripped my hand tightly and pulled me along.

There was a long, dark shaft of corridor that was about sixty feet deep, at which point we came to a fork, offering two choices. Matt turned left, explaining that the bats congregated in the other chamber. Satan stayed by our sides the whole time, not venturing off as he did in the meadow outside. Either he sensed my nervousness or had some of his own. Once we'd cleared the corner to our left, we lost what little daylight filtered in from the mouth of the cave.

The walls near the opening had been cool and dry. The farther entombed we became, the clammier the walls were, and from somewhere I could hear the gurgle of water.

Matt had to use both hands, one to hold the flashlight, the other to feel his way along. Satan and I were right on his heels, my breath coming in short strained gasps, no longer from exertion but from the beginnings of claustrophobia.

The second hallway led us to an inner room, at least twelve by fourteen feet. The ceiling was high enough for Matt to stand up comfortably. A small stream of water creased the floor.

"This is it," he said.

"This is what?"

"Our old fort. This is where we used to play when we were kids. Pretty great, isn't it?"

I couldn't agree. It was dark and clammy and creepy. Maybe you had to be a ten-year-old boy to appreciate the ambiance.

"You don't like it here?"

I shook my head.

"Oh. Oh well. Come on then."

Near the far wall was a huge rock jutting out of the ground, hiding another opening across the room.

Matt slipped through it, followed by Satan and then, reluctantly, me. About thirty feet down the hallway I smelled fresh air. Another thirty feet and another corner, and sunlight flooded in an opening in the wall. We emerged into warmth and fresh air and I breathed deeply, shedding the anxiety that had engulfed me in the caves. We were at a deep bubbling pond surrounded by sand and trees and rocks at our backs.

"Hot springs," Matt said. "Do you want to take a dip?"

I shook my head. "I don't think so."

Millie had neglected to pack me a bathing suit.

The setting was beautiful and relaxing, and we had

a leisurely lunch in the shade. Satan spent most of the time retrieving sticks that Matt threw in the water and splashing around on his own while we ate. It was almost two by the time we were packed up and ready to go.

I was more than a little relieved when he said we would take the long way back, bypassing the caves. The trek back was longer, but easier, mostly downhill, and we took our time, stopping once to finish off Millie's iced tea.

As we approached the house, Matt grew silent and thoughtful, as if he were shedding his personality the closer we got to home. All my attempts at conversation fell on deaf ears. By the time we arrived at his cabin, I'd had enough of being ignored and was grateful to head back to the main house alone.

Opening the door onto the front hallway, I thought I might talk to Ethan before getting cleaned up for dinner. I lifted my hand to knock just as his office door swung open. Glenda let out a shriek of surprise.

"I was just coming to see Ethan," I said.

Hank moved in behind her, blocking the doorway.

"We were just looking for him too," Glenda said. "He's not here."

I thought of pushing past them to see what they were up to but figured I'd get it out of Hank after he'd been to the bar a few times. "Okay. I guess I'll see him at dinner." I turned and walked away.

John caught me at the top of the stairs. "You look wholesome."

"I've just been to the caves." I turned toward my room.

"I know." John stepped in front of me. "Matt seems to be taking up a lot of your time, doesn't he?"

It was a testimony to his charm that he managed to do this without seeming threatening. But the Miller charm, I was quickly learning, was hiding something else beneath the surface.

"Well, it was just something to do," I said.

"That seems to be where he takes all his women."

"Am I supposed to be jealous?"

"*Careful* would be a better word."

"John, *what* are you talking about?"

"Did Ethan tell you Matt was out in the caves with Bonnie the day she was killed?"

"No. Why are *you* telling me this?"

"I thought you might need to know. For your own safety."

"I'll say it again, John, *what* are you talking about?"

"I overheard them out there that day. They were having a terrible argument."

If he wanted to feed me information, I could play along. "What were they arguing about?"

"I think that's when she told him she was pregnant. Matt was livid. From the sound of his voice I was sure he was going to hit her."

I still wasn't sure what John's motivation for this story was. "*Did* he hit her?"

"No—not then, at least—but he said a baby wasn't going to spoil his plans. He wasn't going to quit college, and Bonnie would have to figure out what to do about the baby herself."

When I didn't take the bait any further, John bent down and whispered in my ear, "I told you, Jess, my brother is an intelligent man—capable of many things."

SIX

I THINK I was relieved when Matt didn't show up for dinner that night and not entirely sure why. In fact, I was relieved not to have to interact much with anyone. The trip to the caves had been a good diversion, but there was a cloud hanging over me every time I thought of poor Trisha Chatsworth. And, sadly, it appeared that I was the only one affected by what had happened. I sat at the table while Hank and Glenda pretended I was invisible. Dan and John had both gone into town, and Jolene was in such a foul mood, Ethan spent the entire meal trying to placate her.

After an interminable dinner, Hank started to stand up.

"Trisha's funeral is on Tuesday," I said to the group.

They all looked at me as if I were speaking a foreign language they did not understand.

"I think we should go."

Ethan squirmed in this chair. "I have an appointment Tuesday."

I raised my eyebrows. "And you can't reschedule?"

"Uh, no."

I looked at Jolene.

She cocked her head to one side. "I barely knew the girl."

I cocked my head back at her. "It isn't just about Trisha. I think it would mean a lot to her parents if some or all of us paid our respects."

Hank was inching his way out of the room when I caught him in my sights. "I didn't know her at all."

"Nor did I." Glenda pushed back from the table.

I looked around the room. "So, no one is going?"

"I don't think so," Ethan said.

None of them could be inconvenienced enough to attend Trisha's funeral.

"Fine. I just think it would have been the right thing to do." I excused myself and made my way up to my room, where I spent the rest of the evening.

Monday dawned clear and bright. I hurried through breakfast and went upstairs to my office, eager to get to work. Eager to move forward on some level, in finding out what happened to Bonnie Rawlings—and what happened to Trisha Chatsworth—because deep in my gut, I knew the two were related. Maybe if I could find out what really happened to Bonnie, I could piece together what happened to Trisha.

I wanted to get out of the house before anyone had a chance to waylay my plans. I made a hurried list of articles and documents I needed to get in town then grabbed my car keys, put my cell phone in my purse, in case I got far enough out of the dead zone to use it, and headed for the front door.

Jolene was standing in the front hall, dressed in a yellow silk blouse and formfitting yellow slacks. She looked like a voluptuous canary. I felt dowdy in my tan slacks and white blouse.

"Where are you headed?" she asked.

"Into town." I moved toward the door.

"I think I'll go with you."

Before I could object, Glenda emerged from the parlor. "Are you going into Sedgewick?"

"Yes," Jolene answered for me.

"Maybe I'll go along," Glenda said.

This was getting out of hand. "I have a lot of things I have to do. It could take a couple of hours. You'll probably get bored."

"I don't mind." Jolene grabbed her purse off the hall table.

"Neither do I," Glenda said.

Oh, this was going to be a fun trip. "Okay, let's go."

And we piled into my blue Toyota like girlfriends going to the mall instead of three women who didn't like each other very much.

FIFTY YEARS AGO, Sedgewick, Missouri, must have been charming, with its wide tree-lined streets and a city park just off the main drag. But it was going the way of so many small towns and the signs of impending death were showing. There were empty store fronts on each block and bored teenagers congregated on street corners.

Jolene asked to be let out at the drugstore, pointed me in the direction of the newspaper office and headed off with the promise to rendezvous in an hour and a half in front of the beauty parlor.

I turned toward Glenda. "Where can I drop you?"

"I don't have any plans. I'll just go along with you."

This morning just kept getting better.

The newspaper office was two blocks from where I'd deposited Jolene. I parallel parked near the front door and walked around the car to where Glenda stood waiting on the sidewalk.

The front office of the small brick building was bathed in early morning sunlight. The girl behind the counter smiled as she approached us.

"The Rawlings trial?" she said after I told her what I was after. "I've heard of that. I can show you where our files are, and when you find what you need, just let me know. I'll make copies for you."

She led us down a dimly lit hallway to a door and down rickety wooden steps to the basement and the newspaper morgue, aptly named in this case. It was too much to expect any of this to be online, so I gave her the necessary dates and she came back with the appropriate microfilm. I pulled the faded plastic cover off the reader, fired it up and got started.

The entire case from beginning to end had taken only three months. Bonita was found dead on August sixteenth. By November twenty-second, Tommy Markowski was on his way to the state hospital for the criminally insane. For a small-town paper that only published twice a week, the coverage was quite extensive. Understandably so, apparently, *nothing* ever happened in Sedgewick.

There were articles that hadn't been in Trisha's file, and it dawned on me now that Ethan must have saved those yellowed newspaper accounts from twenty years ago. Why, I wondered.

An hour and twenty minutes later, I had a list of the articles I wanted and had added a few pages to my notes. Gienda had spent the entire time trying to peer over my shoulder and it had been all I could do to keep from sending her back to the car.

At the front office, I handed my list to the young receptionist.

She scanned it quickly. "This shouldn't be any trouble. It's kind of slow around here today. I could probably have these ready for you in a couple of hours."

I thanked her and promised to return later in the afternoon.

We were just emerging into the sunlight when I saw Jolene a block away heading toward us. She sashayed her way up the street, her yellow outfit brilliant against the drab buildings. She was only a few feet from a group of teenage boys when one of them darted toward her. Before I could call out a warning, he grabbed Jolene's purse and tried to wrestle it from her.

With a quickness that shocked him and, I've got to say, delighted me, Jolene snatched back her purse, kicked the boy's feet out from under him and had him on the ground with her stiletto heel all but piercing his Adam's apple.

The other boys fled in terror, either from getting caught as accessories or from Jolene's wrath, I wasn't sure. By the time I reached her side, she was looking down at the culprit, a dangerous smile on her face.

"You won't ever try that again, now will you?"

He looked at her, his eyes were wide with fear. "No, ma'am."

"Because if you do, I'll have to hurt you. Do you understand?"

"Yes, ma'am."

"Do you want me to call the sheriff?"

"No, ma'am. I'm… I'm sorry."

"Do you want me to call your daddy and have him whip you?"

"No, ma'am. Please. Please don't do that."

The smile vanished from her face and she narrowed

her eyes at him. "Then get out of here. This is your get
out of jail free card." She slowly removed her heel from
his throat and the boy rolled over, leapt to his feet and
vanished around the corner.

She looked at her hand. "Filthy, stupid delinquents!
I broke a nail."

She stalked to the car and got in, slamming the door.
"Let's go!"

Glenda and I looked at each other then climbed in
after her.

Glenda cowered in the backseat. Jolene sat fuming
as I drove along in silence. We'd just turned onto Lentil Road when I heard a depressingly familiar thud as I
struggled to keep control of the car.

"What's that?" Glenda shrieked from her perch in
the backseat.

"Flat tire." I steered over to the side of the road and
parked.

"Damn!" Jolene said.

My sentiments exactly.

We exited the car and I found two stones to brace
against the back wheels. I slid the jack under the frame
and pried off the hubcap. Glenda watched as I fought to
loosen the lug nuts. They felt as if they'd been welded
on. Jolene stood tapping her foot. I struggled for several minutes, but the only thing I managed to do was
twist the wrench off.

Finally, Jolene grabbed the lug wrench from me.
"Here, let me try. My nails are already ruined." She pulled
back the jack, used it to brace one end of the T-shaped
wrench then bounced her full weight on one of the arms
until the lug nut came loose with a sharp snap.

She loosened the other four then handed me the

wrench. "You do the rest. I don't want to get any dirtier than I already am."

By the time we made it back to the house, lunch was over. Jolene and Glenda dispersed in opposite directions as I headed for my office.

Ethan, Dan and Hank appeared to be having a conference as I entered Ethan's office.

"Jessie," he said, "how'd it go in town? Did you get everything you need?"

"No. I'll have to go back this afternoon. I never made it to the courthouse to get a copy of the death certificate or the trial transcripts. And I wanted to look over the police reports."

I told him about the attempted mugging on Jolene and the flat tire.

He was actually more concerned about my car than Jolene. "You're welcome to take the Caddy this afternoon. I can have Matt take a look at your car. These country roads can be hard on tires, and you shouldn't be driving around without a spare."

"Thanks, Ethan, but I'll be fine."

After lunch, I headed back into town, where I dropped my flat tire off at a garage. At the county courthouse, I got copies of the trial and death certificate. It was after three by the time I left the newspaper office for the sheriff's office.

Lucky for me, the patronizing sheriff was nowhere in sight. I looked through police reports in the archives. Since an arrest was made at the scene, there had been no detailed investigation, and the reports weren't even worth copying. I asked the young deputy at the front desk how I could get hold of Sheriff Connor, who'd been the officer in charge of the case and was informed that Sheriff Connor had retired five years earlier. The young man then refused to give me Fred Connor's home phone number.

I left the sheriff's office and walked back to my car. I pulled out my cell phone and found phone number listings for two Fred Connors. There was no answer at the first number I tried, which turned out to be just as well, because the second number was the one that belonged to the former sheriff. It took some wheedling, but he agreed to see me. After giving me directions to his house, I told him I was on my way and hung up.

The Connor farm was in a lush, green valley about five miles south of Sedgewick. A split-rail fence enclosed the front yard, and I swung my car through its opening onto a dirt driveway.

Fred Connor stepped off the porch as I came to a stop. He was about six feet tall, wiry and fit. The only telltale signs of his sixty-odd years were the thick gray hair and the hard, callused hands. The clear brown eyes that studied me were warm and friendly, with a glint of humor and intelligence behind them.

"Jessica Kallan?"

"Yes." I smiled and held out my hand. "Thank you for seeing me on such short notice, Sheriff Connor."

"Fred." He returned my smile and took my hand in a firm grasp. "No sheriff anymore, just Fred. Nice shiner, by the way. What happened?"

"Had kind of a freakish accident the other night."

He nodded. "That girl that died up at Ethan Miller's place?"

"How did you know about that?"

He smiled. "You're in a small town now, miss. Word travels."

He led the way to the front porch and we settled into wicker chairs, where we could look out over the newly mowed lawn and flower beds filled with tulips and jonquils.

"So, you're helping Ethan research a book about Bonnie Rawlings' murder," he said after a time.

"That's right. I thought it would be helpful to get a firsthand account from the investigating officer. Do you remember much about the case?"

One corner of his mouth went up in a lopsided grin. "You mean 'cause it was so long ago and I'm so ancient I might be a little addled by now?"

"Yes, to both."

He laughed. "I think I'm gonna like you. Actually, I remember the case very well. We don't have a lot of violent crime around here, except for maybe domestic abuse and that doesn't get reported very often. But even if I'd investigated a hundred murders, I'd still remember Bonnie's."

"Why that one in particular?"

"Because it was never solved. That's just my opinion, of course, but I believe it sure as I'm sittin' here. Oh, we got a conviction, but that boy didn't kill Bonnie any more than I did. What's Ethan's interest in this, twenty years after the fact?"

I probably hesitated too long. "Ethan's come to agree with you. He thinks that an injustice was done."

He snorted derisively. "I'll bet he does."

"Why do you say that?"

"There were a lot of strange things that happened back then, and I always wondered how much was due to Ethan's influence."

"What kind of things?"

"I guess the first thing that hit me was the way John and Hank Amundson were hustled back to school the day after the murder. I'd barely had a chance to question them and they were gone. When I called the school in St. Louis, I found out the fall term didn't even start for another month."

"Well, they were young. Maybe Ethan wanted to get them away from an unpleasant murder investigation."

I didn't really believe this but felt obligated not to air Ethan's dirty laundry in public. I needn't have bothered.

He watched my eyes and I got the feeling Fred Connor might be an astute enough judge of character to see right through me.

"Maybe," he said without conviction. "I used to wonder, too, what John's involvement was with Bonnie."

"She was his future sister-in-law."

"Uh-huh. Your point being?"

"You think John was involved with the girl his brother was engaged to?" I hadn't considered that, but it fit what I knew of him.

"John's always been terribly jealous of Matt."

"That's the feeling I get, too, although I can't figure out what he's so jealous of. John seems to be the golden child."

"Who knows where people get their crazy ideas. But, I've known those boys all their lives and it's obvious in everything John does."

I thought for a minute. "I still don't see what that would have to do with Bonnie's murder. Unless..."

"One or the other of them killed her in a jealous rage?" he finished for me. "Not very original, but it happens all the time."

I liked Fred Connor's long lean face with the years

of his life etched deeply into his bronzed temples. I liked the way his mind worked. Although there was no physical resemblance, there was something about him that reminded me very much of my father. I liked, too, the way his eyes searched mine, seeking, perhaps, the character that lay beneath my own skin.

"What else happened during the investigation that made you wonder?"

"There was the D.A., who was up for re-election at the time and, coincidentally, was able to finance his whole campaign without batting an eye. I always suspected maybe Ethan or his friend Eric was greasing the skids, if you know what I mean."

I knew exactly what he meant and figured he was probably right—a budding realization that made me uncomfortable for reasons I'd yet to admit to myself.

"The D.A. was hounding me to officially arrest Tommy. I'd barely had time to gather any evidence when he was pushing for an indictment. I couldn't understand why he was in such an all-fired hurry."

"But you did have a confession."

He closed his eyes and shook his head. "Thanks to some hot-shot deputy who got to him before I did. Poor Tommy was scared to death of what was going on. You could have convinced that boy that he'd just mutilated his own grandmother."

"His lawyer must have seen what was happening."

Fred Connor snorted. "They had to get his lawyer out of the drunk tank and dry him out first. He was getting ready to retire, and the county was paying his legal fees. All he wanted to do was get through that trial as quick as possible so he could go on another bender, compliments of Sedgewick County."

"Surely someone would have called for a mistrial if it was that bad."

"You've got to understand, miss, that nobody cared— nobody that mattered, anyway. All they wanted to do was get a conviction and the townspeople were satisfied they could let their daughters out of the house again."

"But a jury convicted Tommy?"

"A jury of those same scared townsfolk. With a mo-tivated prosecutor, a defense attorney going through the motions and a confession on record." He looked out across the valley and shook his head. "I suppose I should have done something for Tommy. I try to go visit him sometimes at that place where he lives, but I was just a small-town sheriff. I didn't know what to do."

We stared out over the valley. This was exactly the sort of thing I was hoping for, because I was sure I would find none of this in the official reports.

"So," Fred said presently, "Ethan was afraid one of his kids might have done it and used his money to rail-road Tommy. Why'd he get religion on this all of a sudden?"

"An old friend of his made him promise."

"Eric Amundson?"

I smiled. "Not much gets past you, does it?"

"I don't know. Probably more than I'd like." He watched my face. "And that young girl that died the other night, you were there, right?"

"Uh huh."

"And?"

I shrugged. "The official verdict is an unfortunate accident."

"And?"

"You're not gonna let this die, are you?" I smiled at him.

He smiled back. "Just humor an old lawman."

"I don't know what to tell you."

"Tell me what you think. Gut-level."

"She'd started doing research on Ethan's book about Bonnie Rawlings. I think it made someone very nervous."

"If that's what you feel, then pay attention to it."

I was quiet for a while.

"What?" he finally asked.

"If that girl's death was more than an unfortunate accident, no one's going to investigate it, are they?"

"What do you think?"

I didn't say anything.

"You're looking into a murder that's been covered up for twenty years," he said.

I nodded. "If they could do it once—they can do it again."

He walked me to my car. I thanked him for his help and reached out to shake his hand.

He held it for a long time, watching my eyes. "If you need any more information, just call. I'll help in any way I can. I sure would like to see this thing come out right after all these years."

"I want to meet Tommy."

He nodded. "I can arrange that for you."

He left me standing by my car and walked around the side of the house.

FOR SOME REASON, I didn't feel like going back to Ethan's. All I wanted to do was drive. I was on the county road, heading away from Sedgewick, when I passed the turn-off for Lentil Road. I drove for about another five miles until I saw a sign for a town called Cross Creek. Another mile up the road, I turned left, not knowing where I would end up but not really caring either.

I finally realized what it was about Fred Connor that reminded me of my father. They were both men of integrity, trying to do the right thing in a world that didn't seem to care.

The memories I'd fought to keep at bay since Eric's death came flooding in. It was the year I turned twelve when my world started to fall apart. Until then, every part of my life had been secure. I loved my mother and adored my father. Being an only child, all attention had been showered on me.

My father joined the Omaha Police Department the year before he married my mother. He loved his job almost as much as he loved his family.

One day, on a routine call to Hanscom Park, he saw two of his fellow officers selling drugs to a couple of neighborhood teens. When he went to his superiors with the information, they didn't want to hear it. He was all but told to turn a blind eye to the situation in the interest of the brotherhood of the force. To my father, that was an outrage. He was paid to uphold the law and protect the community. Cops selling drugs to high school kids were lower than scum.

He set out to collect his own evidence. After months of self-directed stakeouts, pictures and interviewing kids and other dealers, he finally felt he had enough to present to the chief of police.

His hard work was met with anger and he was shunned by many of his former friends. The evidence he'd gathered mysteriously disappeared. We started to receive threatening phone calls. The stress was more than he could bear. At thirty-nine, my father had a heart attack and died.

My mother felt disgraced. We were abandoned by the people who had been a part of our lives for so many years. She and I fought constantly. I missed my father but was proud of what he'd done. She was just angry. She'd lost her young husband—for what?

Two years after my father's death, the state police busted the cop drug ring, but it was too late for us. I'd lost my father, and my mother and I had nearly lost each other in the process.

I thought of Fred Connor and how his investigation had been railroaded by powers too big to fight alone— the D.A., Ethan, Eric. Why didn't the good guys ever win, I wondered, not for the first time in my life.

The two-lane stretch of road ambled into Cross Creek. The town was smaller than Sedgewick, just two blocks of main street in the middle of farmland. A small rural town that seemed to accept itself for what it was, never aspiring to be anything more.

I parked the car in one of those cock-eyed parking spaces that was angled so as to be not quite perpendicular to the curb, locked the door and meandered down the sidewalk.

There were a couple of craft shops filled with local works—quilts, handmade goods, woodcarvings and folk art—that caught my interest. In the second shop I entered, I was examining paintings from local artists when I glanced up and saw Dan peering in the window. As soon as he saw me looking at him, he moved quickly out of my line of vision.

I left the shop and walked back out onto the street,

looking up and down the block, expecting to see him. I'd almost convinced myself I'd been mistaken, when I noticed him three doors down, standing in the doorway, pressed up against the building, purposely not looking in my direction.

What was he doing? And how long had he been following me? And was he the one who'd been following Trisha Chatsworth?

I continued on down the block, stopping often, doing everything I could to frustrate him. In the next block, I entered another small shop, taking my time, carefully examining all the quilts and woodcarvings. Out of the corner of my eye, I noticed Dan watching me through the plate glass. After about twenty minutes of dawdling, I approached the clerk and asked if there was a rear exit.

She looked me up and down.

"Please. Someone's following me."

Her look softened as she glanced out the window and noticed Dan. "Him?"

"Yes. He's been following me all over town." I tried my best to sound like a helpless, frightened female, even though "all over town" was a stretch.

"Come on, honey." She moved her girth out from behind the counter and headed for the back of the store. "You can go out this way." She led me through a dusty, cramped storeroom and unlocked a door that led to a narrow alley.

"You want I should call the sheriff?" she asked as I squeezed past her.

"No thanks. I think I'll be fine now."

I followed the alley to the end of the block and peered around the corner of the building, watching in amusement as Dan entered the craft store. I had no doubt the woman who'd helped me would give him a hard time.

I crossed the wide main street and headed back toward my car. There was a small cafe directly across from where I'd parked, and I went in and found an empty table next to the front window.

While I was waiting for dinner, I dug a small notebook from my purse and started making notes of my interview with Fred Connor.

As I nibbled at my hamburger, Dan walked up to my car and looked up and down the street, a bewildered look on his face. By the time I finished eating, he was gone.

In the back of the cafe, I found a pay phone and a phone book where I looked up the address for the only Rawlings listed. I got directions from the waitress when I went to pay my bill.

IT WAS ON one of the dirt roads leading to the Rawlings' farm that I noticed the car behind me. Even from almost half a mile away, it looked unmistakably like Ethan's car—there weren't a lot of beige Cadillacs in the neighborhood. I hadn't noticed it earlier because there'd been more traffic on the highway. Out on the back roads, it became harder to hide.

The farms grew sparser. Small neat homes were interspersed with run-down farmsteads showing weatherworn wood siding and sagging front porches.

Finally, I spotted the shiny silver mailbox with the name *Rawlings*, hand-painted in block letters at the end of one driveway, and I swung my car in, looking for signs of life. I came to a stop in front of the house and looked back in time to see Ethan's car pass by on the road, with Dan at the wheel, staring straight ahead, clearly aware that he'd been spotted.

The Rawlings' yard was neat and flowers bloomed in front of the whitewashed porch. As I approached the front steps, a woman stepped out of the front door and smiled at me.

"Can I help you?"

"Mrs. Rawlings?"

"Yes, I'm Sarah Rawlings," she said, still smiling.

"Are you Bonnie's mother?"

That seemed to catch her off guard. "I was. Were you a friend of Bonnie's?"

I held out my hand and introduced myself. Then I told her why I was there and her smile faded into sadness.

"I don't know what I can do to help you, Jessica. Ethan Miller knows as much as anyone about what happened to my Bonnie. Certainly, more than me."

I was standing next to her on the porch. She was a little taller than me, with a trim figure and thick gray hair cut short and softly framing her high cheekbones and striking green eyes.

"I'd like to know more about Bonnie. I'd like to know who she was. What kind of person she was."

She smiled again with a far-away look in her eyes. "Why don't you come inside."

The white living room was clean and homey, with framed Georgia O'Keeffe prints hanging on the walls. A pale blue couch was at the far end of the room, with two comfortable armchairs opposite it. There was a brick fireplace on one wall, its mantel filled with family photographs.

"Can I get you anything?"

I settled into one of the armchairs by the front window. "I'm fine, thanks."

She settled on the couch. "What do you want to know about Bonnie?"

"Anything you can tell me that would help me know her. What kind of girl she was. Was she good in school? Did she have lots of friends?"

The far-away look was back. "She was a happy child, always good in school. She had a way of—I don't know how to put it—charming her way into people's lives. Things started to change, though, when she was a teenager. She grew restless. It was almost as if life could never be grand enough for her. I thought when she started dating Matt that she would settle down some, but it really didn't help."

"Why do you think she was so restless?"

"I've wondered that many times. I know it was hard on the girls not having their fathers around when they were little, but I tried to do my best to give them a normal life."

The reports mentioned that Bonnie had a sister, Alena, but this was new. "Your daughters had different fathers?"

"I was married twice. My first husband was…well, he was what we used to call a mean drunk. I divorced him when my oldest daughter, Alena, was three. I may have waited too long for that, but I was naïve enough to think I could change him. Alena was fierce. There's no other way to put it. I was never sure if it was something she inherited or something she learned from living with him."

"When did you marry Bonnie's father?"

"Two years later. Alena's father had long since disappeared. And when Jim came along, I think I was so desperate for us to be a family, I jumped at the chance to marry him. I got pregnant with Bonnie a couple of months after we got married."

"But that marriage didn't work out either?"

She stood and walked over to the fireplace, looking at the photographs that tied her to a past that no longer existed. "No. He was a drinker too. A kinder drunk, but still... Most nights I didn't even know where he was. I divorced him when Bonnie was two."

She was right. Missing fathers left a sizable hole behind them, and they'd lost their fathers younger than I had. Alena twice. "Did she have much contact with her father after that?"

Sarah turned to look at me. "On and off. He'd go through periods when he'd sober up and think he wanted to be a father again. He'd come back into her life and buy her all sorts of expensive presents. I tried to tell him that wasn't what she needed, but he must have thought it would make up for all the time he wasn't around—which was most of the time."

"That must have been hard on you."

"It was even harder on Alena. She never saw her natural father, and then Jim would come around and spoil Bonnie and ignore Alena completely. Kids don't understand that sort of thing. I used to think there was a cruel streak in him. He'd get a job working on somebody's car—usually in my backyard, and Alena would stand out there with him for hours watching him while he ignored her. Then Bonnie would come along and he'd drop everything to talk to *her*."

"It's difficult to understand why some people are the way they are." I'd heard enough to hope that Alena got some industrial-strength therapy along the line. "Were the girls very close when they were growing up?"

"Oddly enough, they were." She sighed—a long, heavy breath escaping from deep in her heart. "I don't think I did a very good job as a single mother. I was gone most of the time. I had to be. Alena was the one who was home taking care of Bonnie, almost like a second mother. She doted on Bonnie, I think trying to create the life for her that she never had. Bonnie seemed to be the only stable thing in her life. The only family she felt she had."

Wow. "But you said she was fierce."

"She was, but especially around Bonnie. If anyone hurt Bonnie, she would come down on them like the wrath of God."

"Did Bonnie have many other friends?"

Sarah walked back over to the couch and sat down. "When it suited her. She would have a best friend for a while then drop her when it wasn't convenient anymore. Maybe because she always had Alena. She always had her share of boys hanging around too." There was an odd note in her voice—almost a sound of disgust. "The only place the girls were at all competitive was when it came to boys. Bonnie could flash a smile and they'd come running. Alena had a rougher exterior but was willing to be more…friendly. And she was attractive, in her own way." She closed her eyes and rubbed a long, elegant hand across her forehead. "I guess everything I did was wrong. My girls never learned how to have *normal* relationships with anyone."

"What about Bonnie's relationship to Matt?"

She opened her eyes and looked at me. "Matt was

head over heels in love with Bonnie, and I think she felt the same about him. But they fought a lot."

"What about?"

She thought for a minute. "Everything, I guess. Bonnie was used to getting her own way and having men spoil her. I don't think Matt had a lot of patience with that."

"How did Ethan treat her?"

She smiled. "He was always good to her. Sometimes she'd go up and visit with Ethan when Matt was away at school. He made her feel welcome, like part of the family, I guess. She'd come home saying '*Ethan this*' or '*Ethan that*,' like he was a god or something. Maybe Ethan was like the father she'd always wanted."

"Sarah, there are some people who don't think Tommy Markowski killed Bonnie."

She looked at me without blinking.

"Do you think he did?"

She got up again and walked over to the front window, where she adjusted the drapes to block the evening sun shining in her eyes. "I think I need a beer. Do you want one?"

"Thanks, no."

She made her way into the kitchen, but I couldn't guess what she was thinking, why she needed a break.

When she returned, she seated herself again on the couch and placed the open bottle on the end table next to it. "I don't know what to tell you about Tommy Markowski. In the beginning, I was in shock. The trial was like a very bad dream. My doctor had me on tranquilizers so I could function. I suppose I wanted to believe that Tommy…did that to Bonnie. Somehow, it made it easier if I had someone to blame. But, over the years, I guess I've wondered."

"Why?"

"Maybe it was knowing Tommy. He was such a gentle soul. Or maybe it was knowing Bonnie. When she couldn't get her way, she had a knack of provoking people to do things they might not normally do."

"Then you believe it could have been someone else?"

She nodded.

"Who?" I asked her.

"I have no idea," she said quietly.

"Did you know Bonnie was pregnant?"

She shook her head again. "Not until it came out at the trial. I suppose I should have. I know morning sickness well enough." She looked at her fingers. "And it wouldn't have surprised me, but Bonnie—neither of the girls—ever confided much in me."

I felt that I'd taken Sarah Rawlings as far as she was willing to go that day. I walked over to the mantel and looked at the pictures that filled it.

I picked up a framed photograph. "Is this Bonnie?"

She nodded. "Her high school graduation picture."

For all the files I'd read, it was the first time I'd seen a picture of the murdered girl. She was strikingly pretty, with long blonde hair and big blue eyes, and just enough baby fat in her cheeks to make her look wholesome and innocent. She was dressed in a pink sweater with a necklace at her throat. The necklace was a silver lightning bolt with a streak of blue down the middle that dramatically accented the color of her eyes.

I replaced the photograph and picked up the second one and stared at it closely. There was so much of

Sarah Rawlings in the face of the young woman who looked back at me.

"Alena?" I asked.

"Yes," came the quiet reply.

Alena looked to be in her early twenties. She'd attempted a model's pose that only made her look ridiculous. Her face held none of the wholesome innocence that Bonnie's did. Instead, the eyes were intense.

"Beautiful girls," I said. "What does Alena do?"

Sarah picked up her bottle of beer and took a long drink. "I don't know."

"I'm sorry?"

"I haven't heard from Alena in over ten years. She used to work for Dr. Fischer, in his office in town. Sometimes I wonder if she knew more about Bonnie's murder than she let on—being in a medical office. She was at Tommy's trial every day. I can't imagine what that did to her, she'd just lost the person closest to her in the world. And I was too out of it to be there for her. Again. About a week after the trial was over, she came home one day while I was at work, packed her bags and beat it out of town. I never even got to say good-bye to her—she just left me a note."

"Where did she go?"

"She ended up in California. She was going to be a famous model or something. She sent me postcards over the years. An occasional Christmas present when she was working, but in the past ten years, I haven't heard from her once. I don't know where she is now."

There was so much pain in Sarah's voice I couldn't make her go on. I thanked her for her time and left her there to deal with the ghosts we'd both awakened.

It took over an hour to get back to Ethan's. I got lost

a couple of times and had to do some backtracking. When I pulled into the garage, Matt was there.

He walked over to me as I got out of the car, a dark look on his face. "You've been gone a while."

"I had some things I needed to do. It took longer than I expected." I tried to move past him.

He blocked my way. "You should be careful, Jess. You have no idea what old wounds you're opening up in people's lives."

"Did Dan come running back here to report to you?"

"Dan was concerned about you."

"Well, you can tell him he needn't worry."

He moved a step closer and bent down, his face inches from mine. "Don't be stupid, Jess. Ethan has pulled you into the middle of some very nasty stuff, and I don't think you have any idea what you've gotten yourself into. Look what happened to Trisha."

"I'm not some twenty-two-year-old coed like Trisha Chatsworth. I know what I'm doing." I stepped around him and walked out into the cool night air.

"Just be careful," I heard him say behind me.

SEVEN

THERE WAS NO ONE around when I entered the front hall, or in the parlor or Ethan's office. I decided to head upstairs. There was a note from Millie for me taped to the banister. It said:

Jessica, Fred Connor called and has set up an interview for you with Tommy Markowski tomorrow morning. He'd like you to call him tonight. We missed you at dinner. There's a plate of food for you in the fridge if you're hungry. Help yourself to anything else you can find—Millie.

I went up to my room and plopped on the bed and looked at the note again. Fred Connor must have been serious in his offer to help. I wasn't surprised. I fished his number out of my purse and dialed. "Fred, it's Jess Kallan."

"Did you get my message?"

"Yes. I'm impressed. You move quickly."

"Didn't seem much point in dilly-dallying. I'd wanted to go out there with you, but something's come up and I have to head to Springfield in the morning."

"Nothing serious, I hope."

"As of about two hours ago, I've got a new grandson! I told my daughter I'd be there by noon tomorrow."

"Hey, congratulations!"

"Thanks. I won't stay long. My daughter isn't going to be up for much company. I should be home by Thursday night. If you want to wait until Friday, I can go with you to see Tommy. Otherwise, I talked to his counselor and told him you might come by yourself."

"Thanks, Fred. I think I'll go tomorrow. Not much point in dilly-dallying, I've been told."

He laughed then gave me the name of Tommy's case-worker and directions to the facility that was a two-hour drive from Ethan's.

"We'll touch base when I get back," he said before he hung up.

I stretched and yawned and kicked off my shoes then lifted the receiver again and dialed my mother. I knew she'd been waiting to hear what was going on. I told her about the book, but she was more interested to know about everyone I'd met—most of all Ethan. What I didn't tell her about was Trisha Chatsworth and her mysterious death. No point in worrying her. Twenty minutes later we said good-bye.

My last phone call was to Bob Elliot, my former editor at the *Trib*.

"Hey, stranger. How's it going down there? You and Hank playing nice?"

"You could have warned me."

He laughed. "Honest, Jess, I didn't know until after he was gone."

"I don't believe you. And now you owe me—big time."

"Well, just add it to my tab."

"No, I need to cash in now. I need a favor."

"You didn't call because you missed me and wanted to hear my sexy voice?"

"If I say 'yes,' will it get me that favor?"

"Okay. What do you want me to do?"

"Track someone down for me."

"Text me the details."

"That's not an option. No cell phone reception here."

I heard him rustling paper. "Who and where?"

"As of ten years ago her name was Alena Rawlings. I don't know if she's gotten married since then. Last known whereabouts—California. She'd be about forty now. Used to work as a model."

"Anything else?"

"She grew up in Cross Creek, Missouri."

"Not much to go on. When do you need this?"

"Tonight."

When he was finished swearing at me, I told him *soon* would be good enough and brought him up to date on the Miller household, my new job and the accident the other night.

"I know. I read about it on MSN. Not a lot of detail, like they were trying to downplay it." Bob was quiet for a few seconds. Finally, he said, "I don't think I like the sound of this, Jess. Maybe you should just interview Ethan Miller and head back home. This could get ugly."

"I've been hearing that a lot. But you know I've seen ugly before."

"You've never been in the middle of a murder investigation, where all the potential suspects are in the same house with you. And from what you've told me about that girl, Trisha, I'm not convinced you think it was an accident."

"I'm not convinced. But, Bob, if you had a chance to work on a case like this and collaborate with Ethan Miller, what would you do?"

"Then just watch your effing back." He hung up in my ear.

I went into the bathroom and washed my face, got

out of my clothes, put on a T-shirt and climbed into bed. I lay in the darkness for several minutes, listening to the house settle, trying to figure out what I was feeling.

It was interesting to me that no one I'd talked to seemed to think Tommy Markowski was guilty of Bonnie's murder, even though no one really seemed to have a reason for their belief.

I thought about Eric and Ethan and what they'd done to protect their sons. Ethan covering for Matt and shipping John back to prep school in St. Louis before anyone could tie him to the murder. Eric doing whatever he could to keep Hank out of jail. The guilt and fear they must have carried all these years would have weighed heavily. I tried to put it into perspective and wondered what I would have done if I'd been in their shoes. No matter how hard I tried, though, I couldn't reconcile the fact that they had possibly sacrificed the life of an innocent man in the process. My feelings for them had changed in the past two days, and it would take time to readjust my emotions.

And then there was Trisha. Fred Connor was right, nothing was going to happen in regard to her death and, for all my suspicions, I still didn't know if I was right and, without an active investigation, I probably never would.

I finally drifted into a fitful sleep, waking once, at two, when I heard a car door slam shut in the drive below my window. I rolled over and wandered back into dreamland until my alarm jolted me awake four hours later.

Trisha's funeral was this morning. Part of me wanted to be there for her parents—for her mother—but I felt my time would be better spent continuing my research

for Ethan. If I could find out what happened to Bonnie—
to Trisha—maybe I could bring some kind of closure
to Trisha's family.

I showered and dressed and had a quick cup of coffee
and some toast and was just heading out the front door
when a voice behind me said, "Off to see the killer?"

I turned and looked at Matt. I didn't like the way he
said *killer*, and I didn't like the look on his face.

"I'm going to see Tommy Markowski, if that's what
you mean."

"Do you have any idea what you're doing to people's
lives? Do you even care?"

"What am I doing?" I asked.

"Digging up the past never changes the present."

"Tell that to your father. What if the past is a lie?
What if Tommy Markowski really is innocent? Wouldn't
it change the present for him if the truth came out?
Wouldn't it make his life better today?"

Matt narrowed his eyes. "I think you need to do your
research. Tommy Markowski is better off where he is.
Why can't you just leave well enough alone?"

"The man lives in an institution—how can that possibly be better than having his life back? And you, of
all people, Matt—don't you want to know what really
happened?"

He started to say something then shrugged and went
into the parlor.

I headed out the front door and down the driveway
toward the garage. Dan was coming in my direction,
wiping his hands on a linen handkerchief. I said hello.
He looked at me quickly then at the ground and kept
walking toward the house.

I shook my head. Friendly group. My car was parked

in the middle stall of the darkened garage, but the interior was still sauna hot when I climbed in. I was eager to be on the highway with the air conditioner on and far away from Matt and Dan.

I backed the Corolla out and made my way down the circular driveway toward Lentil Road. I wished Fred Connor was with me, if only to have someone to talk to on the long drive. Radio reception wasn't much better than cell phone, and it was going to be a long, boring ride.

At the top of the hill, I turned and tapped the brake to slow my momentum for the long decline. My foot went all the way to the floor.

I pumped the pedal again, trying to coax it back to life. Nothing. The car was gaining speed and I fought to keep it on the road as I rounded the first curve. The tires squealed and gravel peppered the nearby trees.

A long slow wail came up out of my throat as I yanked the emergency brake handle. The tires started to skid. Then there was a popping sound, and the car began picking up speed again.

I barely made the second curve. I didn't dare take my eyes off the road long enough to even chance a look at the speedometer. My only hope was that I might keep enough control to reach the bottom of Lentil Road, where the terrain flattened out, but even that flat spot did little to slow the car as I flew past the last farmhouse.

A semi on the county road roared into sight. We would reach the intersection at almost the same time, and there was no doubt in my mind who would walk away from that encounter. My hands felt welded to the steering wheel. I looked around, desperate for another option.

Barreling down the road from the other direction as the semi was a full-sized pickup. I was barely fifty feet from the intersection when I pulled the steering wheel hard to the right. The car took flight—off the road, over a gully and across a hayfield. I hit the ground, seconds before the car came to a dead stop, the front fender French kissing the telephone pole that had saved me from French kissing a semi.

The air bags exploded in a cloud of white right before everything went black.

I woke up lying on the cool grass, still wet with morning dew, and two burly men looking down at me.

"Don't move," one of them said. "An ambulance is on its way."

I tried to sit up. Strong hands forced me down.

"Don't move," the other one said. "Really."

I decided not to move, if only to make them happy.

"What happened?" the first one asked me.

"My brakes went out."

"Brakes," the second one repeated, looking up the hill as if to verify what I'd just told him. A red baseball cap covered his head, his craggy face shadowed by its bill.

"Good thing you went off the road when you did," said the first. "Otherwise, you woulda been toast!"

I looked to his partner for comment.

"Dead toast!" he said on cue.

"How do you feel?" the first one asked.

I hadn't really thought about it. When I did, I realized I hurt. My left elbow and the left side of my head were throbbing and my nose felt like someone had punched me. A swatch of pain ran from my left shoulder to my right hip. And I was a little woozy. It was hard to keep my focus on their faces and the conversation.

I told them how I felt.

"Your head probably bounced off your driver's window when the car hit the pole," one of them said.

I could no longer keep track of who was who.

"Probably got a concussion," the other one informed me.

I tried to nod my agreement, but that was a mistake, so I just smiled at him. Sirens blared in the distance, and I was grateful for their timing. I didn't think I was doing a very good job entertaining the two men, and I didn't think I could follow the conversation much longer.

One of them stood and waved his baseball cap in the direction of the county road. The other picked up my hand and patted it, as if to say I'd be okay and he was glad he didn't have to stay there much longer and console me.

THE EMERGENCY ROOM at the county hospital smelled like disinfectant. I lay on scratchy, starched sheets and stared at the fluorescent lights overhead until they became one big blur of white and my eyes started to burn. I closed them, wondering how long it would take Ethan to come and retrieve me. I'd called Millie from the nurse's desk on my way back from X-ray and asked her to tell him.

Southern Missouri wasn't very good for my health. In less than a week, my body had been abused in ways it never had before. First the incident on Ethan's terrace and now this.

The doctor who examined me told me nothing was broken—although, it felt like *everything* was broken.

I had a mild concussion, he informed me, after the ordeal of several hundred dollars' worth of X-rays and an even more expensive CT scan. I should probably rest for a few days and take acetaminophen for the pain was his doctorly advice, then he disappeared behind a pale gray curtain to tend to a woman in labor, whose screams filled the entire first floor of the hospital.

After the doctor left, I peeked down the front of my gown to see the colorful impressions left by the seatbelt across my torso and tummy. Very pretty.

A heavyset nurse dressed in green surgical scrubs came around the curtain and tossed my clothes across my abdomen.

"Ow!" I said.

"A little sore?" she asked in a tone that bordered on sadism. "You can get dressed now."

I'd just finished buttoning my blouse when the curtain was yanked open. Matt was standing there.

"Where's Ethan?"

"On his way to St. Louis." He took a step closer to the exam table. "What happened?"

All of a sudden, I wanted to cry. Tears welled up in my eyes and I looked away. Sterile cabinets and bland curtains swam together in a colorless blur.

Matt waited while I took a few deep breaths and wiped away the tears. "Are you done acting like a girl, now?"

I narrowed my eyes at him. "My car is smashed to hell, I'm bruised in places you couldn't even imagine and I feel like crap. Sorry if it's inconvenient for you if I get a little emotional."

He looked me in the eye for several long seconds. "What happened?"

I started to shake my head but thought better of it. "My brakes went out."

"Brakes don't usually just *go out*. Have you had trouble with them before? Grinding? Lack of pressure?"

"No. They just went out."

He chewed on the inside of his cheek, looking at the wall behind me. I knew what he was thinking, the same thought had crossed my mind. Had whoever found Trisha Chatsworth a threat, found me to be one also?

"I'm fine, by the way," I said.

"Good. Let's go."

I climbed slowly off the table, careful not to jar any of my delicate innards and walked over to the corner where my purse lay on the floor like a lifeless rag doll. I bent to retrieve it and the linoleum did a little dance before my eyes. I grabbed the wall and took a few more deep breaths, determined not to throw up all over myself.

Matt must have noticed. He came over to where I stood, bent down and lifted my purse off the floor. With the purse in one hand and me in the other, he led me out to his truck. I climbed gingerly into the cab and closed the door. Matt inserted the key in the ignition and looked over at me.

"Put your seatbelt on."

"No."

He pulled the key out. "We're not going anywhere until you put your seatbelt on."

"Do you have any idea how sore I am from my seatbelt? I have a rainbow tattooed across my abdomen from it."

He glared at me. "That seatbelt saved your life. If it weren't for that seatbelt, we'd be peeling you off the highway like road-kill. So, quit whining and put on your seatbelt."

I yanked the seatbelt across my chest, let out a yelp of pain and snapped the stupid thing into place. "Happy?"

"Ecstatic." He started the motor.

I glared at him as we pulled out of the parking lot.

We stopped at the drugstore on the way out of town, and Matt went in to get some acetaminophen. I counted each agonizing second until he returned so that I could get back to my room and rest.

He drove slowly over the potholes as we inched our way to the highway. At the bottom of Lentil Road, a gasp escaped my lips as I looked at the telephone pole I had encountered on my way into town a few hours ago. It was leaning to one side, snapped partway through.

He looked over at me. "You okay?"

I wasn't sure if he meant physically or emotionally. "Yes. Where's my car?"

"It was towed to the garage."

"When will I get it back?"

The Dodge slowed as he steered over to the side of the road and brought the truck to a stop.

He turned and looked at me and spoke very slowly. "Jess, odds are you won't be getting your car back. Ever. They had a bear of a time pulling it off that telephone pole."

I didn't say anything.

"Do you even realize you're just lucky to be alive?"

THE TYLENOL HELPED ease the pain, and I fell asleep only marginally aware of the throbbing in my head. I awoke with a groan when I rolled over in my sleep and a jolt shot through my rib cage.

I rolled gently onto my back and stared at the ceiling, willing myself to go back to sleep. It didn't work, I was feeling edgy. Maybe it was the reaction to the accident, but I knew the longer I lay there with nothing to do, the worse it would get.

I sat up and paused to see what my stomach would say about that. After a couple of minutes with no word, I stood, swayed, grabbed one of the bedposts then made myself focus on the chair on the other side of the room. After a few tentative steps, my body seemed to remember how to do this, and my head cleared. I was doing okay.

I made my way to the dressing table, trying not to look at my reflection in the mirror, ran a brush gently through my hair then headed for the door, looking for something to take my mind off the way I felt.

There was no one around as I headed for my office and seated myself behind the desk. It would probably be a day or two before I was ready to drive again, and I couldn't sit around wasting time. If I couldn't make the two-hour trip to see Tommy Markowski, then I'd have to figure out my next move. I booted up the laptop, remembering from middle school, how painfully slow dial-up could be.

My first step was to find out if I still had a car. There was an old phone book on one of the bookshelves, I reached for it and looked up the number for the sheriff's office. The deputy who answered the phone said my car had been towed to Medford's Garage and told me to ask for Cliff.

I dialed Medford's Garage and got Cliff on the line.

"Lady, that car is headed for the tin graveyard in about two days flat."

"There's nothing you can do to get it running again?"

"Oh, I could replace everything north of the dashboard and get it running, but it wouldn't be worth your money or my time. Just call your insurance company and get a big fat check out of 'em."

"Have you had a chance to look at the brakes?"

He laughed. "Yeah right. What's to look at? The whole front end looks like an accordion, and everything underneath's all ripped to shreds."

"Thanks." I hung up.

Great. I was stuck. Ethan was gone and the only distraction I had was the Rawlings murder case and questions about whether Trisha's fate would soon be mine. A hell of a note.

I looked at the papers in front of me and tried to focus. According to Fred Connor, Tommy Markowski's trial had been a travesty from start to finish. Who else besides Fred would have inside information on the case?

Tommy's lawyer, if he was even alive, probably wouldn't remember much if he was half the drunk Fred said he was. I thought about the jury members who'd had ringside seats and thumbed through the file until I found a yellowed newspaper clipping—a grainy photograph taken on the day the jury had been dismissed following Tommy's sentencing. They'd deliberated for only two hours.

Members of the jury were trailing down the courthouse steps. I looked closely at each grainy face, trying to get a sense of what they'd been thinking. Most of them looked weary. A few showed elation...or maybe it was relief. Then I noticed a young woman standing off to the side. Even in such a poor-quality photo, I recognized the face immediately. The hair was darker, the skin seemingly unlined, but the features were the same—they'd scowled at me often enough over the past year.

Glenda Burke looked considerably older than her twenty-seven years. The picture showed a face much too old for such a young woman. It had taken two decades for her to grow into her features.

What was Glenda doing at the trial? Did she have some connection to this place and these people? And why hadn't Ethan mentioned any of this to me? The list of things Ethan hadn't mentioned to me was getting longer, and I felt more and more like I was being played. But why? None of it made sense.

I didn't know much about Glenda. Hank had hired her shortly after Eric's death. She was mediocre as a secretary and a joke as a receptionist. But where had she come from?

I picked up the phone, dialed the number for the *Trib* and punched in the extension for my friend, Sue, in Human Resources. When she answered, I asked her to fill me in on what she knew about Glenda.

"Why do you want to know?" she asked.

"Trust me, you're better left in the dark on this one."

She was silent for a minute. "This could get me fired."

"Please, Sue. It's important."

"How important?"

"Very," I lied.

She put me on hold. I sat staring off into space until she came back on the line. "Got a pen?"

"You're a doll," I said after she'd finished.

According to Glenda's personnel file, she graduated from high school and had been employed as a low-level office clerk at Hy-Vee grocery store in Cross Creek, Missouri, until about eighteen months ago. There was a blank period of time from the end of her former job until she started at the *Trib* a little over a year ago. She now lived in the Dundee neighborhood in Omaha in a high-rise condo building I knew I could never afford. Pretty upscale digs for someone who'd worked for years in the back office of a chain store.

Was Glenda an old family friend, or did she know something that Hank wanted to keep hidden? Was she blackmailing him? Preying on the guilt of a very unstable man?

My head started to throb until it was impossible to think. I left my desk littered with papers and made my way up to my bedroom, where I took two more Tylenol, crawled into bed and fell into a deep sleep.

EIGHT

THERE WAS A light tap at my door. Through bleary eyes, I looked at the clock. Eight a.m. The accident had wiped me out more than I realized.

"Come in."

The door eased open and Millie poked her head in. "Oh, good. You're awake." She had a bed tray in her hands with coffee, juice, eggs and toast. She smiled as she set it across my lap, then brushed the hair off my forehead. "How're you feeling this morning?"

The kindness of her gesture touched me. "Better than I expected."

She produced a cordless phone from the big kangaroo pocket on her apron and handed it to me. "Ethan wants to talk to you. He started calling about six—but, I told him you needed your rest." She straightened the blankets on the side of the bed and left the room, closing the door behind her.

I took a fortifying swig of coffee then picked up the phone.

"Jessie," Ethan roared in my ear. "How do you feel? Are you all right?"

Until that moment, I'd been feeling good, except for my bruised ribs and a few stiff joints. His volume made my head start to ache and a wave of nausea swept through me. I sipped some more black coffee. "I'm fine. A few bumps and bruises, but I'll survive."

"That's not what Matt told me. He said you had a concussion and you slept all day yesterday."

"*Mild* concussion. And, yes, I slept all day. But I'm feeling better and I should be back to normal by the end of the week."

"I think you should take it easy for a while. Tell me about the accident."

"Not much to tell. I was headed down the hill toward town and my brakes went out. I hit a telephone pole in preference to hitting a semi, and my car is totaled."

"Had trouble with your brakes before?" he asked.

For some reason, I wasn't ready yet to deal with that question for the day.

"Not on this car. Maybe I should have had them checked before I left Omaha, but I didn't think about it."

He was silent for a moment…actually, several moments.

"Ethan, are you still there?"

"Yes. Listen, I think you should lay low for today at least. Take it easy, get your strength back."

"Ethan, when can we talk? I have some—"

"I'll be home tonight. We can talk then."

"But—"

"And could you do me a favor?"

"Sure. What?"

"Spend some time with Jolene today. She usually gets bored with too much time on her hands. It would be good for her if she had someone to talk to and do things with."

Aw no! Instead I said, "No problem."

I ate all of my breakfast and drank the whole carafe of coffee before I climbed out of bed, showered, slipped on some shorts and a T-shirt and headed off to find Jolene and spend quality time with her.

The air was thick, and my clothes were clinging damply to my body by the time I found Jolene sunbathing out by the pool, the top of her white string bikini draped across the deck chair, where she lay on her stomach soaking up cancer-ridden ultraviolet rays.

I stretched out in the deck chair next to hers, hoping to catch a hint of a breeze, trying to catch my breath. The trek up the hill had been harder than I thought it would be.

Jolene lifted her bleached-blonde head and looked me up and down. "You look like hell."

"I feel like hell."

She rested her chin on her arms and watched my face. "Matt said you really did a number on your car."

"It's totaled. What are you doing today?"

She shrugged. "Sometimes it's so god-awful boring around here, I just want to crawl right out of my skin. I hate it when Ethan goes away and leaves me here with nothing to do."

"What's he doing in St. Louis?"

"Some publicity thing for his book or something."

We stared at each other for several long seconds and I searched for something to say.

"How did you and Ethan meet?" I finally asked.

She propped herself up on her elbow, exposing two perfectly formed breasts. I couldn't help but look. There were the faintest scar lines underneath each one. She saw me watching but didn't seem to mind. "We met at a party in Beverly Hills."

"No kidding? When was that?"

"About a year ago, at a cast party for a movie a friend of mine was in…a really bad movie. Nobody worthwhile was in it. I didn't think anybody who was anybody would be there."

She rolled gracefully to a sitting position and reached for the top to her suit. "Then about ten o'clock Ethan showed up. He just swept me off my feet. I let him drive me home—and…you know."

"Pretty romantic." I couldn't help wondering what would have drawn Ethan to Jolene and why he'd even be at a party where he was the most famous person there. On the other hand, maybe that did make sense.

"When did you move out here?"

"About six months ago. I wanted Ethan to stay in California, but he wouldn't hear of it. He can be very stubborn. Somehow he talked me into coming back here with him." She stood in one fluid movement, turned toward the pool and dove in.

Jolene was swimming laps, her bronzed body gliding through the water, when Glenda trudged up the hill, sweat beading on her forehead. She flopped into Jolene's chair and stretched out her thin, white legs—her eyes focused on the pool.

I would get some work done after all. "Hi."

She turned her head and forced a smile. "Hello."

"Do you swim?"

"No."

"What brings you down here?"

"To the pool?"

"No—to Ethan's. Are you and he friends?"

I could tell she didn't know what to say.

"No," she finally said. "I come down here with Hank."

"Oh? That's interesting."

"What's interesting about that?"

"I guess I didn't realize you and Hank were…close."

Her eyes got big. "Well, we're not! Not like that."

I suppressed a smile. "Like what?"

"Well, whatever you're implying."

"I really wasn't implying anything. It's just that..." I glanced out at Jolene.

"What?"

I shrugged. "Most secretaries don't travel with their bosses unless they're you know, involved."

She moved quickly to an upright position and swung her legs over the side of the chair. I braced myself for a lunge.

"Well, we're not!"

Okay, now that she wasn't thinking clearly, time for the investigative reporter to ask the questions. "Why else would you be here with him?"

She huffed and puffed for a few moments—loud breaths escaping through her nose. "Business."

I raised one eyebrow. "What kind of business?"

"If you must know, Hank and Ethan are often in negotiations and it's my job to take notes."

"Negotiations for what?"

"That's none of your concern! And if you go around telling people lies about me—I'll... I'll make you very sorry."

"I'm sorry. I didn't mean to pry. Let's drop the subject."

Guarded relief swept over her features.

"We could talk about the Rawlings trial instead."

I think she actually stopped breathing for a moment. A semblance of color crept up her neck and into her cheeks, giving her a momentary lifelike look. "I don't know anything about it. You'll have to ask someone who was here at the time."

"I have a newspaper photograph sitting on my desk

that shows a very good likeness of you outside the courthouse the day the sentencing concluded. Would you
like to see it?"

She stood up and hovered over my prone body.
"I don't have anything more to say to you." She was
breathing erratically through her nose again. Then she
huffed her skinny little body down the hill.

Jolene lifted herself out of the pool, her elegant form
a mocking contrast to Glenda's retreating back. "Did
you piss her off?"

"That obvious?"

She nodded, picked up a towel and began rubbing it
down her long legs. "She's always been an odd duck.
Kind of spooky. The first time she showed up with
Hank, I asked Ethan what she was doing here. He told
me not to worry about it—but I don't like the way she's
always sneaking around."

For the rest of the morning, I watched Jolene swim
and sunbathe and practice her tennis serve. She didn't
need a playmate as much as she wanted an audience.
By the time we got around to watching Jolene paint her
toenails, I went to my room.

I stripped out of my sweat-soaked clothes and headed
for the bathroom. The accident the day before had really put a crimp in my plans. I had to talk to Tommy
and if I couldn't get to him, I could talk to his family.

I toweled myself off, grabbed a pair of jeans and a
clean cotton blouse and slipped them on. I found Millie in the kitchen preparing lunch. "Millie, can I use
your car?"

"Are you sure you should be driving?"

"I'll be fine. The doctor didn't tell me I couldn't drive.
He said I needed to rest, which is what I've been doing."

She retrieved her purse from a hook by the back door, fished out a set of keys and handed them to me. "It's the Festiva on the west side of the garage. Please be careful, Jessica."

"Trust me, Millie, your car will come back in one piece."

"It's not the car I'm worried about," she said.

I stood for a moment, my hand on the car's door handle, telling myself it was okay to drive again. Taking Millie's car had been a spur-of-the-moment decision. Even though no one knew what I was doing or where I was going, I couldn't get in until I bent down and looked under the vehicle for any escaping brake fluid pooled on the ground. It was wise to be a bit precautious now.

I PARKED THE red Festiva on the gravel road and approached the splotchy white house with the sagging front porch. The woman inside must have heard me coming. She pushed open a screen door patched with electrical tape and watched me make my way across the brown grass, her arms folded across her large stomach.

Her eyes were small and beady-looking and one front tooth was missing. Even from six feet away, I detected an unmistakable body odor.

"What d'ya want?" she asked as I approached, trying to keep a smile on my face.

"Are you Mrs. Markowski?"

"Who wants to know?"

"My name is Jessica Kallan. I wanted to speak to Mrs. Markowski about her son, Tommy."

"Tommy?" That caught her off guard. "You ain't here from the state?"

"No. I'm working for Ethan Miller, and I'm doing

some research on Bonnie Rawlings' death. Are you Mrs. Markowski?"

The mention of Ethan's name produced a glimmer of interest in her dull eyes, "Yeah."

"Tommy's mother?"

She nodded. "What does Ethan Miller want to know?"

"He's writing a book about the murder."

"A book?" Her interest increased. "He must be paying you a lot of money."

I picked up my cue and pulled my billfold out of my purse. I took out a couple of twenty-dollar bills as she looked at me and the contents of my billfold. The expression on her face didn't change until I took out another twenty and handed her the bills.

"Well now, isn't this nice?" She tucked the money into the pocket of her stained blouse. "Why don't you come on in and we can talk."

The inside of the house was even worse than the exterior implied. A yellow film covered the windows. There were dirty dishes and empty beer bottles on almost every flat surface. It smelled like cigarettes and grease. I took the least offensive chair in the room and sat down.

Mrs. Markowski brushed a heap of soiled clothes to the floor and plopped herself onto the sagging couch opposite me. "Well, what do you wanna know?"

"As much about Tommy as you can tell me. I'd like to know him from your perspective."

She shrugged her shoulders. "What's to know? He ain't smart." She reached for a beer bottle on the table, shook it, found it empty and put it back.

"I know Tommy worked for Ethan sometimes."

"I guess that's what he did. I never paid no attention."

A big mangy gray cat wandered into the room and

rubbed up against my leg. It was all I could do to keep from pushing it away.

She nodded toward it. "He don't like everybody, you know."

I wasn't thrilled I was one of the chosen ones. I tried to shift my legs so they weren't touching him, but he flopped across my feet and began to purr. "Mrs. Markowski, do you think Tommy killed Bonnie?"

"How would I know?"

"Do you think Tommy had any reason to kill Bonnie Rawlings?"

"She was one of those hoity-toity girls, real full of herself. Shoot! I could've killed her."

"Did Tommy ever talk about her?"

She was silent for a minute. "Not that I can recall. My husband, Bill, did, though. Said she was a real tease."

Okay, that fit with what I knew already. "Did she ever come on to Tommy?"

She snorted a laugh. "How would I know? All I can say is if she did, she was dumber than he was."

I had a feeling I wasn't going to get my money's worth. "Your son was convicted of rape and murder. Don't you have any opinion about whether or not he's guilty?"

She looked at me hard, her eyes squinting into narrow slits. "Well, I know for a fact he didn't rape her."

"How do you know that?"

"Because he couldn't."

"Couldn't what?"

"He couldn't rape nobody. The doctor told me he was sterile."

"The two aren't necessarily… I mean, a man can be sterile and still have…sexual…function."

She dismissed me with a wave of her hand. "All's I know is what the doctor said."

"What made him sterile?"

"Tommy had the mumps real bad when he was about thirteen, and that nosy social worker at the school made me take him to the doctor. Must have been a real bad case 'cuz the doctor kept him right there at his own house for two weeks. I guess he thought Tommy might die." She must have forgotten that the beer bottle on the table next to her was empty when she picked it up and shook it again.

"Anyway, when he came home, he kept sayin' how his crotch was always hurtin'. The doctor said that would pass, but then he told me Tommy was sterile. Which was just fine with me, him bein' slow and all."

"Did you tell this to anyone during the trial?"

"Told his lawyer. But you know what? Just because he didn't rape her, don't mean he didn't kill her."

She had a point. "Who was the doctor? I'd like to talk to him."

She shook her head. "Name was Plante. He kind of specialized in people like Tommy, I guess. Used to work at the state hospital. But you ain't gonna be talking to him. He's dead."

"Who else would have Tommy's medical records?"

"There's another doctor took his place name of Fischer. He saw Tommy a couple of times."

"Do you ever go visit your son?"

She snorted again. "You kiddin'? I'm not going into that place they got him locked up."

"You don't seem very upset by any of this."

"All's I know is that ever since he went off to that nut hospital, somebody brings me money couple times a month, so that's just fine with me."

"What are you talking about?"

"Every couple weeks, just like clockwork, somebody puts a couple hundred dollars cash in my mailbox."

"Who?"

She started to laugh. "Somebody with a guilty conscience."

I stood to leave and the screen door slammed behind me.

"What's so funny?" asked a raspy male voice.

"Aw nothin', Bill." She wiped her eyes.

The man moved around in front of me. Her husband, Bill, was dressed in dirty clothes, and the sneer on his face looked as if it had been carved there.

"Who's she?"

"Name's Jessica something or-other. She works for Ethan Miller. He's writing a book about Tommy."

"Why? Ain't nothin' special about him."

"Ethan Miller thinks there is," she said.

He looked at me, his face inches from mine. "You can tell Ethan Miller we don't want him messing in our business. I want my lunch," he said to his wife. Turning back toward me, he said, "We don't have nothin' more to say to you."

I wanted to run for my car and lock myself in, but I made a point to walk slowly, feeling his eyes boring into my back.

NINE

I PUT THE car in gear and pulled away from the side of the road and the patches of brown grass that covered the Markowski lawn. As much as I didn't like Tommy's mother, I did learn a couple of things. Even if Tommy hadn't raped Bonnie, he might have killed her. And whoever had been giving her money every month had a very guilty conscience.

I glanced in the rearview mirror and could have sworn I saw Ethan's Caddie parked at the other end of the block. I focused my attention back on the unfamiliar road I was driving and when I looked back in the mirror, the car was speeding away in a cloud of dust. Strange neighborhood for a Cadillac.

There was a gas station about a mile from the Markowski house and I stopped to put gas in Millie's car. While the tank was filling, I pulled my cell phone out of my purse and looked up the phone number for Dr. Fischer's practice. I dialed the number and was told Dr. Fischer was out of town until the next day, so I got back in the car and pointed the Festiva in the direction of Ethan's house and headed out of town, mulling over what I knew and didn't know about Tommy Markowski.

I parked Millie's car on the side of the garage and was just rounding the corner when Matt stepped in front of me.

I let out a yelp. "God! You scared me."

He raised an eyebrow and folded his arms across his chest.

"Yes? Did you want something?" I asked.

"Where were you just now?"

"Why do you ask?"

"You've been to see the Markowskis."

"Ah, I thought I was being spied on. Again. You know you and Dan seem to have a real problem minding other people's business."

"Stay away from them, Jess. You could end up in more trouble than you're already in."

"I didn't realize I was in any trouble." I tried to move past him on the narrow path.

He stepped in front of me again, thwarting my escape. "How stupid are you? Trisha is dead and there have already been two attempts on your life. How many does it take for you to realize how ugly this whole thing is?"

He was trying to scare me, but why? I could think of two equally possible reasons. Either he cared or he was worried about what I'd find. Given the way he'd been acting so far, it was hard to believe the former. I tried to move around him again.

He took another step to block me.

I stared him in the eyes. "Will you please get out of my way?"

"Will you please get the hell out of Sedgewick before you get yourself killed? Do you want to end up like Trisha? And if you don't care that much about yourself, then think about what you're doing to other people for a change."

I took a deep breath. "Okay. Apparently, you have

some speech you want to make. Why don't you go ahead and make it."

He took a step forward. "I can't believe how stupid you are. You don't have a clue what's going on around here. You don't have any idea what kind of people you're dealing with."

"I'm not afraid of the Markowskis."

"I'm not talking about the Markowskis. When Bonnie died, don't you think that had some effect on us? Don't you think someone or some people may not want you running around trying to figure out what happened?"

I looked at him. "Are you one of those people?"

"Don't be an idiot. Stop what you're doing and get out of here before it's too late. How many times do I have to say it, look what happened to Trisha."

I walked past him.

My head was starting to throb again, and I wondered if Millie was right. Maybe I shouldn't be up and around so much.

John intercepted me on the way to the house. "I've been looking all over for you," he said, then must have noticed my grim look. "Are you all right?"

"Your brother's an ass."

"Well, yeah, I've known that for years. Maybe what you need is a night out. Have some fun. Are you up for it?"

I was about to refuse when I realized that an evening alone with John might give me more answers than all the interviews I'd had so far. Especially if he was drunk—which seemed a pretty safe bet from what I knew of him. "Sure. Why not?"

"Great. Six o'clock. Wear something pretty."

I lay down for an hour and fell asleep. By the time I woke, the throbbing in my head had disappeared and I hunted through my closet, trying to find something appropriate to wear for an evening with John. I had a summer dress with spaghetti straps in a pastel print with a matching jacket, that wasn't too wrinkled from the drive down.

I wrestled with my conscience and my wardrobe choice for twenty minutes. I might never have another chance like this, and I had to make the most of my investment.

Spaghetti straps won.

At five minutes to six, I was standing in front of Ethan's office, waiting for John, when the front door opened and Matt came in.

He ran his eyes over my outfit and raised his eyebrows. "I didn't realize dinner was formal tonight."

"I'm going out."

"My, my, don't you work fast?"

"I'm going out to dinner with John."

"Seriously? That's the best you can do?" He turned and went into the parlor.

I paced the front hall for ten minutes, waiting for John. Finally, I went back upstairs and turned down the long corridor where his bedroom was. I knocked on the first door on the left.

"Come in." He was sitting on the edge of the bed, slipping his feet into leather loafers. He looked up and looked me over. "Very nice."

I'd made a good choice. "Thanks. Are you ready to go?"

"Yes. Do you want to grab my keys and wallet off the dresser over there?"

I walked over to the cherry wood chest of drawers, picked up his car keys and found his wallet buried under a pile of credit card receipts. There was a lone picture on the dresser, a beautiful young woman wearing a dress that would have been in style thirty or forty years ago.

I picked it up. "Who's this?"

"My mother. When she was younger."

The resemblance to John became obvious as soon as he said that, from the blue eyes to the captivating smile. A softened version of his handsome features. Her hair was as blonde as her son's and there was a glint of mischief in her eyes. She wore a white dress and, at her throat, was a sapphire necklace in the shape of a lightning bolt, exactly like the necklace Bonnie Rawlings had been wearing in her graduation picture.

The necklace was so unique it was hard to believe there were two of them floating around Sedgewick, Missouri. I started to ask, but something told me now was not the time.

I turned to John. "She was beautiful."

He nodded. "Still is. Let's go."

John owned a red Corvette, naturally, and I learned quickly that he liked to drive fast. Even so, we were on the road for an hour before we arrived at a small town that looked like a booming metropolis compared to Sedgewick, although the sign at the edge of the city limits declared the population to only be about twenty-three thousand.

There was a cafe on the river, where we ate dinner at a table on the terrace overlooking the water. John asked about the research I'd been doing and, during cocktails and salads, I told him about my visit to the Markowskis' home that morning.

"I can't believe you went there alone. I wish you'd told me where you were going."

While we ate, John told me stories about prep school and the practical jokes they used to play on Hank. I'm not normally one for practical jokes. There's usually a cruel streak to them and someone gets hurt. And even though Hank wasn't one of my favorite people, a bunch of spoiled rich kids taking pot shots at him seemed anything but funny.

One of the stories happened the summer they were seventeen, when John talked Hank into going with him one night to follow the school's headmaster to a cheap motel, where he met his secretary in the parking lot.

"Whatever possessed you to do such a thing?"

"It was a dare. Everybody knew they were doing it, but nobody had any proof."

"What happened when you got there?"

"We were supposed to take pictures. We went around behind the building and found a back window to their room where we could see all the action. Then we realized we'd left the camera back at the dorm."

"And?"

"You have to remember we were two horny teenage boys. Neither one of us wanted to leave to go get the camera. Finally, they both went into the bathroom and I told Hank we had to do something to prove we'd been there."

"What did you do?"

"We slit the screen on the window, crawled into the room and stole their clothes. Hank almost got us caught. He kept whining the whole time about how much trouble we were going to be in."

"*Did* you get caught?"

"Well…we would have been fine if we'd just taken the clothes, but the Headmaster's car keys were in his pants and I just couldn't resist a little joyride. Stupid part was—I drove the car back to school and got busted by security. I thought Hank was going to pee his pants when those flashing lights came on behind us."

"What did they do to you?"

"The headmaster couldn't expel us without explaining why, and he wasn't about to do that. But we spent most of the summer in St. Louis doing detention—working the grounds, cleaning bathrooms. Everyone else was gone and we worked our asses off for two months, and I thought Ethan was the meanest bastard in the world for making me stay there."

"That was the summer Bonnie was murdered?"

"Yeah. Some summer, huh? I was barely home a month and then Ethan was shuttling me off to school again."

Wow! Apparently, the whole world revolved around John. He emptied the last of the champagne into his glass.

I made my move. "You know what I learned yesterday?"

"No. Tell me." He leaned in for a sloppy kiss. His lips tasted like alcohol.

"Glenda was at Tommy's trial. I found a picture of her standing outside the courthouse."

"Not real exciting news. A lot of people were at Tommy's trial."

He didn't seem to grasp the impact of what I was saying. "But what was she doing there?"

"Most of the county was there. No big deal. Glenda was also at the house when Bonnie died."

This was new information. "What was she doing at your house?"

"Ethan used to hire town girls to come out and help Millie clean. Glenda was there that day."

"I didn't see her name listed in any of the newspaper articles."

"Who cares? It's all old news." He leaned in again for another kiss.

I put my hand against his chest and held him off, hoping he wasn't so drunk I'd missed my opportunity for some valuable information. "Why wouldn't she have been questioned?"

"She was probably cowering in a corner somewhere. She was just help." He slid his hand under my dress and up my thigh.

I had one hand on his chest and the other on my thigh, trying to stop his progress. "Okay—maybe, but…"

He slumped back in his chair, annoyed that I had other things on my mind. "This is Sedgewick, Missouri, Jess. *Nobody cares.* Nobody cares if we follow the rules. Nobody cares if we don't go by the damn book. Nobody. She's such a mouse. I'm sure she ran away when the cops came."

I was wondering if now was the time and decided to go for broke. "The necklace your mother was wearing in that picture was quite unique."

John reached for my glass and gulped down what was left, which was most of it, since I wasn't sure I should be drinking with a concussion—I'd only had a sip. "Ethan had it made for her." He was starting to sound bored. "My mother has a temper like a lightning bolt. Ethan gave it to her one time as a make-up present after one of their more dramatic fights. That was about six months before they got divorced."

"Bonnie was wearing a necklace just like it in her graduation picture."

I thought he faltered slightly—or maybe it was the alcohol. "The day my mother walked out of that house, she ripped off the necklace and threw it on the floor. It was her way of making a statement. I kept that necklace because it was one of the few things I had to remind myself of a time when we were still a family."

"Did you give it to Bonnie?" I asked.

He looked out over the river then back at me. "Bonnie didn't have much going for her. I gave it to her to let her know that someone cared."

That sounded like a bunch of crap. I maintained my smile as the reporter in me wanted to ask more questions.

"Let's get out of here." He stood and pulled me to my feet. "There's got to be some action going on around here somewhere."

He nuzzled my neck and slobbered on my ear as we made our way back to the car and refused to let me drive. He took winding two-lane county roads, faster than was prudent under any circumstances, and I realized when I was thrown against the door for the third time I should have taken his keys. My already-sore shoulder was on fire with renewed pain.

We stopped at two roadside taverns on the way back, places where John was well known. Easy to see why when he started buying drinks for everyone.

By the time we left the second bar, John was not only drunk but increasingly obnoxious. In the parking lot, I told him to hand over the keys.

A mushy smile formed on his lips. "No."

"I'm not getting in the car with you."

"Then you'll just have to stand here all night."

"Fine. I'll call Ethan to come and get me."

I turned to go back into the building, and call for a ride. John grabbed my arm and swung me around. "I was just kidding. You can have the keys." He dropped them down the front of my dress.

As I walked around to the driver's side of the car, trying to fish them out of my bra, I realized just how much John was still a horny teenage boy—afraid of his father, playing borderline-cruel practical jokes, with absolutely no brakes on his impulses. As we headed back onto the highway, John's hands were all over me, and he kept trying to nibble my ear and kiss my neck. It was annoying as hell. The stick shift was the only thing keeping him on his side of the car.

The road was unfamiliar and, except for the light from an occasional farm or passing car, it was dark as pitch. By the time we reached Ethan's, all the muscles in my neck were strained and my head was throbbing again.

The drive back hadn't done much to sober John up. He suggested we go skinny-dipping by the light of the moon, and I pictured him drowning in the pool, leaving me to explain to Ethan why I was wet and naked and his youngest son was dead.

"John, I just want to go to bed. Alone."

"It's too early for bed."

"I'll see you in the morning."

He grabbed for me as I turned toward the house. I sidestepped his miscalculated lunge and hurried up the front steps.

The lights were on in the front parlor and I looked in to see Matt sitting there, his long legs stretched out in front of him.

"Come in and talk to me," he said.

I stepped into the room but didn't sit down.

"Have a nice evening?"

"Lovely, thank you."

"Really? And what made this particular evening so lovely?"

There was an empty glass in his hands, and I wondered if all of Ethan's sons were drunk tonight. "The company."

"Touché, Ms. Kallan."

"Thank you. Now, if you'll excuse me, I'm going to bed."

"I'd like to talk to you."

"Matt, it's late and I'm tired. I have a splitting headache and I ache all over from the accident."

"Then perhaps the evening wasn't quite as lovely as you led me to believe."

I was just about to turn away when John's car started up out in front.

"John's going out," I said quickly. "You have to stop him. He's really drunk and shouldn't be driving."

Matt just sat there and shook his head. "I can't. I decided a long time ago I can't chase after him every time he does something stupid."

"That's a very nice speech, but he could kill himself or someone else in the meantime."

He passed a callused hand over his eyes. "Jess, you don't understand what—"

"Would you *please* do something."

"I've been through this before. Every time I try to

help John, he just resents me more and more. If I tried to follow him right now, he'd turn it into some kind of game, which would be even more dangerous."

"Matt—"

"At some point, John's lifestyle is going to catch up with him. But it's something he's going to have to figure out for himself. I can't babysit him twenty-four hours a day." He watched me for a while. "Now, will you sit down and talk to me?"

I didn't move from the doorway. "What do you want to talk about?"

"What did you and Sarah Rawlings talk about?"

"Why do you want to know?"

"Did she mention me?"

Okay, not what I expected. "Why would she?"

"Just curious." He tried to sound nonchalant, but he was watching me with an intensity that made me uncomfortable.

I was silent for a minute.

He looked away. "I can't believe Ethan is doing this."

"Looking for the truth?"

He looked up again. "Putting us through this again. Like it wasn't bad enough living through it the first time."

"Do you think Tommy Markowski is guilty? I should think you, of all people, would want to know what really happened."

He winced. "You know about Bonnie and me. I was young and naïve and absolutely crazy about her. And to answer your question, no, I don't think Tommy murdered her. I don't believe he's capable of that."

"Who do you think really did kill her?"

"I honestly don't know and, after all this time, I don't

think we'll ever know. It won't bring Bonnie back and it won't give Tommy back his life. You met the Markowskis. You saw where Tommy came from. He might be better off where he is."

"I don't think that's your decision to make. Tommy has a right to have *some* kind of life."

"He'll never have much of a life living with his parents."

"Even if that were true, you're wrong that the truth won't make any difference." I came in and sat down in front of him. My earlier suspicions began to seem a little silly. He looked sad, not guilty, but my evening with John had brought a few things to light for me. I wanted to articulate them, and he needed to hear them.

"Ethan hasn't written up to his full potential since Bonnie died. John's stuck in some time-warp from high school. You're devoting your life to your greenhouse. This whole family has been twisted out of shape by whatever happened in that guesthouse twenty years ago. And now it's happened again. Another young girl is dead. It's got to be better to know the truth, for everyone's sake, especially you, Matt. You not only lost Bonnie, but your baby too."

His jaw muscles tightened and he grew silent for several long seconds. I figured the conversation was over, and I'd said what I wanted to say. I started to stand up, when he spoke again. "I have to go away for a day or two. Please be careful."

TEN

THE FIRST THING I did the next morning was check the garage for John's car. It was sitting there intact and I breathed a sigh of relief knowing he hadn't killed himself out on the highway the night before.

I made my way back to the house and knocked on Ethan's office door before I opened it and poked my head in. He was seated behind the mahogany desk, papers in hand, already working.

"Have you got a minute?"

"Of course." He shoved the papers into a desk drawer and looked me over. "How do you feel?"

"Mostly okay. Some sore spots, a few colorful bruises and a headache that seems to make an appearance when it's least convenient. I guess I'll live."

He furrowed his brow. "I've been thinking that maybe we should put our research on hold for a while."

"Why?"

"So you can recuperate. Go home for a few weeks. Then when you're feeling up to it again, we can talk."

"I'm fine, Ethan. Really I am. Besides, I think I'm making some real headway on this case and I don't want to quit now."

"This book has waited twenty years. Your health is more important. I wish you'd reconsider."

"I'd like to stay and finish what I've started, and

you're forgetting one very minor detail when you think I can go home and just lounge around for a month."

"What's that?"

"I have no job and I have no paycheck and at the moment no car."

"What's going on with the car?"

"It's still at Medford's Garage. An adjuster is supposed to look at it today."

"I can help you with the money part—and the car," he said.

"Thanks, but I'd rather stay and do the work you're going to pay me for."

He looked at me for several seconds. "Okay."

"Good. Now that we've agreed on that, can we talk about business?"

"What have you learned?" He passed a hand over his face and I realized how tired he looked.

"Did you know that Tommy Markowski was sterile from a childhood bout with the mumps?"

He shook his head. "No. Do you think that's pertinent?"

"I'm not sure yet. I would like more information."

"Okay, go on."

"Bonnie seemed to be in possession of the sapphire lightning bolt necklace you'd given to John's mother."

"I know. I'd seen her wearing it. At first I couldn't imagine how she'd gotten hold of it until I questioned John."

"Did that bother you?"

He was silent a moment. "Not in the sense that you might think. I had no need for the necklace. My wife was long since gone, and John could do with it whatever he pleased. I just thought it was inappropriate for John to be giving such an expensive gift to his brother's fiancée."

"Do you know why he did?"

"I suppose he told me at the time, but it was probably an impulsive act, which is characteristic of my son."

"Ethan, why didn't you tell me Glenda was working here that day?"

He looked at me blankly for a moment. "I didn't?"

"No. Her name wasn't in the police reports either."

"Glenda was a mouse of a girl. I'm sure if she thought there was trouble brewing somewhere she would have hightailed it for the hills." He forced a laugh. "Do you think she's the killer?"

I couldn't read his face. Ethan had been remarkably open with his feelings about the murder and about his concerns for his sons' possible involvement. But I also sensed there was a part of him holding back. I had tried to bring up Trisha's accident but he was quick to downplay what happened with that incident as well.

"I have no opinion about Glenda at this point," I said, "but, if I'm going to find out anything about Bonnie's murder, I need all the facts."

"I understand."

I felt his guard going up.

"What do you want to know?"

"Tell me about Glenda."

"I'm not sure what I can tell you. I didn't know her very well back then. I used to hire girls from the area to come and help Millie clean the house. Well, that's not true—Millie hired them, I just wrote out the checks. Glenda was here when she was supposed to be and I guess she did her job. I never paid much attention to all that. That's about all I know. Glenda hardly ever spoke to anyone and seemed uncomfortable when we spoke to her."

He was silent, searching the recesses of his brain for threads of information about a nondescript girl from twenty years ago. "I think she had a crush on Matt."

"What makes you think that?"

"She seemed to always be wherever he was. Now, I remember!" He slapped his hand on the desk, a spark of memory in his eyes. "That's why Millie finally got rid of her. She was always following Matt around instead of doing the chores Millie had for her. If Matt was in the parlor, then she cleaned the parlor, whether it needed to be cleaned or not."

"What did Matt do?"

"I doubt Matt even noticed her He was always in a world of his own."

The door behind me opened and Jolene walked in. "I thought you were taking me shopping this morning." She positioned herself by the side of the desk halfway between the two of us.

"I haven't forgotten," Ethan said. "Is there anything else you need right now, Jessie?"

"Can we talk again when you have more time?"

"I'll make a point to touch base with you." He stood behind his desk.

I picked up my cue and stood as well. "Thanks for your time. Have fun shopping, Jolene." I moved across the room and felt for the switch in the bookcase to open the wall to the hidden staircase. As soon as the wall closed behind me, their voices rose as they began their bickering for the day.

I stood at the window in my office looking out at the hills bathed in the light of the morning sun, feeling a weight settling over me as I wondered what I was doing and why. Matt was right. Someone apparently wanted me, if not dead, at least frightened enough to back out. And yet, here I was, with no intention of leaving. What was driving me to stay I wasn't exactly sure. I didn't like this feeling of not knowing.

I thought again of my father. Did I have the strength of his integrity to find the truth, no matter what the cost? I didn't know for sure. The question only added to the weight of my confusion and I pushed it aside.

I sat down behind my desk. Could I have missed something in the police reports? The newspaper articles? Where had Glenda been during all that was happening? I scanned each document, searching for her presence. She wasn't there, and I wasn't even sure it mattered. I doodled names on a notepad, looking for some thread, some hint of clarity. Nothing came. After five minutes, I gave up trying to figure things out. I had to get out of the house. I dialed Fred Connor's number.

"Hi, Jess. I was just going to call you."

"How's that grandson?"

"He's a keeper. My daughter done good. Say, have you had breakfast yet?"

"As a matter of fact, no."

"Why don't you meet me in about twenty minutes at the truck stop on the edge of town."

He gave me directions, promised to bring baby pictures and we said good-bye.

Millie was in the kitchen and, less reluctantly than the day before, retrieved her car keys for me from her purse hanging on the hook by the back door. I promised once again to return it in one piece.

"I'm not worried about the *car*," she said, "I'm just not sure you should be up and around so much."

"Millie, I appreciate your concern, but I would go absolutely batty if I had to stay in bed all day. You wouldn't want that, would you?"

She agreed she wouldn't, but I wasn't convinced.

As I pulled the car into the driveway, I tapped the brakes several times, just to make sure...

I parked the Festiva in the gravel parking lot of the truck stop, locked the doors and entered the small building. Fred Connor wasn't there yet so I nabbed a table toward the front of the diner when a brawny truck driver got up to pay his bill.

I was looking out the window, thinking of Tommy Markowski, and hoping Fred would take me to see him today, when I sensed someone standing over me. I looked up to see Sarah Rawlings, dressed in a sage tunic blouse that accentuated her high cheekbones and green eyes.

"Mind if I join you?"

"Please. Sit down."

She slid gracefully into the booth across from me.

"I'm waiting for someone, but you're welcome to join us for breakfast."

"Just ate," she said. "Have to be at work in about twenty minutes. I was just wondering how things are going?"

"You mean my research? Not much to tell you. I'm just learning bits and pieces as I go along."

"I've been thinking a lot about you, ever since we talked. I've been thinking a lot about a lot of things."

"Bonnie?"

She nodded and tears filled her eyes. "Yes, Bonnie.

And Alena. And myself. And what a terrible mother I must have been to allow all that to happen."

"Sarah, blaming yourself now won't bring Bonnie back."

"I know." She took a tissue from her purse and dabbed her eyes.

"Sarah, do you remember the necklace Bonnie was wearing in her graduation picture?"

"The sapphire lightning bolt? Of course. It was a beautiful piece of jewelry. Bonnie loved it."

"Did she say why John gave it to her?"

"John?" She looked surprised. "John didn't give it to her. Ethan did."

It was my turn to be surprised. "John and Ethan both said John gave the necklace to Bonnie."

We stared at each other in silence. Sarah finally shook her head. "No. I remember distinctly. Bonnie told us Ethan gave it to her. The reason I remember so well is that the day she brought it home Alena and I both oohed and ahhed over it. It was so incredibly beautiful. I could tell right off that it was going to bring trouble. Alena asked Bonnie if Matt gave it to her and Bonnie said, no, Ethan did."

"Did you believe her?"

"I had no reason not to."

"Why on earth would Ethan give a valuable piece of jewelry to a child?"

She chewed on her lip. "Now that you mention it, it does seem strange. Maybe…"

"Maybe what?"

She shook her head again. "I told you how competitive those girls were when it came to boys. Alena was very jealous when Bonnie and Matt got engaged. Alena

Jo always had big dreams of being rich and famous. In her eyes, marrying into the Miller family would have been like marrying into the Kardashians. Maybe if Bonnie said John gave her the necklace, we wouldn't have thought much of it. John never had a lick of sense about anything. But if she made Alena *think* Ethan gave her the necklace, it would be just one more dig that she would one day be a Miller."

"What did Alena do when Bonnie said the necklace came from Ethan?"

"She went nuts. She called Bonnie a whore, tore the necklace off her neck and threw it on the ground. Then she slapped Bonnie and ran out of the house."

"Wow."

"Bonnie was inconsolable that the necklace was ruined. I ended up taking some money out of my savings to have it fixed. Alena never got over it, though."

I thought for a minute. "There's got to be more to it than that. I mean, if Bonnie was going to marry Matt, she would have been a Miller."

Sarah chewed on her lip. "I think Alena was having an affair with Ethan. I was never sure, but I think Bonnie knew about it and wanted to one-up her sister."

"Why?"

"That's just the way she was. Maybe it had something to do with Matt. I don't know. Matt and Alena dated for a while, but that didn't seem to go anywhere. Maybe Bonnie was jealous of that."

"Whatever happened to the necklace?"

Silence hung in the air between us. "No one knows for sure. I always thought Tommy stole it."

"Why Tommy?"

"When I had to identify the body, there was a red

mark around Bonnie's neck as if someone had yanked it right off her."

"Was it ever found?"

"No."

She looked at her watch. "I've got to run. Call me if you need to, Jessica."

She left the diner just as Fred Connor walked in. He spotted me right away and came over and planted himself opposite me. "Thought I'd beat you here. I didn't see your car in the parking lot."

"I had a little accident the other day." I told him about the brakes and my trip to the hospital.

"Are you all right?"

"I'm very colorful at the moment, but I'll live."

He gave me a look that told me he thought there was more to the story, but he let it drop. We talked about his grandson and looked at baby pictures until our breakfast arrived. Then over omelets and hash browns he turned the conversation to Bonnie's murder.

"So, old lawmen never retire," I said.

"Neither do old reporters. Your day will come."

I brought him up to date on everything I'd done—my research in town and meeting Sarah Rawlings and the Markowskis. He seemed very interested in Tommy's sterility and the necklace that made the rounds of the women involved with the Miller men.

When I'd finished, he sat there for a while, looking at his coffee. "Sounds like you're on the right track. You're certainly finding things the original investigation missed. What next?"

"I'd like to meet Tommy. That's where I was headed the day my car was totaled. Will you take me there?"

"I wish I could, but I got a call just as I was leaving

the house. A friend of mine in St. Louis is in the hospital. He had a heart attack last night. They're doing a bypass today. I'd really like to be there. He used to be in the department with me. He's one of the good guys."

"I'm so sorry. You definitely have to be there. I'll figure some other way to get out to see Tommy."

He smiled his lopsided smile. "I knew you'd say that. You're good people. If all goes well, I'll be back again in a few days. If you can wait, I'll take you then."

"If I can't make other arrangements, I'll wait for you."

"Fair enough. What now?"

"I think I need to talk to Dr. Fischer and see what he knows about Tommy's sterility. Might as well find out now if it has any bearing on the case."

"Yup." He picked up a paper napkin, took a pen from his shirt pocket and scribbled directions to the doctor's office. Then he paid for my breakfast and walked me to Millie's car.

He took a scrap of paper from his shirt pocket and handed it to me. "This is my cell phone number and the number where I'll be staying in St. Louis. Call if you need to. Even if I can't help, maybe you can just bounce ideas off me. Got to use this old noodle for something."

I gave him a hug. "Be careful," he said, his face serious.

"Don't worry about me. You have enough on your mind right now."

"And I don't want you added to my list." He turned and headed toward his Ford Ranger.

It took maybe nine minutes to get across town. Dr. Fischer's home office was a couple of blocks off the main drag. It was a big sprawling, two-story, turn-of-the-century house painted a pale yellow, with white shutters around the upstairs windows. A wide verandah wrapped around the front. There was a sign on the lamppost outside, with his name and office hours. A side door off the parking lot led to a parlor that had been converted to a waiting room.

An older woman resembling a little round pixie sat behind the reception desk. "May I help you, dear?" Her plump cheeks dimpled into a smile.

I told her I'd like to see Dr. Fischer.

She smiled again. "I'm sorry, dear. The doctor is semi-retired. He isn't taking any new patients. I could refer you to one of his colleagues."

"Oh, I'm not a patient. I'm a reporter and I need his help with some research I'm doing."

Her eyes lit up. "A reporter? How exciting. Where are you from? St. Louis? Kansas City?"

"Omaha."

She let out a squeal of excitement. "He'll be done with the patient he's with in a few minutes. I'll tell him you're here." She wasn't much taller standing than she was sitting. She hurried across the room and disappeared behind a pair of sliding doors. Returning seconds later, she led me across the wide front hall into the doctor's private office, settled me into a chair and brought me a cup of coffee.

After she left, I got up and wandered around the room, read his diplomas and studied the Monet prints he had on the wall. I glanced out the front window once, just in time to see a Cadillac make its way down the street. It was difficult to identify the driver, but I was starting to wonder just how many beige Cadillacs there were in Sedgewick, Missouri.

A door opened behind me and I turned as a large man with thick white hair and round, pink cheeks entered the room. I introduced myself and explained the purpose for my visit.

"How can I help you?" He settled his bulk behind the desk.

"Did you ever see Tommy Markowski as a patient?"

"I know the Markowskis. I saw Tommy a couple of times many years ago."

"What did he come to you for?"

His clear blues eyes locked me in his gaze for several long seconds. "Tell me what kind of information you're looking for. And bear in mind I have to honor my patient's privacy."

"I'm familiar with HIPPA regulations."

"Good. Let's keep that in mind as we proceed."

"Do you remember Bonnie Rawlings' murder?"

He nodded.

"Some of the people I've interviewed seem to think Tommy was wrongfully convicted. I've talked to Tommy's mother and I think there might be something in his medical history that could be pertinent to his case."

"Such as?"

"Mrs. Markowski implied Tommy may have been sterile. If that's true and sperm was found in the semen from Bonnie's autopsy, then it could be proof of his innocence."

"Well, it would be proof he didn't rape her."

"I understand, but at least it would be proof of something. Do you have any records on Tommy that might indicate whether or not he really was sterile?"

He pursed his lips, caught up in some inner debate. "Dr. Fischer. I understand your situation, I understand the laws, but if there's any thread of hope here for Tommy, don't you think we should pursue it? Twenty years of his life have already been taken from him, and from what I understand, I don't think he's someone who can fight for himself."

"Why is Ethan writing this book now, after all these years?"

The question, of course, was valid. It wasn't the first time it had been asked. "He thinks Tommy may have been convicted of a crime he didn't commit. I guess he wants to set the record straight." The more I repeated that, the flimsier it sounded. It made Ethan look like an avenging knight, albeit one who showed up twenty years too late.

Dr. Fischer rubbed his forehead. "I didn't know Tommy well. I only saw him a couple of times. A likable kid— well, man, I should say." He stopped and scrunched up his face.

I could almost see the wheels turning in his head. He was thinking about something that seemed disturbing to him. I let the silence drag.

"I'd only been in Sedgewick a few years when Bonnie Rawlings was killed. After working the ER in St. Louis, my wife thought being a GP in a small town would be a great stress-reliever. I took over Dr. Plante's practice when the old coot finally decided to retire." He looked at me again. "It took years to undo the damage done by that old quack. Those first few years here were a medical nightmare."

I still didn't jump in. I was curious to know where he might be headed with all of this.

"Do you know anything about Plante?"

"I'd never heard of him until just the other day."

"He was an ignorant old country doctor—born in the early nineteen-hundreds, thought he had the right to play god with other people's lives. He was the only doctor in this town for almost six decades. Thought he knew everything and was as stubborn as a Missouri mule."

"What does this have to do with Tommy?"

He got up from his chair and opened a cupboard behind his desk, each shelf packed with books. He reached up to the top shelf and took one down, crossed in front of his desk and handed it to me. "This is the kind of man we're talking about."

The book was old and covered in a blue cloth binding, the title too worn to read. I looked at the doctor.

He settled himself against the edge of his desk, only two feet in front of me. "Look inside."

I turned to the table of contents. "Is this what I think it is?"

"Eugenics. Not uncommon in the early part of the twentieth century."

I glanced at the hand-drawn illustrations. "It's barbaric."

He nodded and walked around behind his desk, resting his large frame in the big leather chair.

I read a chapter heading, "Involuntary Sterilization of Indigent Women."

"This is unreal."

"A hundred years ago, eugenics was common practice—castrating or sterilizing the developmentally delayed and the mentally ill. It was even sanctioned by the Supreme Court. I'm sure the medical community thought they were doing society a favor, trying to rid us of defective genetics. But, the practice had long since died away by the nineteen seventies."

"And you think Dr. Plante did this to Tommy?"

He raised his eyebrows. "I can't respond to that," he said. But I knew by the look on his face that that was exactly what he thought.

I sat for a minute, trying to digest this new information. "Okay. So, if *someone* was castrated, would that man be physically capable of rape?"

"Hard to say. Castration definitely lowers the libido and may make a man unable to have an erection. But there's no guarantee. Back when the procedure was used on sex offenders, it was usually in tandem with medication to keep the sex drive in check."

I looked at the cloth-covered book again. "It is possible, though, that a castrated individual would be incapable of sexual function."

He nodded. "Yes, that's certainly a possibility. And as you said before, if sperm was found in the semen at a crime scene, it would be proof that, uh Bonnie, wasn't raped by a castrated individual."

"Did you say anything during the trial?"

"What could I say? It was all supposition on my part. Plante was dead and had destroyed many of his medical files by the time I took over his practice."

"Wouldn't they have tested for DNA?"

He shrugged. "I'd have to read the coroner's report, but I think that would have been presented at trial if anyone had bothered to check."

We sat looking at each other for a while. "Sarah Rawlings told me that Bonnie's sister, Alena, used to work for you."

"She was my first secretary when I set up practice

here. I should say receptionist. She worked part-time and did my typing for me. Updated medical files for patients. Smart enough girl, but she had a chip on her shoulder bigger than Rhode Island and seemed to take a lot of time off from work. I wasn't sorry to see her go."

"When did she quit?"

"Shortly after the trial she came in here, picked up her last check and told me she was leaving town."

"Did you know Bonnie was pregnant?"

He nodded. "She came to see me that very morning for the results of her blood test."

"How did she take the news?"

He was silent for a moment. "Actually, I'd say she was ecstatic."

"Not the typical reaction of a young unwed mother."

"No. I have another patient in five minutes. Is there anything else you need to know?"

"I can't think of anything. Thank you so much for your time, Dr. Fischer." I stood to leave and held out my hand. It disappeared between his two large ones.

"Let me know if there's anything else I can do for you."

"I will."

I was reaching for the doorknob when he spoke again. "Do you know what they used to call it?"

I turned to look at him.

"A therapeutic castration. I wonder how many young men were grateful for *that* therapy?"

ELEVEN

ETHAN WAS GONE when I entered his office and made my way upstairs. Dan was sitting at his desk and glanced at me over the top of his glasses, then back at the papers in front of him. I didn't bother to say good morning. What was the point?

I didn't know what to do with myself—I was at a loss. I spent the next several hours going through files, hoping for insight that didn't come.

About one o'clock, I heard Dan go downstairs. Fifteen minutes later, Glenda came through the door from Dan's office then stopped short when she saw me.

"Oh good. I've been looking for you."

"You've found me. What do you want?"

She stood there looking at me from across the desk, her blue-veined hands fidgeting with the front of her blouse. "I think you should stop what you're doing."

"I'm not doing anything at the moment."

Her lips pursed. "Don't be obtuse. You're upsetting a lot of people around here and you know it."

Obtuse? I don't believe anyone had ever accused me of being obtuse. I would have to add that to my list of character flaws. "Glenda, what are you talking about?"

She sighed—probably at my obtuseness. "This book of Ethan's is a big mistake. And the way you've been running around talking to people has been very upsetting to this household."

"Why should you care? You're not part of this household."

"Well, because…well, to be honest, I'm, uh, quite fond of everyone here. I hate to see them in such turmoil. You're dredging up some painful memories."

"And are you one of the ones in turmoil?"

"No. It's those other people."

"Really? You seem pretty turmoiled to me."

"No. Absolutely not! It's them I'm worried about."

"Glenda, were you working here the day Bonnie was murdered?"

I watched her face as she responded. "Where did you hear that?"

"Doesn't matter. Were you here that day?"

"I don't recall."

"How could you not recall if you were working here on the day a girl was murdered? How could you not remember something like that?"

"Maybe I was here that day."

"What time were you working that day?"

"I don't remember."

"Glenda, you know exactly when you were here that day and now I do too. You wouldn't be this evasive if you had nothing to hide. It would be easy enough to check."

She looked down at the floor and then her hands and started fidgeting with the buttons on her blouse.

Finally, she looked up at me never really making eye contact. "Okay. I was here. I was working that afternoon. I didn't know what was happening, though. I never went near that guesthouse. You have to believe me."

I watched her face and said nothing.

"You *have* to believe me. I was cleaning upstairs and I heard the sirens and knew there was trouble somewhere. I just got scared and took off through the woods. I was so scared. I didn't want to be in the middle of any trouble."

"Why would you be so scared if you didn't even know what happened and you had nothing to do with it?"

"My husband."

I never knew Glenda was married. I shook my head to clear the cobwebs. That was a mistake. It was just enough movement to start my head aching again. "I didn't know you were married."

"I'm not. I'm divorced."

"What does your ex-husband have to do with all of this?"

"Earl never liked me working up here, thought the Millers were too uppity. And he certainly didn't like anything that would disrupt his life. I didn't know what was going on when the sheriff's deputies came racing up here, but I knew it was trouble and if I got in the middle of any of it, Earl would have beat me."

"He would have beaten you for something that didn't even involve you? That's awful." I readjusted my opinion of Glenda.

She clenched her jaw and looked me in the eyes. "I don't need your pity."

"Oh my God, Glenda. What are you talking about? I just think wife-beaters are lower than sewer life, and your husband had no right to treat you like that."

"*Ex*-husband. And it's none of your business."

With my head starting to throb in rhythmic precision, I couldn't keep up with this. I looked at her levelly. "I'm going to finish what I've started. I'm doing a job for Ethan and I don't intend to quit."

She stood there for a minute, apparently deciding on a different approach, because she tried to smile yet she looked as if she might be in pain with the effort it took. "Jessica, don't be foolish. You're young yet. You don't understand how these things work. People have to look out for each other—care about one another's feelings."

"I don't think we have anything else to discuss. I'm not going to change my mind and you're probably not going to change yours either." My voice was firm and it took her by surprise.

"Well, just think about what I said." She left the room and I almost shook my head again. What had that been about?

After she left, I stared at my desk for ten minutes. I felt like I could make no more progress until I talked to Tommy Markowski, and I couldn't get to Tommy Markowski because I had no effing car.

I stared at the stack of papers in front of me, hoping one of them might jump up and say *look at me*. When no jumping paper presented itself, I took my hand and spread them grandly across the desk in an attempt to conjure up some enthusiasm, but enthusiasm was beyond my grasp at the moment.

My headache came on with a vengeance then, and it was impossible to think. I left the unruly papers on my desk and made my way up to my bedroom, where I took some Tylenol and climbed into bed.

I didn't emerge until dinnertime. An uncomfortable vibe had settled over the parlor and I felt it as soon as I walked into the room.

Ethan sat alone in a corner, glaring at Jolene. Glenda

was glaring at me. Hank refused to look in my direction. John looked at me occasionally, but his blue eyes were as cold as ice. Dan was on the couch looking into his glass, perhaps hoping a genie might appear and remove him from the group of people who surrounded him. Even Millie was subdued when she came to announce dinner was ready.

Things stayed grim around the table. Ethan and Jolene were clearly on the outs about something. They snapped at each other periodically throughout the meal, and I had no intention of getting involved.

As soon as dinner was over, all parties dispersed in different directions. I made my escape out the front door. The sun was still out and it was too early to go to bed.

I wandered aimlessly, trying to soak up the quiet beauty that surrounded me, determined for the time being to put Trisha Chatsworth and Bonnie Rawlings out of my mind. The door to the greenhouse was locked. As I was turning away, Satan came bounding around the corner. He let out a yelp when he saw me and came charging at me, tongue readied for greeting.

I knelt down and let him lick my face as I hugged him around the neck and petted his big black skull. I finally struggled to my feet and he whimpered pathetically. "Do you miss Matt?"

At the mention of Matt's name, his ears perked up and he started to dance around my feet. Then he took my hand in his big slobbery jaws and tried to pull me away from the building.

"Where are we going?"

Satan ran ahead then turned back and barked at me. I followed but stopped when I realized we were on the path leading to Matt's cabin. Satan ran up to me again, taking my hand in his mouth and pulling me along. After a few feet, he dropped my hand then ran ahead, stopped and looked back at me expectantly.

"Okay, I'm coming."

Before I knew it, we were standing on the front porch of Matt's cabin. Satan pawed the door and whined. He wanted in. Matt had been gone all day and wouldn't be back until tomorrow or the day after, but Satan wanted to go home, to be in his own house.

"He's not there," I said.

He looked at me then pawed the door again and whined. He was breaking my heart. Besides, at that moment, he seemed like the only friend I had in the world.

I turned the doorknob and opened the front door. Satan bolted in then sat in the middle of the living room and barked at me. We were beginning to understand each other a little too well.

I stepped into the cabin. The drapes were open and the evening sun bathed the room in a soft golden glow. Satan led me into the kitchen and sat down in front of one of the cupboards. When I didn't respond, he scratched the cabinet door and looked at me.

I opened the cupboard door and found the treasure he was waiting for—doggie treats. I poured an assortment onto the floor and filled his water bowl and food dish. Then while he was busy with his gourmet feast, I wandered back into the front room.

The cabin was homey, the walls paneled in dark wood and the carpet and drapes in earth tones. Matt must have been an amateur photographer, for the walls were filled with framed pictures of lakes and sunsets and close-ups of plants in bloom.

In one corner sat a rolltop desk, the top pushed back, papers cluttering its surface. I walked over, snooping brazenly, looking at the odds and ends of Matt Wheaton's life. Many of the papers had to do with the research he was doing for the Department of Agriculture and were too technical to warrant my interest.

I picked up a stack of canceled checks and thumbed through them. Nothing much of interest there. Another pile held letters, most of them from the University of Missouri. There had to be more to Matt Wheaton than I was seeing. I opened the top right-hand drawer. A stapler, blank envelopes, pens, pencils and rubber bands.

I was determined to find out something—anything— about Matt. He was an enigma to me. Process of elimination brought me to pay dirt in the bottom drawer on the left where Matt kept the pieces of his personal life.

Steamy emails from a woman named Christine, written five years earlier, were printed out, clipped together and pushed to the back of the drawer. His Life-Saving certificate and Boy Scout badges were crumpled up in a corner. There must have been ten or twelve daily planners stuffed in the back of the deep drawer.

My hand reached to the bottom and lifted out a hefty stack of receipts from various businesses. The top ones were the most recent, most of them from the local sporting goods store, some coupons for pizza from the Bar & Grill in Sedgewick. I went through each one curious as to where Matt spent his time.

I was almost to the bottom of the stack and getting bored when I opened up a tattered, hand-written receipt from a pawnbroker in Cross Creek. The paper was well worn and faded with age.

In fact, I knew how old it was—twenty years. It was

a receipt for two hundred and fifty dollars for the hock of a sapphire lightning bolt necklace.

Was this the receipt that had been taken from Trisha's desk? The one she'd told her mother someone stole when they went through her research papers? I stuffed it quickly in the pocket of my jeans.

Just then Satan barked and I jumped, dropping the entire stack of papers on the floor. They fanned out in every direction. I was on my hands and knees gathering up the pieces of various colored paper, when that familiar voice said to my backside, "I see you've gotten tired of peeking in windows and taken to breaking and entering."

I bumped my head on the desk in an attempt to right myself and my cheeks grew hot. "The door was unlocked." I put the receipts on the top of the desk as nonchalantly as possible. "Satan invited me in." I pointed toward the kitchen, hoping that would justify my presence.

At the mention of his name, Satan came tearing out of the kitchen and almost knocked Matt over in his greeting. After they'd said hello, Matt looked back at me and raised his eyebrows.

"Seriously, he led me here. I was worried about him and wasn't sure how long you would be gone."

"Millie feeds him when I'm not here." He was gazing at the papers on the desk behind me.

"Well, good. As long as he's taken care of, I won't worry."

I inched my way toward the door, said good night and hurried down the front steps. As I made my way up the trail, I looked back once to see Matt standing in the doorway watching me. I felt my headache coming back.

TWELVE

JOHN WAS LEANING up against a tree as I rounded the corner of the greenhouse, hands stuck deep in his pockets, a peculiar look on his face. "Been down to see Matt?"

"I was out walking and got waylaid by Satan." I tried to move past him.

He reached out and took hold of my arm. "May I walk you back to the house?"

"Okay."

We started strolling toward the house.

His hangdog look didn't change. "I think I should apologize for last night. I behaved badly and I'm sorry. It's just that I thought you were…interested."

We stopped walking and I looked at him. "John, drunk is so not sexy."

"Yeah, I know. I just got carried away. I'm sorry."

"I appreciate that."

"Friends?"

"Sure."

It felt good to have that resolved.

FRED CONNOR CALLED the next day from St. Louis. His friend had come through the operation well, but Fred decided to stay on a bit longer. Would I mind waiting a few more days to go see Tommy?

Okay. Plan B. That afternoon I asked Millie if I could once again borrow the Festiva. I drove into Sedgewick, found the hardware store and had duplicates made of her car keys.

If I could only find out who was making those payments to the Markowskis, maybe it would help me piece things together. There was no way the payments were being made in broad daylight...too much risk of discovery. I decided to simply keep watch.

For the next six nights.

I found a spot on the balcony at the far end of the second floor and positioned one of those butt-numbing, wrought-iron chairs so I had a good view of the garage. And there I sat. In the dark. Swatting mosquitoes, ducking low-flying bats, mulling over everything I knew so far and getting nowhere. At dawn, I dragged myself off to bed and slept until noon, barely able to function for the rest of the day.

Night two was simply a repeat of the night before. Dark. Mosquitoes. Bats.

During the day, I tried to work on my notes, played tennis with John and went swimming with Jolene. She must have realized, at that point, I was no threat to her relationship with Ethan. Or maybe she was simply desperate for a playmate. And Ethan seemed thrilled to have her out of his hair.

Every night at dinner I was seated next to Matt. And every night I braced myself for some kind of confrontation. He must have noticed I had disturbed his personal files, and he must have been mad as hell. But he said nothing to me. I kept waiting for the fallout that never came.

At midnight on the sixth night, I got out of bed, slipped on a pair of jeans and a long-sleeved shirt, along with some thick socks and my hiking boots. If I was going to be mosquito bait, I would not submit willingly.

I stuffed Millie's car keys in my pocket, hoping I would finally have to use them, opened my door and looked up and down the hallway. The corridor was vacant. I made my way to the end, unlatched the French doors and slipped outside. I sat down and propped my feet on the balcony railing.

The hours plodded by. I did everything I could to stay awake, starting with naming the fifty states and then trying to name them in alphabetical order. Four hours later, I'd exhausted my repertoire of mental exercises, again, and was mindlessly keeping a tally of how many mosquitoes I'd killed in the past half hour.

At four thirty, the garage door slid open and I was instantly on my feet.

A car started up and backed out onto the gravel driveway, turned sharply and headed down the long circular drive toward Lentil Road.

It was impossible in the morning darkness to see who was driving and, even though I recognized the car as one I'd seen parked in the garage, I had no idea who it belonged to.

I took the narrow side steps from the balcony to the brick walkway two at a time and hurdled a small white fence. Eighth grade gymnastics finally paid off.

By the time I reached Millie's car, I was out of breath, my head throbbing from landing hard on the other side of the small fence. It wasn't until I reached the bottom of Lentil Road that I saw the other car again, about a mile ahead of me on the county road headed for Sedgewick.

I kept my lights off. There was enough of a moon to drive by, if I aimed straight down the middle of the road and kept a certain distance between us.

By the time we were out of Sedgewick, I was getting a

little antsy and closed the gap between the two cars. We were about half a mile from the Markowski house, and I wondered what the other driver would do if he noticed another car behind him? Would the mission be aborted? I couldn't do any more nights alone on the balcony.

The car in front of me slowed and I did too then pulled off to the side of the road and switched off the ignition. The other car pulled up beside the Markowski mailbox and switched off his lights. All I could make out in the darkness was an indistinct silhouette.

The driver slid across the front seat and reached out the passenger window, an arm extended to the mailbox by the side of the road. The arm stretched and fumbled for a few seconds and then must have realized the car was parked too far from the mailbox.

The door finally opened, the overhead light went on and Dan stepped out, looking up and down the road, before he walked the few feet to the mailbox and stuffed a thick envelope inside.

He drove his car down the road past a few driveways before he swung into one and turned around. He headed back toward me, his bright lights glaring in the darkness. I slunk down in the seat until he passed and hoped he hadn't been paying attention. He would have known Millie's car well enough.

I realized too late that even if Dan didn't notice Millie's car when he passed it on the road, he would surely notice it missing when he pulled into Ethan's. Great!

I didn't want to meet Dan face to face, so I drove slowly, trying once again to figure out what was going on here. I thought finding out who was making the payments would tell me something, and it did, but not enough. *Why* was Dan paying off the Markowskis?

Guilt? And just how much was Ethan involved? Dan could have been acting on Ethan's behalf, and Ethan could have been acting on behalf of one of his sons. And even if he believed one of his sons was the killer, that didn't mean he was right.

Dammit! Why didn't these people ever talk to each other?

I was too tired to think anymore.

I sat at the bottom of Lentil Road for a good ten minutes before I started up the hill. By then Dan's car was in the garage, but he wasn't around. I would deal with the consequences later. Right now, I needed sleep. There was a thin pale finger of dawn on the eastern horizon as I dragged myself up the stairs to the second-floor balcony.

WHEN I WENT downstairs for lunch, Dan was seated at the table. He didn't look at me, but then, he never did, and his body language gave no clues as to what he might be thinking. Maybe he hadn't seen me that morning.

Later that afternoon I was in my office trying to work, despite my lack of sleep, and Dan was in his, but we hadn't said a word to each other all afternoon.

I looked again at the police reports. Dan's name wasn't in any of them. If he hadn't even been around at the time of the murder, there went his motivation for paying guilt money to Tommy's family on his own behalf.

About three o'clock there was a light tap outside my doorway. I looked up.

Millie was standing there with a thermos and a plate of cookies. "Am I interrupting?"

"No. Come in."

"I brought you some coffee and cookies. I've been worried about you. You look so tired. After your accident, you shouldn't be working so hard." She set the plate and thermos on the desk in front of me.

"I just…haven't been sleeping too well these past few nights."

She looked at the papers in front of me. "Is it any wonder? All you think about all day long are these terrible things."

"I really don't think that's the problem. I'll be fine in a few days."

I unscrewed the cup from the top of the thermos, poured coffee into it and offered it to her.

She declined the coffee but took a cookie and sat across from me. "Maybe I'll just get off my feet for a little while."

We talked about the weather and our families and friends until I shamelessly steered the conversation around to Ethan and his new book. All of a sudden, it was as if a curtain dropped between us.

"I'll never understand why Ethan is doing this after all these years," she said. "We were all doing just fine the way things were."

"I'm not so sure that's true."

"But it was all settled. There was a trial and a conviction." As if it were that easy. Or maybe she just needed to believe it was that easy.

"Millie, there's a good chance that Tommy was physically incapable of rape. And if he didn't rape Bonnie, someone else did. And someone has been paying off the Markowskis all these years. Why would they do that if Tommy was really the murderer? Do you suppose they know Tommy is innocent? And what about Trisha? Did she uncover something that made someone nervous?"

I watched her face as she tried to process this new information.

"There's someone in this house who knows the truth about Bonnie's murder." What I didn't add was that someone in this house was quite possibly a killer.

"Who?"

"I wish I knew. Millie, did your husband ever say anything about what happened at the guesthouse that day? He worked outside. Maybe he saw someone. Did he ever mention that to you?"

She looked at her hands, tightly folded in her lap. And my heart began to race. Had the answer really been in front of me all along?

"Millie?"

When she looked at me, there were tears in her eyes. "After that first day, Paul and I never discussed it. He wouldn't talk about it 'til the day he died."

"Why?"

"He was absolutely devoted to Ethan and those boys. I guess he thought he could protect them if he didn't talk about it."

"Protect them from what?"

A tear ran down her cheek. "I don't even know anymore." Her voice sounded small. She walked out of the room, her shoulders hunched under the weight of two decades' worth of silence.

I put my head down on the desk. I thought, perhaps, I had finally found the one person who might be able to tell me who was with Bonnie that day. But whatever secrets had been left uncovered seemed to have been buried with an eighteen-year-old girl more than twenty years ago.

THIRTEEN

THE RAIN STARTED that night. Just a persistent drizzle at first that turned to a relentless downpour by morning. At seven a.m., I was sound asleep when there was a pounding on my bedroom door. When I didn't respond, the door flew open and Matt walked in.

"Get up," he said.

I raised my head and squinted at him through sleepy eyes. "Huh?" was all I could manage.

"Get dressed. You're coming with me."

I rolled over. "Go away."

He leaned over me and rested his hands on each side of my head then bent down and whispered in my ear. "If you're a good girl, I'll take you to see Tommy Markowski."

I pushed him out of the way and jumped out of bed. "Are you serious?"

"Yes."

"When do we leave?"

"Half an hour." He didn't move.

"Go away."

"Really? That's the thanks I get for doing you the biggest favor of your life?"

"Well, first of all, it's not the biggest favor of my life. And secondly, I have no intention of getting dressed with you standing there watching."

He shrugged. "Oh well. I'll be parked out front." He left, closing the door behind him.

It took me thirty-five minutes to shower and get ready. My hair was still wet as I climbed into the cab of his pickup after telling Millie where I was going and who with.

He looked at his watch. "Close enough. Actually, I thought it would take you an hour."

Satan ran up to the truck and scratched at the door. Matt rolled down his window. "No. Go home."

He had to repeat the command twice more before Satan moved away from the truck. I watched out the back window as we drove away. Satan was sitting in the driveway, looking like he'd lost his last friend.

When we reached the county road, we turned east, heading in the opposite direction of Sedgewick. Neither of us spoke for the first ten minutes.

Finally, Matt reached down on the seat beside him. "Breakfast." He handed me a thermos and a box of doughnuts.

I poured a cup of Millie's coffee. "Why are you doing this?"

"I told you, I'm taking you to see Tommy. I thought you wanted to meet the killer."

He'd called Tommy a killer once before, and there was something in his tone I found disturbing.

"I thought you wanted me to go home."

He turned and looked at me for a few seconds then back on the road. "I don't like what Ethan's doing. I'm not even sure I understand it, but whether I like it or not, you're not going to quit until it's finished. Maybe Tommy can tell you what you need to know."

"Thank you. I appreciate that."

"You're also not very good at undercover work, and I figured you might as well finish your research before you get yourself killed." He glanced over at me again, a definite smile on his lips.

"I have no idea what you're talking about."

"Really? Then, might I suggest that the next time you search someone's residence, you make sure the occupant doesn't come home and catch you in the act."

Finally. I kept my eyes on the passing scenery. "I told you I was concerned about Satan. He wanted inside and something to eat."

"And the next time you do late night surveillance, pay attention to those minor details, such as disappearing cars. Dan was really pissed when he got home and saw Millie's car gone."

"Dan told you that?" I didn't realize they talked to each other that much. Why would Dan tell anyone what he'd been doing? Unless Dan and Matt were somehow in this thing together. I was feeling better about telling Millie where I was going. I was pretty sure that, whatever was going on, she wasn't a part of it.

"Did Dan also tell you where he went and what he was doing?" I asked.

He shook his head. "No, he didn't. It's none of my business. Just like it's none of yours."

I decided to enlighten him about what exactly Dan had been doing during our early morning rendezvous. I told him about the anonymous money that had been delivered to the Markowskis every month over the last twenty years, watching his face for some kind of reaction.

He looked at me once but, other than that, he kept his eyes on the road and his mouth shut.

We rode the rest of the way in silence. It took two hours to get there and the rain didn't let up once.

The residential facility, where Tommy had spent the past fifteen years, was twenty miles from the nearest town, set on acres and acres of green rolling hills. The buildings were low, one-story brick structures connected by covered walkways, like the threads of a spiderweb.

Matt parked in front of the main administration building, where we had to sign in, and we were issued visitors' badges. I followed Matt out the back door and down a covered sidewalk to the last building in the complex.

Inside, the dorm was cool and bright. Some of the residents were watching *The Price is Right* on a large screen TV. A few were playing pool. One of the counselors came out of the office and told us Tommy was outside with his work crew. We were sent through another door out onto a cement patio off the back of the building, where we made our way up a hill to a vegetable garden being readied for planting. The workers were wearing rain slickers, pulling weeds from the muddy brown soil.

Matt walked over to a covered pavilion, where he talked to the counselor overseeing the project. The man nodded, tapped one of the workers on the shoulder and pointed to the pavilion. Tommy turned and ran toward Matt, slipping in the mud, a smile filling his damp face.

"Matt! Matt!" He jumped up and threw his arms around Matt's neck and kissed him on the cheek.

Matt hugged him for a minute and laughed as he tried to struggle free from the enthusiastic embrace.

"Come here often?" I asked.

"I've been here a few times."

"Did you bring me something?" Tommy asked, looking hopeful.

Matt fished in his pocket and pulled out a roll of Lifesavers. Tommy took them, tore open the wrapper and popped three in his mouth. Then, as an after-thought, he offered one to Matt. He shook his head and told Tommy to put them in his pocket.

"Who's she?" he whispered to Matt.

"Her name's Jessica," Matt whispered back. "She's a friend of mine. She wanted to meet you."

Tommy put his head down and looked away.

"Aren't you going to say hello?" Matt asked.

"'Lo," Tommy said under his breath.

I took his hand and shook it. "Hello, Tommy. It's nice to meet you."

He looked at me, his middle-aged face crinkled as he smiled through yellowed teeth.

The hood of his rain slicker slipped off his head and he ran a hand through greasy dark brown hair, peppered with strands of gray. He wasn't much taller than I was, nor any more muscular. There were a few careless whiskers on his face, but he lacked a full beard. His voice was a mild tenor, caught somewhere between a woman's voice and the deeper bass of other men his age.

Were these the effects of possible castration? A perpetual boy caught in a time warp between the beginnings of puberty and the aging body of a man closing in on his fifth decade of life.

I looked at him closely, wondering if this was the man who strangled Bonnie Rawlings. And, for what reason, if all sexual motivation had been removed from the violent attack?

Matt and Tommy moved to one of the picnic tables, sheltered from the rain underneath the pavilion roof, and I went over and sat across from Tommy, looking for any signs of malice in his guileless face. He watched me closely out of the corner of his eye.

"This is a nice place," I said.

He nodded and ran a hand through his hair again. "I got a airplane collection in my room. You can see it if you like."

"I'd like that, but maybe later What kinds of planes do you have?"

He started to name every type of plane I'd ever heard of. Then he asked if I'd ever been on a plane. We spent the next several minutes talking about airplanes and all the places they could take you.

Matt finally interrupted. "Tommy, Jess wanted to meet you because Ethan is writing a book about Bonnie Rawlings, and she wants to ask you some questions about the day Bonnie died."

It wasn't the most graceful segue.

"No!" Tommy shouted, jumping up from the table. "No! Don't talk about it. I don't want to go back to jail. I don't want to go back to that other place!"

Thanks, Matt. I tried to make my voice as reassuring as possible. "Tommy, you don't ever have to go back. I just want to know what happened, that's all, so I can write it in the book. I want to know what you remember."

He looked at Matt and then at me. "I don't have to go back?" He didn't seem sure I was reliable.

"No. I promise," I said. "You won't have to go to jail again or to the—that other place. No one can make you. It's against the law."

He seemed to relax a little.

"Okay." He rubbed his forehead with long narrowed hands. He sat down, but he was back to watching me out of the corner of his eye.

I didn't know enough about Tommy's capabilities to know how much I could trust his memory, but it was important I hear his account of what happened that day.

"Tommy, do you remember the day Bonnie died?"

He nodded.

"Could you tell me what you remember about that day?"

"It was hot." His gaze darted around until it settled on the dirty picnic table. "It was hot because it was summer. It gets hot in the summer. And I went to Ethan Miller's house 'cause I had a job. I had lots of jobs 'cause I did good work. Mr. Paul always said I did good work."

I slipped a notebook and pen out of my purse and started making notes. For some unfathomable reason, Tommy relaxed completely then. Maybe it made him feel important or because he finally had something to focus on, as my hand moved across the page.

"What kind of job did you do for Ethan?" I asked.

"Worked for Mr. Paul. I pulled weeds and stuff. Sometimes he let me drive the big lawn mower. Sometimes we painted stuff. But, Mr. Paul said, come at one o'clock. So, I went there at one o'clock."

He paused as I made a few more notes on the page.

"What happened then, Tommy?"

"Couldn't find Mr. Paul. I looked everywhere. I went to the kitchen and Miss Millie said to wait. But I had to find Mr. Paul."

It was amazing the details we remembered. Even

one as limited as Tommy had threads of memory that were of no particular consequence.

"I waited, but then I had to go find Mr. Paul, 'cause I had a job to do."

"Did you find Mr. Paul?"

"No. That door at the guesthouse was open, and I thought maybe he was there." He stopped and looked at me. "You want I should tell the rest?" he asked softly. "It's bad. Real bad."

"I know it is, Tommy, but I need to know everything you remember."

He was silent a minute. "I went in the guesthouse and it was a mess. Some of the furniture been knocked over. And Bonnie, she lied on the floor and she looked like she was hurt bad. She didn't move or nothin', and she was almost...naked." He said the last word in a whisper.

"What did you do?"

"I got scared and ran away. Matt was coming down the hill. He says what was wrong and I says Bonnie was hurt real bad and he made me go back there and show him." This was all said in a jumble of words, as if he relived the incident in his mind.

I had to strain to understand it all. I looked at Matt and caught his gaze. He got up from the picnic table and walked up the hill, his black hair glistening in the rain.

"I didn't want to go back," Tommy went on, oblivious to Matt's absence. "But Matt made me go. When he saw Bonnie, he sat down and cried. That scared me more than anything, so I ran away and then the police came and made me go to jail."

"Did you hurt Bonnie in any way? Did you touch her at all?"

His eyes grew wide. "No! I wouldn't hurt her. I

wouldn't hurt her," he almost sobbed as he repeated himself.

"It's okay, Tommy. I believe you. Do you remember seeing anyone else that day? Did anyone else go into the guesthouse?"

Deep in thought, he sat for a minute then nodded. "John and Bonnie went in. Then Alena, she was Bonnie's sister. She was pretty, but I didn't like her."

"Why not?"

"She called me bad names."

"Did you see anyone else?"

"Ethan Miller and that other guy."

After some probing, I figured out that the *other guy* was Hank. Tommy wasn't sure of his name, but the description fit.

For the next couple of minutes, I tried to force the exact chronology from him, trying to get him to remember in what order the others had entered the guesthouse that day. He told me that John and Bonnie entered the guesthouse and how Hank stood outside, looking through the window while the two of them were in there together. John left alone and Hank went inside. Hank was mad and crying when he came running out of the cottage minutes later. John returned for a few brief minutes and left, carrying his shoes.

Then Ethan came along, went into the guesthouse then later returned to the main house. Alena, Bonnie's sister, arrived with Hank in tow. Hank waited outside again while Alena went inside. Then Tommy went again to look for Paul Gunderson but couldn't find him. When he got back to the cottage, he went inside and found Bonnie dead.

It frightened him and he didn't know what to do so

he went running out of the small bungalow straight into Matt.

"Did you tell the police what you saw?" I asked when we'd gotten the sequence of events out to Tommy's satisfaction.

"They told me not to tell nobody 'cause nobody would believe me."

"What about Sheriff Fred?"

"He says I should tell that man at court...but they never listened to me."

Matt hadn't returned and I had no idea where he'd disappeared to, so I went with Tommy to his room, where he showed me the model airplane collection he was so proud of. I left him to go back to his work in the garden and tracked down his counselor in the office.

"Do you have a minute?" I asked.

"Sure," said the young man, smiling up from the desk. "You're saving me from state reports. I've got all the time you need."

"Our tax dollars at work?"

He laughed. "What can I help you with?"

"Did Fred Connor explain to you why I wanted to meet Tommy?"

"It's about the murder, right?"

"Yes. I'm doing some research about it."

He shook his head. "It's hard to believe Tommy could be involved in anything violent. He's a very gentle person."

"What I'm wondering is, how much of what he says can I believe? He seemed to have a pretty clear picture in his head about what happened that day. It was twenty years ago. How accurate could he be?"

"Oddly enough, it's probably pretty accurate. I don't

know if you've read any files on Tommy—he's a savant. Do you know what that is?"

"Dustin Hoffman in *Rainman*?"

"Similar. There are varying degrees and specialties involved, but the effect is the same. For some reason—no one is quite sure how it works—people like Tommy with limited capabilities excel in certain areas. Tommy's area seems to be details. He could probably tell you what he had for lunch two weeks ago last Tuesday and what I wore to work that day."

"How reliable is this gift?"

"It wouldn't hold up in court, if that's what you mean. But if you spent enough time around Tommy, you'd be surprised how uncanny it is." He paused for a second. "Was he able to help you?"

"I'm not sure yet. Can I ask you another question?"

He waved his hand over the papers in front of him, "You can ask me questions for the rest of my shift if you'd like."

"Are you familiar with Tommy's medical records?"

He thought for a moment. "I'm not sure where you're headed with this. I've only been here a few months. I read all the files for my caseload when I started but I don't recall any significant medical information about Tommy. Why?"

"I have reason to believe he was castrated when he was younger."

His eyes opened wide. "Ouch. I don't remember reading anything like that."

"Could you check his file?"

"Sure." He got up from the desk and walked over to a gray metal filing cabinet, where he retrieved Tommy's file. He thumbed through it, shaking his head. "I don't see anything like that in here."

"Is it possible that information is missing?"

"Anything's possible. The residents aren't given routine physicals. They're sent to the doctor when they're sick or hurt. Tommy's usually pretty healthy."

"Is there any way we could find out?"

"Not short of giving him a strip search. Unless we have good cause, we can't do anything like that without his consent. And I can tell you right now, he would *not* consent. He's a very modest man."

I thanked him for his time and left to find the missing Matt Wheaton. I found him out front, sitting in the cab of his truck.

"Well, what do you think?" Matt asked after I climbed in and he started the ignition.

"I think he's innocent."

He turned out of the parking lot, back onto the highway. "Any particular reason?"

"A gut feeling."

"How trustworthy is your gut?"

I looked at him. "It's saved my hide more than a few times. Besides, I had an interesting conversation with Dr. Fischer the other day."

"About what?"

I told him Dr. Fischer's theory about the therapeutic castration performed on Tommy by the late Dr. Plante. Matt took his eyes off the road long enough to look me in the eye.

He let out a low whistle. "Really?"

"Dr. Fischer's pretty sure that's what happened to Tommy."

"Wow. That explains a lot. Like why my mother always took me out of town when I had to see a doctor."

"That's lucky for all of us. We certainly wouldn't want any of the Miller men walking around as eunuchs. What would the women of Missouri do without their pulsing virility?"

He didn't think that was funny.

It took us three hours to reach Ethan's. The rain was torrential and the driving slow. Visibility was limited to about thirty feet and the defroster kept going out. I ended up sitting next to Matt, a handful of Kleenex ready for whenever the windshield started to fog up. At one point, we had to pull over to the side of the road and wait out a particularly bad downpour.

By the time we reached the bottom of Lentil Road, the muscles in my neck and shoulders were tense and strained. I couldn't even see the farmhouses as we made our way up the hill. As we crossed over the small wooden bridge, I noticed the water in the riverbed had risen to about twice what it had been when we left that morning.

"Thank you for taking me to see Tommy," I said when we were safely in the garage and he'd turned off the ignition.

He turned to look at me. "I wish you'd quit now, Jess. You're pretty sure that Tommy is innocent."

"Which means someone else is guilty. It's a short list, and you're related to most of them. Matt, why are you so against this book of Ethan's? I understand how hard it is to have those memories dredged up, but don't you think it's important to find the truth? You don't believe Tommy is guilty and I have a feeling you never did."

He was quiet for several long seconds. "I never

thought Tommy was guilty. I've known him for longer than I can remember, and I think I always knew he could never do something like that. If you'd seen him that day…"

"Then why are you fighting Ethan on this?"

This time he shook his head. "Ethan and I have… issues. We have for years. It took us a long time to get to where we are—to have a relationship again. If I felt he finally wanted to find the truth, then—okay, let's do it. This book feels like he's manipulating us all over again."

I wasn't sure I totally understood. There was definitely a dynamic between Ethan and his sons that wasn't healthy. "Matt, do *you* want to know who really killed Bonnie?"

He took a deep breath and let it out slowly. "I don't know."

"Why?"

"What will it change? Tommy *is* better off where he is, no matter what you say. And us? Well, I'm not sure we would survive the fallout."

"Meaning?"

"Meaning, you're right, I might very well be related to a murderer."

There was no delicate way to put it and we were way past tiptoeing around the issue. "John?"

He held my gaze and nodded, but there was something he wasn't saying.

"And?" I asked.

"And, Ethan is doing what Ethan does best, making people dance to his tune. He put Trisha, and now you, right in the middle of this—whatever it is. Whoever is guilty has hidden his tracks for twenty years. He'd have a lot to lose, being exposed now. This could get dangerous before it's over. It's already gotten dangerous."

He watched my face. "I don't suppose it would do any good to tell you to pack your bags and get out of here tomorrow, would it?"

"No," I said, for reasons that I knew, somewhere inside, were way beyond working with the great Ethan Miller.

"Then—"

"I know," I said, "I'll be careful."

FOURTEEN

IT WASN'T QUITE THREE and there was one more stop I wanted to make that day. I waited until Matt disappeared down the path toward his cabin and then headed for the garage. I didn't even bother asking Millie if I could borrow her car. The Festiva and I were on a mission and the fewer people who knew, the better.

Twenty-five minutes later I stood in front of Fillmore & Sons Pawnbrokers on Main Street in Cross Creek. What were the odds that a pawn shop in a backwoods corner of Missouri would have records dating back twenty years? Still, I had to try.

A barrel-chested young man dressed in a white shirt and green tie stood behind the glass display case at the register. "Can I help you?"

I doubted it. He probably wasn't much older than the paper I held.

"I hope so. I found this old receipt in my grandmother's papers. It was for a necklace I remembered from my childhood. It was a family heirloom and it meant a lot to all of us. I don't know why Grandma would have hocked it, but I was wondering if you would have any records on it. Maybe who bought it? I could track it down and see if maybe I could buy it back."

He stared at me without blinking, with a look of boredom. The story needn't have been so elaborate, because he really didn't seem to care. He'd probably heard it all before.

"Let me see the paper." He put out a large callused hand. I gave it to him and he raised his eyebrows as he read it. "This is twenty years old."

"I know. Is the owner around? Anyone? Anyone who might be able to check your old records?"

"I'm the owner here now." He puffed out his massive chest.

"Do you have records that go back that far?"

"Maybe. I don't know. I think there are some in the basement and some in the attic. I never looked at them. It would take weeks to find what you're looking for." He handed the paper back to me.

I thought I was beaten. "What about the previous owner?"

"That would be my dad. We could ask him, I guess."

"Would you? It would mean a lot to me?" I was getting sick of my own performance.

"Just a minute." He picked up the phone and dialed then briefly explained the situation to the person on the other end. He handed me the receiver. "He wants to talk to you."

I got on the line and did an instant replay of my earlier performance, trying to inject a more pathetic tone to my voice. It must have worked. Mr. Fillmore senior agreed to come down to the store. When he arrived less than twenty minutes later, he introduced himself, shook my hand and took the receipt from me. A brief examination of the paper brought a smile to his face. He was an older, miniature version of his son. Same features and hands—but shorter and not quite as broad.

He looked up at me. "I remember."

"Are you sure it's the same necklace? It was twenty years ago."

"Miss, I know a quality piece of jewelry when I see one. That one was exquisite. Beautiful. Worth much more than I was able to pay for it. I told the young lady that. I told her she should go to St. Louis or even New York City. She was cheating herself by selling it to me."

"A young woman brought it in?"

He nodded. "I thought maybe she'd stolen it, but I had no police reports on it so we made a deal."

"Whatever happened to the necklace?"

"I waited sixty days—in case she returned—then I sold it to a buyer in Memphis for ten thousand dollars. I would have felt bad about that, but I tried to tell her."

"Do you have any other records on the necklace?"

"Come with me."

I followed him through the back of the store, past shelves filled with the paraphernalia from other people's lives. We went down a wooden staircase into the basement, where metal file cabinets lined two walls on opposite sides of the building.

"Good thing you called," he said. "The boy would never have been able to find this for you. He's a good kid, but not much upstairs, if you know what I mean."

All the filing cabinets were clearly marked and in chronological order. If the boy couldn't have figured that out, then he indeed didn't have much upstairs.

Mr. Fillmore walked down the row on the left-hand wall until he came to the appropriate year, opened the drawer and pulled out a thick manila folder for that month. He rifled through papers until he found what he was looking for.

"Here." He handed it to me.

Clearly documented was the sale, the description of the item, the amount and the signature of the claimant—Alena Rawlings.

The sapphire necklace was like the kids' game *Button, Button; Who's got the Button?* It was passed from one hand to the next and it seemed a mystery as to where it might end up.

Alena had taken Bonnie's necklace and hocked it to finance her trip out of town. I wondered if Sarah Rawlings knew what her oldest daughter had done, weeks after her sister was murdered. And how had Matt come into possession of the receipt?

The rain had stopped while I'd been in the store. I pointed the Festiva in the direction of Ethan's house. I'd almost made it to the top of Lentil Road when something hit the side of the car. The metal reverberated loudly and I swerved on the wet road.

I pulled over to the muddy shoulder, switched off the engine and opened the door to investigate, not really in the mood for another flat tire. There was a second impact against the left front fender—the clear and distinct sound of a gunshot. Crap!

I slammed the door closed, slid down in the seat and turned the key, praying the shots hadn't hit anything vital in the motor. As soon as the engine kicked over, I threw the car into gear and sped the rest of the way up Lentil Road—tires squealing—mud flying—until I screeched to a halt right in front of the door.

Ethan came bursting out of the house and pulled me out of the car. "I heard gunshots. What happened? Are you all right?"

I couldn't speak.

Dan rounded the corner of the garage as Matt came

crashing out of the woods, hair and shirt plastered to his body.

I tried to breathe.

"What happened?" Dan asked. "Is she okay?"

"Someone tried to shoot me," I said, Ethan still clutching my arm. "The car…gunshots…tried to kill me." I hoped he understood—I couldn't make any more sense than that.

He grasped my arm tighter. "Who? Who tried to kill you?"

All I could do was shake my head.

"I heard it too, Ethan," Matt said through labored breaths. "I was out walking Satan and saw someone out there with a rifle. Tried to chase them. Couldn't make it." He bent over, putting his hands on his knees, taking in big gulps of air.

"Who the…" Ethan started to say then looked at me again. "Are you all right?"

I started to nod then realized I really wasn't all right. Someone had just tried to kill me again. My knees started to buckle.

"We need to get her in the house," Dan said.

I found myself in Ethan's office, sitting in one of his big overstuffed chairs with a glass of brandy. Ethan kept urging me to drink it, but I couldn't focus on putting the glass to my lips long enough to get the liquid down.

"We need to call the sheriff," Dan said.

Ethan looked at him, the color gone from his face. He stood there for the longest time, thinking. "Okay."

Matt picked up the phone and dialed.

By the time the sheriff had come and gone, I had regained my composure. An eerie sense of peace had

settled over me, and I wondered if this was what it felt
like to be in shock.

Sheriff Stevenson was as cocky as he'd been after
Trisha's death. He questioned Matt and me, took a cursory look at Millie's car and went out to the scene of
the crime to see if he could find anything.

Back at the house, his official verdict to us was
"Poachers."

I don't think any of us in that room thought it was
that simple.

"How do you know the shots weren't intended for
Miss Kallan?" Dan asked.

The sheriff laughed. "Why would anyone want to
kill her?" As if I might not be important enough to be
murdered. Just like Trisha.

Ethan explained about the research I'd been doing,
about the people who might want to silence the questions I'd been asking.

"Only problem," Stevenson said, "is they already
got Bonnie Rawlings' killer locked up in a nut-house,
two hours away."

There was nothing we could do to convince him—
it felt like déjà vu and the night he came out when Trisha died. He left to write his report and tell the guys
at the office what a bunch of lunatics there were up at
the Miller house.

Ethan sent Dan and Matt away and we were alone
in his office.

"The sheriff's not taking this seriously," I said.

Ethan sat down behind his desk. "I know."

"Do you think someone tried to kill me?"

He lifted his shoulders in a heavy sigh. "You've been
uncovering a lot of dirt and asking a lot of questions."

"Just like Trisha did?"

"Just like Trisha did."

"What do we do now?"

He looked me right in the eyes. "We quit. I'm not willing to have you killed for this. It's not worth it. I'm going to send you home."

I wasn't willing to die for it either, but somewhere inside I knew that wasn't the answer. "Ethan, *if* someone was trying to kill me, they must think I know a lot more than I do. If I leave now, who's to say they're not going to follow me home?"

He passed a hand over his face. "You may be right, but you'll be safer in Omaha than you are here." He turned back to look at me. "Why don't you go pack your things while I make arrangements to get you out of here."

The suitcase lay empty on the bed. In an hour's time that was the most I'd accomplished. I was starting to feel trapped by a murderer whose identity I didn't know. And I didn't like it.

The voices in my head of Eric and my father kept telling me to do the right thing. Only I didn't know what the right thing was. I paced. My father had died trying to bring some justice into this world. Would I endure the same fate? And was it worth the price?

I felt my honor slipping away and didn't know how to hold on. What I *did* know was that someone had tried to kill me. Just like they'd killed Trisha Chatsworth. There were no poachers. Only a faceless person who'd hidden his or her crime for so long they weren't willing to let anyone destroy the facade they'd created. No matter what it took, they would do whatever they needed to do to protect themselves. If Bonnie and Trisha were disposable, so was I.

I dialed the number in St. Louis, hoping Fred would be there. I needed to hear a clear voice of reason. No one answered and all of a sudden, I felt very alone and very vulnerable.

I couldn't wait for Ethan to decide my fate. I slipped downstairs and out the front door. Millie's car was sitting exactly where I'd left it. I got in and headed down Lentil Road.

I wasn't sure where I was going and was surprised to find myself sitting in Fred Connor's driveway. It must have been the only safe place my subconscious could think of. I got out, walked up to the covered front porch and sat in the same chair I'd sat in the first time I met Fred. There was something comforting about being at his house, something protective that calmed my nerves and soothed my errant thoughts.

I looked out over the yard and watched the rain begin again, trying to sort things out in my head. Something didn't sit right and I couldn't put my finger on what it was. Something was bothering me. What?

The fact that there were so many suspects didn't help.

Rain pelted Fred's garden, the daffodils awash in a sea of mud, straining under the force of the downpour. I don't know how long I sat there curled up in the chair, waiting for a spark of insight.

I didn't know who killed Bonnie. I didn't know who'd pushed a cement vase over a railing at an innocent young girl. And I didn't have a clue who'd fired a gun at me. All I knew at that moment was I couldn't run. I could never run far enough. It wasn't just the fact the faceless someone would find me. I knew I could never escape the fact that Tommy Markowski was being punished for a crime he didn't commit. That Rhonda Chatsworth was counting on me to do what the sheriff refused to see. Or that Sarah Rawlings would never be free from the loss of her daughters, that she would live with her pain and guilt forever unless I could put right what had taken her family from her. Or that Ethan's family, and his career, were still bent and broken. I could never escape the faith that Eric had in me, how he'd treated me more like his child than he did his own son. And I could never escape the loss of my father or do justice to his memory if I ran away.

Was this what my father must have felt? Was this what had pushed him on, when he knew it would be safer for him to quit?

I sank deeper into the chair, not wanting to leave the illusion of security I felt sitting on Fred Connor's front porch, hoping I could change my mind. I waited another half an hour then walked slowly to Millie's car, not sure if I was strong enough to deal with what lay before me. Not certain if I would even be alive when it was all over.

FIFTEEN

I NEEDED TO talk to Matt. A friendly but familiar bark greeted me as I walked up the front steps to the cabin. Satan came bounding up behind me, ready to pin me to the doorframe with a wet slobbery kiss. I moved just in time to avoid the collision.

The front door opened and Matt stood there looking at me. "I should have known it was you." He moved to one side to allow me to enter. "No one else gets him that excited."

I stepped into the living room.

"Are you okay?" He looked at me with those penetrating gray eyes.

Something about his look made me want to cry, but I knew from past experience that wouldn't be well received.

His hand reached up and touched my cheek. "*Are you okay?*"

I shook my head and the tears came. "I don't know."

His arms went around my waist and he pulled me close, my head buried in his shoulder. I don't know how long I cried, how long we stood there holding onto each other. His breath brushed my hair, he kissed my ear then my neck. When I lifted my face to look at him, he bent down and kissed me firmly, passionately, on my mouth. My already muddled thoughts were blurred with new images, new sensations. The easiest thing in the world at that point would have been to let myself go completely.

To let him take me to a place blissfully removed from the ugliness outside of me and the fear within.

I pulled away. "I can't," I said with more resolve than I felt. "I can't."

He looked at me again, reading my face, searching my eyes, then stepped away. "Why are you here?"

We were still standing by the front door and I knew we wouldn't enter any farther into his domain. I couldn't risk it and he must have decided he wouldn't allow it.

"I needed to ask you about the pawn receipt," I said. "Where did you get it?"

"What pawn receipt?"

"The one I found on your desk the other day for a lightning bolt necklace. Where did you get that?"

"*On* my desk or *in* my desk?"

"Dammit, Matt! People are shooting at me. I don't have time for games. *Where* did the receipt come from?"

"Okay. You're right. I found it in Trisha's desk about a week before you got here. She had a folder with articles about Bonnie's murder. I took it from there."

"Why?"

"I'm not really sure. For some reason, it seemed important at the time. What difference does it make?"

"I don't know. I was coming back from the pawnshop when I was shot at. Where did Trisha get it?"

"How should I know?"

I sighed. I thought he might have turned into an ally. Now he was just pissed off at my rebuff and we weren't going to get anywhere.

"Thanks for your help." I turned and walked out the door.

I trudged up the long circular stairway to the second-floor hallway, very aware of the hunger pangs in my stomach. There was about half an hour until dinner, and I really wasn't in the mood to talk to anyone. I stood at the top of the stairs and glanced down the hall toward Ethan and Jolene's open bedroom doors, directly across the hall from each other.

Why not? I poked my head into Jolene's room. The walls were a comforting pale blue accented with flowered borders and maple furniture. The dresser and makeup table held every cosmetic and potion imaginable that could make a beautiful woman even more beautiful. The reading material on the nightstand was six months' worth of *Cosmo* and *People* magazines. Her dresser drawers were crammed full of low-cut sweaters and lingerie, thongs and Wonder bras.

Ethan's room was almost Spartan in comparison—everything neatly in its place. I pulled open a drawer in the nightstand next to his bed. A cream-colored photo album was its lone contents. I picked it up and opened the cover.

The first picture was a very naked Jolene, air-brushed enough to qualify for any men's magazine. The pages that followed were Jolene at various ages and in various stages of undress posing for a talented photographer. It was interesting to see her cosmetic transformation over the years and I wondered how she'd financed all the surgery. But, on second thought, no I didn't.

I replaced the album, glanced around the room and then wandered downstairs, hoping the night would pass quickly.

I made it to the dining room just as a sullen-faced Millie was serving dinner. I very much needed not to be alone. I wouldn't be an easy target in the company of others.

It was a dreary evening, with the rain pelting the house

in an endless staccato and the trees scraping against the windows every time the wind gusted. We were confined to the house and we weren't happy campers. Maybe it was the barometer, or the storm that held us all captive, insulated from the world on Ethan's mountaintop. Or maybe it was the fact that, once again, a murderer had been unleashed in the midst of their lives and now in the center of mine. Whatever the reason for the tension, it was as palpable as the storm that raged outside.

Ethan gave me a sour look as I slipped into my chair next to his. He leaned toward me. "Where did you disappear to?" he asked in a low voice, so the others couldn't hear.

"I needed some time to think, so I took a drive."

"I've made arrangements—Dan's going to drive you to Springfield tonight."

I shook my head. "I'm not leaving tonight."

I sensed an argument brewing just as Jolene took hold of his arm and shot me a withering glance. "Your intimate conversations are becoming tiresome," she said.

"We'll talk about this later," Ethan said to me.

I looked around the table, trying to gauge the atmosphere. Jolene was now obviously annoyed with me. Glenda seemed on edge, jumping every time the thunder roared in the sky and shook the house. Dan picked at his dinner and kept his gaze on me throughout the meal. Hank was well on his way to pickling himself as he bolted back bourbon like there was no tomorrow. Matt seemed characteristically preoccupied and John was mopey.

Even Millie was subdued as she served the various courses, retreating quickly to the sanctuary of her kitchen.

When dinner was over, Matt, John and Ethan left to make sure the house was secure for the night and to check if there had been any damage done to the structure in the gale-force winds.

"We'll talk as soon as I get back," Ethan said to me. "I'll be in my office."

I excused myself from the others and headed upstairs. Sitting behind my desk, I stared blankly at all the way-too-familiar papers spread out in front of me. There had to be an answer somewhere in that jumble of information.

A feeling of terror crept up my spine. What was I doing? Maybe Matt was right. Maybe I should have gone home a long time ago. I hoped it wasn't too late. If I worked through the night, I could consolidate all my notes and somehow get them to Fred. His trained eye might be able to see what I could not.

But even as I formulated the plan, somewhere in the back of my mind, I knew I wouldn't carry it out. I wasn't ready to let go. There was enough evidence to exonerate Tommy, or at least get him a new trial. But there were still too many missing pieces. There would be no justice for Trisha or Bonnie or Tommy until the murderer was found. And, there would be no safe haven for me until the person responsible was behind bars.

Thunder crashed outside and rattled the window behind me. The storm was really starting to get on my nerves. I reached for the phone and dialed Fred's number in St. Louis, wanting desperately to make contact with the outside world. I wanted someone to know I was alive and, temporarily, still sane.

Relief flooded through me when I heard Fred's voice.

It was as if I'd been lost at sea and someone had thrown me a lifeline. "Fred, it's Jess."

"I was just thinking about you. I saw a weather report on TV. Some storm you're getting."

"The storm is the least of my worries right now."

"That doesn't sound good. Tell me what's going on."

I wasn't sure where to start. I already knew what his response about the shooting would be, so I skipped that detail. "I went to see Tommy Markowski today."

"And?"

"I liked him."

"So do I," Fred said, "but that doesn't mean anything. There have been a lot of likable murderers over the years. Look at Ted Bundy."

"The difference is that Ted Bundy was a very intelligent man, calculating in his behavior. Tommy doesn't have those skills. Who he is, is what comes through."

"True. But, personalities aside, a court needs something more substantial to go on."

I told him what I'd learned from Dr. Fischer. At first, I thought the line had gone dead when he didn't respond for a while.

"Son of a bitch," he finally said.

I told him everything I'd learned from the sapphire necklace to the monthly payments Dan had been delivering to the Markowskis for twenty years. I told him Tommy's account of the people he'd seen entering the cottage on the afternoon of Bonnie's death and Glenda having been on the estate that afternoon and fleeing the scene.

"I had no idea how much the original investigation missed," he said when I was through. "But we were fighting an uphill battle at the time, with Ethan and

Eric leading the charge for the other side. Have you got any motives?"

"That's where I get stalled. There were plenty of animosities between different people, but nothing that seems strong enough."

"Sometimes you have to find the most plausible scenario and build on it. Let's go through the list together. Maybe something will jump out at us. Let's start with John."

"The only thing I have on John is his jealousy of Matt." I thought for a minute. "He hasn't ever held a job. He drinks too much and plays too hard."

"The boy who never grew up."

"What's his deal with Matt? I don't really understand it."

"I'm not sure I do either, but he's been jealous of his brother all their lives." Fred paused, then asked, "What about Hank?"

"For motives? My suspicion is that Glenda's been blackmailing the Amundsons, but I'm not sure what it is she's been holding over their heads. The only thing I really know about Hank is that he was a big loser when he was a teenager and he grew up to be an even bigger ass."

"Point taken. Which brings us to Matt."

I was suddenly uncomfortable. I think I'd known all along that the most damning implications pointed to Matt. A week ago, that wouldn't have bothered me. But I'd seen him with Tommy. There was a gentleness about him that touched me.

"Jessica," Fred said, when I'd hesitated too long, "what're you thinking?"

"What I know about Matt."

"And?"

"He had the perfect motive—jealousy of the woman he loved. I think she was two-timing him with John. What were the two of them doing together that day in the guesthouse? Why did John give her such an expensive necklace? Matt said Bonnie was dead when he found her—but what if she wasn't? It would be his word against Tommy's. Who do you think people would believe?"

"We both know who people would believe, but let's not get bogged down yet. What about Dan?"

"I haven't a clue about Dan. Certainly, his movements are suspect. But, I can't think of any real motive he had. Besides, he wasn't listed in any of the police reports, I'm guessing he wasn't even around."

"Maybe you should spend a little more time trying to find out more about him. What about Ethan?"

"What about him?"

"Motive?"

"Ethan? Seriously? What possible threat could a poor eighteen-year-old girl be to Ethan?"

"Don't be naïve, Jessica. When you start closing your eyes to any possibility, that's when you start making mistakes. And a big enough mistake could be fatal."

There was a sick feeling in the pit of my stomach. Yeah. I was well aware of that.

Fred was quiet for a while. "I don't have a good feeling about this anymore. You've been doing a lot of solid work, talking to the right people, asking the right questions. Whether you know it or not, somewhere in that brain of yours, you've got the key to this whole thing. It could make someone very nervous."

It already had, I wanted to say. What I told him was, "I'm leaving in the morning."

I think he was hoping for a more immediate response, but he didn't press it. We talked for a few more minutes. I told him I would get my notes in order for him to review and I'd come back to visit him when he got home.

When we finally said good-bye, I hung up the phone reluctantly, hesitant to let go of the contact with someone who wasn't connected to this house.

Half an hour later I was busy sorting my files, trying to weed out the extraneous paperwork from the pertinent material I needed. I had a pile with my notes, trial transcripts, newspaper articles, medical reports and the death certificate. Everything else was going in the wastebasket under the desk.

I heard lumbering footsteps on the staircase leading to Dan's office and froze. They didn't sound like Ethan's.

A few seconds later, Hank appeared in the doorway, drink in hand. "I see you're working."

"Uh-huh."

He stepped into the room, swaying slightly, looking around. He let himself drop into the chair on the other side of the desk and started to fidget. He patted his hair, straightened the crease in his pants, drummed his fingers on the desk, obviously agitated by something other than the alcohol that was corroding his liver. He chewed on his lower lip as his gaze roved the top of my desk.

I was hyper-aware of his every movement.

"I understand you went to see that Markowski fellow today," he finally said.

"Yes."

He coughed and fidgeted some more. "How…how was he?"

"He's fine." Why did he care? "Did you know Tommy?"

He shook his head and looked away. "Not really. I used to see him around here sometimes, but I, uh, I never talked to him."

Hank got up and paced the small area of the room, moving unsteadily. I watched, waiting for him to stumble and fall, taking books and bookshelves along with him, but somehow, he managed to stay on his feet. There wasn't much space in which to move, and after a couple of minutes, he was, once again, in the chair opposite me, looking unsure as to how he'd gotten there. He looked at me and seemed startled by my presence.

"Was there something you wanted to talk to me about?" I asked.

"Yes. Uh, no. Uh, I don't know."

"Hank, *what* did you want to talk to me about?"

His eyes focused on mine for a minute, then he said quietly, "That Markowski fellow didn't kill Bonnie."

He said it with such authority that it took me by surprise. I went into alert mode, not sure where this conversation was headed. "You seem pretty sure. How do you know Tommy didn't kill Bonnie?"

He looked at me as if I'd missed the obvious. "Because I did."

The panic I was feeling went right over the top. I was more frightened at that moment than I was when I realized someone was shooting at me. It wasn't so much what Hank said as the way he'd said it. The words were barely out of his mouth when his personality changed. His voice took on an odd tone and there was a wild look in his eyes.

He laughed. "You didn't know that, did you, Jessica? No one knew. No one. I haven't told anyone in twenty years, not even my father. Oh, he wondered all right. But he never knew, because I never told him. *She* told me not to."

Oh Lord, had Hank been getting messages from Bonnie from beyond the grave?

He started pacing again, not with the lumbering gait he'd had before, but with an agitation and purpose even more disturbing. There was no way I could make it to the door without passing within inches of him. The room was too small. A cry for help would never be heard. I was too far removed from the others, hidden away in the depths of the house—confined in a room that had been built for concealment.

The only hope I had was to try to calm him as best I could. Bring him back to his senses. I honestly didn't think he'd come to do me harm. I didn't even think he'd come to confess. But, he was in such a state now, I wasn't sure he knew what he was doing.

I forced my voice to remain steady, trying desperately to keep him from feeling threatened. "Why don't you tell me about it, Hank?"

He laughed again. "You'd like that, wouldn't you, Jessica? You'd like me to tell you all about it. You think you know everything." He was looming over me, swaying and clenching his fists. I was blocked in behind my desk.

He wasn't in very good physical shape, but I had no idea what he was capable of in his present state.

So, I kept talking. "Hank, I'm not sure I know anything at the moment. But, I do think you need to talk. You've kept that ugly secret for so long that you need to let it out. I don't believe you meant to hurt Bonnie, did you?"

He was quiet and he shook his head sadly.

"Of course you didn't. It must have been an accident."

Tears were running down his cheeks. "It *was* an accident."

I rose from my chair and took his arm. "Tell me about it, Hank,"

He went willingly, as I led him back to his chair, and he sat down stiffly, wiping his eyes with the back of his hand. I'd hoped to make it to the door, but he reached up and gripped my arm tightly.

"Bonnie," he started and his voice shook. "Bonnie and John."

I waited for him to go on. I had no choice.

"Bonnie and John were together that day. I was there too, but they didn't pay any attention to me, unless they were making fun of me. They were flirting and laughing and I could tell John was really getting turned on. He whispered something to Bonnie and she said, 'Yeah, let's go to the guesthouse.' I just followed along. I can't believe how stupid I was! But when we got to the front door, John told me to wait outside."

"And did you?"

His grip was growing tighter and my fingers started to tingle.

"Oh, I waited all right. But, I could hear them inside, laughing and then I went and looked in the front windows. They were right there in the living room, for God's sake! Bonnie was prancing around nude—wearing nothing but that stupid necklace John had given her. I couldn't believe how beautiful she was!

Finally, John got up and closed the curtains, but it was too late. I knew what they were doing." He stopped, lost in thought.

"John didn't care that Bonnie was engaged to Matt?" I tried to keep him talking. As long as he was talking I figured I was safe.

Hank shook his head. "John probably wanted Bonnie *because* she was engaged to Matt. Just another trophy for him."

"How long did you wait?"

"Until they were, uh, through. I can't believe how stupid I was. The longer I waited, the madder I got. And I decided John wasn't the only one who was going to get lucky that day. John finally came out with a big smile on his face and headed up the hill."

He passed a hand across his forehead. "When he left, I went inside, and Bonnie was standing there still stark naked. She looked me up and down with an awful sneer and said, 'What do you want?' When I told her I wanted my turn, she laughed. Then everything happened so fast. I hit her and she screamed and started cursing at me, and I hit her again—I don't know how many times—maybe three or four. I didn't mean to hurt her. I just wanted to make her stop. The last time must have been pretty hard. She fell against the coffee table and hit her head."

Oh, my God. It was as simple as that?

He lifted his free hand to stare at it. "She didn't move. She just lay there, and I knew—I *knew*—she was dead." He stopped talking, just looking at his hand.

"What did you do then?"

He looked at me, but his eyes didn't seem to focus. "Hank?"

"I ran. I was so scared, I wanted to get as far away from there as possible. Glenda was on her way to clean the guesthouse, and I actually knocked her over. I just kept running."

"Then it was an accident, Hank, just like you said."

"Do you think anyone is going to care at this point?" His emotions were rising again. "I've kept it hidden for twenty years. Markowski was convicted in my place. No one is going to care if it was an accident." He was fidgeting again and, at random, picked up a stack of papers from my desk. "What are these?"

"My research for Ethan." The mood swings were getting harder and harder to follow. The agitation followed too quickly on the heels of remorse.

He scanned each document. "Well, you're good, I'll give you that. My father taught you well. Did you know Glenda wanted me to find a way to stop your research?"

"Why?"

He shrugged. "To protect the lifestyle she's acquired, I guess. If I'm in jail, she'll have no one to blackmail. I can't believe how I've listened to her all these years. She was the only witness to what I'd done. I had to keep her quiet."

He threw the papers back on the desk and looked at me, his eyes wide. "Oh my God! Oh God! I need to be alone now. I need time to think. Go away." He started pacing again, a frown creasing his face.

When I didn't move, he looked at me again. "Go away!"

It might be my only chance to make my escape, and I meant to take it. As I moved toward the door, he reached out and grabbed my wrist again. "Don't tell anyone.

Please. Promise me you won't tell anyone tonight. Not even Ethan. Just for tonight. Will you promise me that?"

I didn't answer right away and his grip grew tighter. "Promise me, Jessica."

"All right, Hank. I promise."

"Thank you. I know I can trust you." He let go of my wrist and I hurried through Dan's office and down the stairs.

The front hall was deserted. Out of the corner of my eye, I thought I saw a movement, but when I turned to look, no one was there.

My promise to Hank hadn't been the least bit noble; I was merely trying to save my own hide by buying a little time. It didn't matter one way or the other, because I couldn't find a living soul to share my secret with. I went from room to room in desperate search of another human being. There was no one in the parlor, the library, the TV room or the dining room. Millie wasn't in the kitchen, and I felt very frightened and alone. All I wanted to do was lock myself in my bedroom and wait for morning.

As I went back through the front hall, I heard Hank in Ethan's office, moving about, talking wildly. I ran all the way up the stairs and straight to Ethan's bedroom. I pounded on the door as loud as I could, when there was no response, I threw it open and went in. The room was empty. Great.

I made my way quickly down the hall to my own room, where I closed the door and slid the lock into place. It was going to be a very long night.

SIXTEEN

MY PLAN WAS to sit up all night. I feared that Hank would eventually come to his senses and, realizing what he'd done, come looking for me. Or worse yet, he would *not* come to his senses and still come looking for me. Either way, I wasn't about to be caught off guard.

Normally, I wouldn't find Hank much of a threat under any circumstances. But his guilt and fear had been festering for twenty long years and I had no way of knowing what it had done to his already warped psyche.

As I began to calm down a bit, and the house remained quiet, I realized there was something off about what Hank had said and I couldn't figure out what it was. If Bonnie had submitted willingly to John, then she hadn't been raped.

How much time had elapsed between the time Hank ran from the guesthouse and the time Tommy came across the body? Had someone else found Bonnie lying on the floor and gone to call the police? If so, who? And why had that person chosen to remain anonymous?

Which brought me back to John and, reluctantly, to Matt.

What if Bonnie hadn't died from Hank's blows? Had John bragged to his brother about his conquest and Matt, in a jealous rage, taken his anger out on the girl who was to become his wife?

What had Ethan been doing in the guesthouse that day? And where were Eric, Paul Gunderson and Dan?

There were too many unanswered questions. The rain pounding against the house didn't help my mood. In the midst of my turmoil, however, I came to one conclusion. I would still leave in the morning. Hank's confession answered the question of what happened to Bonnie. Someone else would have to find out who killed Trisha Chatsworth.

First thing in the morning, I would head for home. Maybe I would interview Ethan some other time. Maybe not. It was time I started looking for a job and getting on with my life. A sense of relief washed over me, having come to that decision. I lay on the bed, exhausted. If I only closed my eyes for a few minutes…

The next thing I knew, there was a tiny sliver of light, struggling to break over the horizon. The rain and wind hadn't abated in the few hours I'd slept. If anything, the weather seemed worse.

As consciousness dawned, I sat up in bed, suddenly aware Hank hadn't killed Bonnie. Either Hank had believed a lie all these years or he had purposely tried to dupe me last night to throw me off the trail. But why? His performance had been so agonizingly painful, it was difficult to believe it was an act.

I grabbed a pair of jeans and a blouse from off a chair and slipped them on then pulled open the bedroom door and headed for the stairs to find the evidence that confirmed what I knew.

The house was still partially dark, and I moved quietly down the hallway, not sure what to expect. The hidden entryway to the spiral staircase was as black as pitch. I passed through quickly, leaving the doorway in the wall open to provide light from Ethan's office to filter in, allowing me to find the bottom step.

I took the stairs two at a time and was in Dan's office in a fraction of a second. I moved through Dan's office and into my own and reached for the pile of papers on my desk. I went through them one by one... and then again.

Crap! The death certificate was gone.

It didn't matter, though, I knew what it said. And I knew that was why Hank had sent me away last night. He'd seen the death certificate. Which said Bonnie had died by strangulation.

I knew I had to wake Ethan. No one was safe anymore.

I retraced my steps through Dan's office, and if I'd been paying more attention to what I was doing, I probably wouldn't have fallen going down the stairs. But my foot caught on the fourth step from the bottom and, in my attempt to right myself, I ended up spiraling off the bottom of the wrought-iron staircase and careening off into the corner of the little room.

I landed with a sickening thud onto a well-padded surface, and I screamed as I raised my head and looked straight into Hank's dull and lifeless eyes.

As I struggled to my feet, I got my first real glimpse of Hank slumped in the corner, an ugly hole in his chest, his hand stubbornly clutching the crumpled copy of Bonnie's death certificate. I turned and ran.

SEVENTEEN

OF COURSE, no one heard my screams. The wind was too loud and the house too well built. I probably should have run to the nearest phone and summoned the sheriff before I went tearing through the house, yelling for help, but I was operating on fear, fueled by the adrenaline coursing through my veins. The only thing I wanted to do at that moment was to get as far away from Hank's pallid stare as quickly as I could.

I backed into Ethan's office then turned and fled, sliding across the ceramic tile in the front hall and running up the front stairs and down the length of the second-floor hallway.

Ethan's bedroom door was closed. He must have heard me coming, because when I pushed open the door, he was standing there, bare chested, tousled hair, trying to zip up his pants.

"Jessie! *What* is going on?"

I spluttered something about Hank being behind the wall.

He squinted at me and took hold of my arm. "What is going on?"

"Hank!" was all that came out of my mouth.

A door opened across the hall, and I felt Jolene move in behind me. "What's going on?" Her voice was husky with sleep.

"I don't know yet." Ethan gripped my arm tighter.

John, dressed in a T-shirt and jockey shorts came barreling into the room, almost colliding with Jolene. "Dad, I heard someone yelling. What's going on?"

"I don't know yet! If everyone will just shut up for a minute, I'll try to find out! Jessie, *what* is going on?"

"Hank. He's... I think he's dead."

I hadn't noticed Glenda's arrival, but I heard a shriek. I looked over my shoulder. She was standing behind John, dressed in a hideous pink housecoat.

The stress of the past twenty-four hours finally took its toll. A torrent of hysterical laughter welled up from inside and I couldn't hold it back. Seeing everyone standing there in various stages of dress and undress seemed like the funniest thing in the world.

Ethan, holding me by both arms, shook me gently.

"Why don't you just slap her?" Jolene said.

For some reason, that made me laugh even harder.

"Do something, Ethan," John said.

"What do you suggest?" He shook me again. "Jessie! Stop it right now."

The laughter subsided as quickly as it had started. The brief hysteria had broken the nervous tension that had been building ever since the shooting. My head was starting to throb again, but oddly enough, I felt very clear-headed and in control. "You're hurting me, Ethan."

"Oh, sorry." His hands dropped away, but he watched me closely, waiting for the lunacy to return.

"Hank is dead," I said. "I found him a few minutes ago in the stairwell leading to Dan's office. By the way, where is Dan?"

"His room is on the other side of the house," John said.

"No," Ethan said. "Are you sure he's dead? What happened?"

"He's very dead," I said. "Someone shot him."

Glenda started screaming.

"Get her out of here. Then go find Dan," Ethan said to Jolene. "John, come with me. Jessie, call the sheriff and an ambulance."

No one moved for a few seconds.

"Now!"

Jolene grabbed Glenda's arm and turned her back in the direction of her bedroom. John followed his father down the stairs. I followed too, not wanting to be far from Ethan, thinking his presence would keep me safe. I could call the sheriff from his office.

Ethan hesitated outside his office door. John pushed past his father, kneeling next to Hank's body and searching for a pulse. He looked at Ethan and shook his head. "Nothing."

Blood stained the front of Hank's custom-made shirt, circling the wound like a bull's eye.

Ethan, visibly shaken, turned away from the body. "Close up this doorway," he said to John. "Where's Dan?"

"I'm here," Dan said from the hallway and Ethan jumped. He was dressed in slacks and a blue shirt, his hair combed into place, Harry Potter glasses perched on the bridge of his nose.

Dan went over to the body and made his own cursory examination. When he moved away, John closed the door behind him.

Ethan slumped in a chair. He looked up and saw me standing there. "Did you call the sheriff?"

I hadn't. I picked up the receiver and looked at Ethan. "The phone's dead."

He reached out and took the receiver from me. He

held the instrument to his ear for several seconds.
"Dammit! This storm has knocked out the phone lines."

The first thought that popped into my head was that
someone had cut the lines to the house, leaving us all
helpless. When my gaze met John's, I could tell the
same thought had occurred to him. If ever I missed my
cell phone, it was at that moment.

"Dan, you're going to have to go into town and roust
the sheriff," Ethan said. "Get him up here right away.
John, go tell Matt what's happened. I want you and him
to search the grounds. And for God's sake, put some
pants on!"

Dan was on his way before Ethan had even finished
talking. Jolene appeared at the open door with Millie
behind her. Millie's face had lost all color.

"Ethan, you can't wait in here until the sheriff
comes." Jolene took him by the arm and led him toward the hallway. "Millie, why don't you go make us
some coffee."

Ethan clicked the lock on his office door and closed
it behind him. We all filed into the dining room, and
Millie disappeared into the kitchen and returned a short
while later with a pot of coffee. She offered to make
breakfast, but no one was very hungry. Without something familiar to occupy her, she sat next to me and
started to cry.

"I'm sorry," she said after a while, taking a tissue
from her pocket and drying her eyes. "I'll be all right
now." She tried to smile, but her effort lacked the conviction that she or anything would ever be all right
again.

Then, just as things started to get calm, Glenda
popped up and leveled a finger at me. "This is all her

fault! Hank's death is on her head! If she hadn't been poking her nose into everyone's business, this never would have happened. I hope you're satisfied!"

"Glenda," Ethan said, with equal amounts of weariness and sternness in his voice, "sit down and try to control yourself. That kind of behavior isn't going to get us anywhere. We have to sit tight until the sheriff gets here and let him sort it all out."

The look Glenda leveled at him was as hateful as the words she had hurled at me, but she did as she was told and sat back down and kept her mouth shut.

The sad thing was that Hank had finally learned the truth that would set him free from decades of guilt. And now he was dead. He might have knocked Bonnie unconscious, but it was strangulation that killed her.

At some point after I'd left him, Hank must have figured it out and confronted the real murderer— someone who'd entered the guesthouse after him and killed Bonnie. Had that same person also killed Trisha Chatsworth? And had they tried to silence me?

I looked at Ethan and saw sadness in his eyes, the weight of his own personal loss. He'd lost his godson, the son of his best friend. A man he'd watched grow from boyhood, who'd played and gone to school with his own sons. No matter what he felt for Hank, the irreversible fact was he'd lost a part of his life, a part of his past.

And maybe he was feeling his own sense of guilt, because, like it or not, Ethan had been the catalyst in Hank's death, far more than me, by pursuing Bonnie's murderer. In fact, to be honest, Ethan had manipulated them all.

His hair still tousled from sleep, he sat at the head of the table, his gray eyes tired, the lines around his mouth evident beneath the whiskery stubble that covered his jaw. He would have to find his own way through his grief, and, I knew from experience, it was a journey he would have to make alone. But, grief would not be his only journey. At some point, he would have to confront his guilt.

We sat in sullen silence for what seemed like an hour before we heard someone moving through the kitchen. Dan appeared in the doorway, water dripping from his raincoat and his bare head. Mud covered his shoes and trousers.

"The bridge is out," he told Ethan. "And your Caddy is up to its hubcaps in mud."

Ethan shook his head and got up slowly. "I'm going to get dressed. When Matt and John get back, we'll figure out what to do."

Jolene followed Ethan out of the room, while Dan stood in the doorway, dripping water and mud all over the floor, wiping his glasses on a paper towel.

"Then there's no way down the hill?" I asked.

Dan shook his head. "The creek has risen so high, it's overflowed its banks."

A twinge of panic crept up my spine. It hadn't been so bad when I thought help was on the way, but knowing we were stranded made me realize how vulnerable we all were. How vulnerable *I* was. Did Hank's murderer think I knew more than I actually did?

Millie disappeared into the kitchen and returned carrying towels for Dan. While he went to shower and change, she started cleaning up the mess he'd made.

Ethan was back in twenty minutes, looking more presentable, but no less weary. He was pouring himself a cup of coffee when John came through the kitchen, wearing a rain slicker that he slipped off and threw over the back of a chair.

"The bridge is out," he told his father as he reached for a cup and the coffeepot.

"I know. Did you and Matt find anything outside?"

"I didn't find anything," John said. "Not even Matt."

"What does that mean?"

"He's not here, Ethan. He's not in his cabin or the greenhouse. He's gone and so is his truck."

EIGHTEEN

ETHAN DIDN'T BELIEVE Matt was gone, and I hoped with everything in me he was right—even though John insisted he'd checked everywhere.

I followed Ethan to the mudroom off the kitchen, where miscellaneous rain gear was stored, and grabbed a hooded poncho off a hook as I ran out the door after him, trying to keep up with his long purposeful strides.

We checked the garage first. Matt's truck was gone. Then we cut across the back lawn and over a small rise, where the path led to the cabin. The wind was blowing so hard the hood of my poncho kept sliding off my head, and my uncovered face was dripping by the time we reached the cabin.

There were no lights on as we approached and Ethan threw open the front door. He walked through every room, bellowing loudly for Matt.

One thing gave me hope—Satan was still there, ready as always to offer me a slobbery kiss. Matt wouldn't have gone far without him.

I made sure Satan had food and water and let him outside to take care of his personal business before I closed him up again in the cabin and hurried off up the hill after Ethan as he headed for the greenhouse.

Matt wasn't in the greenhouse either. Ethan turned on his heel, slamming the glass-paned door after him and strode off, tight-lipped, in the direction of the house.

Millie was there at the door to take our wet ponchos. "Maybe he went into town last night and couldn't get back home again."

Ethan struggled out of his coat, turning one of the sleeves inside out. Rain from the sleeve splattered Millie in the face. "Maybe. I need a drink."

I followed him into the front parlor, where he poured himself a glass of brandy.

Dan was sitting on the couch watching us over the rim of a porcelain cup as he sipped his coffee. He waited until Ethan had downed his first shot. "What do we do now?"

"How should I know?"

The look he gave Ethan was almost compassionate. "I recommend we sit down and relax. We'll figure something out."

"Relax? I have a dead man in my office, we can't get hold of the sheriff and my son has disappeared."

"And standing up isn't going to change any of that. Sit down for a minute."

To my surprise, Ethan obeyed.

"We're all under a lot of stress right now," Dan said, "but getting yourself all worked up isn't going to help the situation. I don't think we're in any immediate danger, and if we keep our wits about us, we'll be able to get through this thing."

It was the longest speech I'd ever heard Dan make. Ethan relaxed somewhat.

"What you've failed to point out, Dan," John said from the doorway, "is that either my brother is a cold-blooded killer or one of us is. Either way it doesn't look good."

"Oh, shut up, John," Ethan said.

John clenched his jaw, biting back whatever retort was on his lips. After a moment he said, "This house was locked up as tight as a tick last night, Ethan. And I checked all the doors and windows this morning. There was no forced entry. It was either Matt or one of us."

Ethan stalked out of the parlor. When I caught up with him in the hallway, he was heading for his office. Then he must have remembered what was in there and turned toward the TV room.

I followed and stood behind him as he looked out the window at the valley. "Are you all right?"

"No."

"Do you want to talk?"

"No."

I stood there for a minute. "I think it's time we did."

He turned wordlessly to face me.

"It backfired on you, didn't it?"

He didn't respond.

"You set a trap and someone wound up dead. Two people, if you count Trisha."

He shook his head. "You don't have any idea what I've done."

Our gazes met and all of his defenses, all of his carefully constructed persona, dropped away. For several long seconds, I felt as if I were looking into the soul of Ethan Miller. And it made me sad.

"I think I do," I said. "You orchestrated all of this, didn't you?"

He cocked his head to one side and the defenses all snapped back into place. "What are you talking about?"

"You've pulled everyone back to the scene of the crime. All the players are in place—except the ones who couldn't make your command performance."

He studied my face.

"Of course, Eric and Paul Gunderson were unable to attend," I said. "And Tommy's unavailable. Alena Rawlings disappeared years ago. But everyone else who was here the day of the murder has been lured or cajoled back into your house for one last performance."

He closed his eyes and nodded. "How did you know?"

"All the suspects back together again? That can't be coincidence. Besides, you feel so responsible for Hank's death, and deciding to research this book can't generate that kind of guilt. You've done something more—you've brought everyone together again, including the killer."

His body sagged under the weight of what he'd done. "I thought I had everything under control. I never expected anything like this."

"Were you the one who got Glenda her job at the *Trib*?"

"No. That was all her. She thought she had something on Hank and Hank must have thought she did too."

"And Matt? Did he realize that you pulled him away from his real job to play out this fantasy for you? How long have you been planning this? It's not something you could do overnight."

"A year and a half ago. Right after Eric died, I'd promised him I would make everything right." The sadness in his voice almost broke my heart—but only for a second. I had to remind myself of the lives that had been ruined because of what he'd done. Twenty years ago, and then now.

He shook his head. "At first, I didn't know what to do. I didn't know how to make it happen. Then, at the funeral, when so many of us were together again, I thought that if I could gather all the suspects together and put some pressure on them, someone would slip. I thought they'd give something away, or even just demonstrate obvious guilt. I thought we might even get a confession. None of them is a natural killer, and the guilt must have been riding them for the past twenty years. I thought… I don't know what I thought."

"And I was the pressure?"

"You were the pressure. Well, originally, it was Trisha, but she was moving so slowly and didn't have the experience you do. I'm so sorry, Jessie, I didn't think someone would try to kill you. And Hank…and that poor girl… I thought I could keep things under control."

I wanted to tell him he hadn't been the one who pulled the trigger. But, truthfully, he might as well have.

"I need to be alone for a while, Jessie. Please go away. I need some time to think."

I didn't move. Only hours before Hank had told me the same thing and now he was dead. What would happen if I left Ethan alone?

"Please, Jessie, go away."

There was nothing I could do. As I made my way back down the hall, I heard him sobbing.

I headed up the stairs to my room and had my hand on the bedroom door when someone whispered my name. When I turned around, Millie was standing there.

"I don't want to be alone right now," she said. "Can I sit with you for a while?"

"Sure. Are you okay?"

She shook her head and started to cry. I led her into my bedroom, closing the door behind us. She sat on the edge of the unmade bed, another reminder of our confinement. There would be no outside help coming today to do the daily chores that I'd come to take for granted. I felt like sitting down next to her and crying too.

"I'm sorry," she said when she regained control of herself. "I have to stop doing that."

"Under the circumstances, it's allowed."

"This is just like the last time. It's all so ugly. So senseless."

"I know. And my fear is it's going to continue until we find out who did this." What I left unsaid was that I was most probably the next likely candidate. "Millie, is there anything you can tell me about the day Bonnie was murdered? Anything that would help us now?"

She shook her head. "I don't know what to tell you. I was in the kitchen most of that afternoon."

"And your husband never said anything?"

She looked over at the window. "I'm pretty sure Paul saw a lot more than he ever told me about. I don't know how to make you understand Paul's devotion to Ethan and those boys. If he saw something—anything—that would have been incriminating, he would have kept it to himself. After that first day, we hardly ever spoke of it."

"Would he have helped to cover up a murder?"

She looked up at me and her eyes filled with tears. "I don't know."

"What did he actually see?"

"I know he saw John and Bonnie together. It was pretty obvious what was going on. Knowing John, there was little that surprised Paul. He said Hank stood outside the guesthouse while the other two were inside. Just about everyone else went into the cottage that day. Bonnie was the only one who never came out."

She looked at me with sadness in her eyes. "I wish I could help you, Jessica, I really do. But you probably know more than I do at this point." She took a deep breath and stood. "I can't talk about this anymore. I need to keep busy. I think I'll make us some lunch."

After she left to try to salvage something normal from her day, I walked to the window and looked out over the front lawn. The rain was coming down harder than ever—the trees bent low in the wind. The sky was still dark, with no visible break in the clouds. The tulip beds were drenched in water, the flowers floating in a thick muddy soup.

I was surprised to find that I missed Matt. A lot. Where had he disappeared to in the middle of the night? And what had been so urgent to drive him out into this storm? Unless.

I couldn't do this anymore. I crawled into bed, too tired to think and too depressed to do much of anything else. When I finally woke, it was early evening. I lay in the darkened room, staring at the ceiling.

The long nap had given me a brief reprieve, and it had also brought with it a clarity that had, until now, eluded me. Fred Connor was right. Somewhere in the muddle of everything I'd learned, I held the answer to Bonnie's murder. I just wished I knew what it was.

Cocooned in the fading light, I was suddenly, painfully aware that Ethan was the father of Bonnie's unborn baby. My perspective of Ethan had changed dramatically in the past week, and this new realization was just one more piece of his grandiose behavior, and it made me sad.

Ethan never seemed far from female companionship. Why did he need to seduce an eighteen-year-old girl? Was his ego that big? Was he that needy? But the bigger question was—how could he do that to his son?

I wondered if or when Matt had figured it out. The night I'd mentioned the baby to him, he'd recoiled as if I'd slapped him. Was that loss or betrayal? Or both?

He must have known. He'd been at the university all that summer picking up extra classes. Bonnie was two months pregnant when he came home in August. And during June and July, John was in absentia too, doing penance at prep school for stealing the Headmaster's car.

Bonnie wasn't exactly a nun. Her dalliances could have included any boy in the county. But she wasn't stupid either—she wouldn't have wasted her time on a boy headed nowhere. She'd set her sights much higher—higher than Matt Wheaton, who would live out his days on a professor's salary. Ethan was the only one who could give her the life she wanted. And that was her fatal mistake.

NINETEEN

I WANTED TO take another look at my notes. There had to be something I'd missed. I threw back the covers and searched in the dark for my shoes.

Then I remembered Hank. I couldn't get to my office without going past his body. Again. The concealed little room was the only way leading to the circular staircase and the private offices…overlooking the guesthouse.

I ran out the door and down the stairs.

John was passing through the front hall and I grabbed his arm.

"Nice hair," he said.

"What? Oh, I forgot to comb it."

"So I see."

"Where's Dan?"

"I think he's at Matt's cabin."

"Is Matt back? How did he—"

John shook his head. "Matt's not back. I don't know what Dan's doing down there."

I grabbed a yellow raincoat off the coatrack and headed for the door. John said something before the door slammed shut behind me, but I didn't stop to find out what it was.

The raincoat was about two sizes too big. The sleeves kept sliding down over my hands and the bottom hit me about mid-calf. I felt like I was wearing a lead suit as I sloshed through the wet grass.

My bare head was soaked by the time I was halfway to the cabin, and cold rain slithered down my back. The cabin lights were on and it glowed in the darkness like a Thomas Kinkade painting. Satan, wet, muddy and happy, ran toward me as I approached the front porch. He lunged at me playfully.

"Not now," I said firmly, patting his head as I went up the steps.

Dan was at the kitchen table—tools and gadgets spread out in front of him. He barely glanced in my direction. "What are you doing here?"

I sat down across from him, pushing my wet hair off my forehead. "You saw everything that happened in the guesthouse, didn't you?"

He didn't say anything, but his hands froze in midmotion.

"You know everyone who went in there that day. The police never questioned you because you were hiding in your office and they didn't even know you were in the house. But your office window—you can see everything from there."

He let his breath out slowly and looked at me. "Yes, that's true—but, there's nothing I can tell you that's going to change anything. I've been over that day a thousand times in my head and I get nowhere."

"Who are we all running from, Dan?"

"I don't know!" He took a deep breath. "That's just it. I genuinely don't know. I've probably suspected all of them at one time or another over the years. But I've never known for sure and I've never wanted to know, which, I guess, makes me just as bad as the rest of them."

"Tell me what you saw. Maybe we can piece this thing together."

"I really don't think it will help."

"We have to try."

He closed his eyes. "I was in my office and happened to look out the window just as John and Bonnie were going into the guesthouse. There was no doubt in my mind what they were going to do. Hank stood outside for almost thirty minutes, looking in the window, while the two of them were in there together."

"Did Hank ever go in during that time?"

He shook his head. "Not that I was aware of. I went back to my work and must have looked again just as John left—alone. Hank went in then and came running out of the cottage several minutes later. John returned for a few brief minutes and left carrying his shoes."

"Did John and Hank run into each other?"

"No. Hank took off down the driveway. John was coming from the other direction. Shortly after that, Ethan entered the cottage. He spent almost ten minutes with Bonnie before he left and returned to the main house. Then Alena, Bonnie's sister, came along, with Hank in tow. I could see Hank was visibly upset, even from my vantage point. Alena motioned to Hank to stay put while she went inside."

"What did Hank do while Alena was inside?"

He was silent for a moment, as if conjuring up a lost memory. "He paced back and forth in front of the cottage. At that point, I got a phone call. The next time I looked back, Tommy was running out of there."

"Was he upset?"

"Almost hysterical. That didn't mean much to me at the time. He was a sensitive kid, anything could have happened to upset him. Bonnie could have laughed at him or teased him. But when he returned with Matt, I knew something was wrong. Matt had to force Tommy to return to the cottage. That's when I started to get worried."

"What did you do?"

"I headed down there. By the time I reached the guesthouse, Tommy was gone again. I found Matt sitting on the floor, holding that girl's dead body. Just sitting there crying and rocking her back and forth as if she were a child."

He paused in his narrative and I waited for him to go on. "You see, I never knew for sure if Matt had killed her. Or Ethan, for that matter. I didn't want to believe that either one of them had. Matt denied it, of course, but I could never be quite sure. And to be perfectly honest, I really didn't want to know."

"Why?"

He looked a little wistful. "Matt was a remarkable boy. I like to think that if I'd ever had a son, he would have been a lot like Matt. I grew very fond of him over the years, and if I found out he'd killed Bonnie, I'm not sure what I would have done. I still would have protected him, I guess."

"And Ethan? Would you have protected him?"

"Yes, I guess I would have. I've had a very good life because of Ethan. He lured me away from a magazine in St. Louis, and I've never regretted it for one minute. I know I must not seem like much to you—just a lackey. But I'm very good at what I do. A lot of Ethan's early recognition was due to my efforts."

"Bonnie was carrying Ethan's baby, wasn't she?"

"I believe she was," he said quietly, as if he had moved beyond the point of being shocked by anything Ethan did.

"Did Matt know?"

"He must have figured it out. He wasn't stupid, and he certainly knew his father well enough to know anything was possible. But, I never asked him and he never told me."

There it was again, the impenetrable silence that kept the Miller household in check. And kept getting people killed.

"What I don't understand is how Matt could have fallen for a girl like Bonnie. She certainly wasn't the kind of girl you brought home to meet your mother."

"It is strange, isn't it? But Bonnie was beautiful and incredibly manipulative. And, at that time, Matt was more than a little naïve. He was so focused on where he was headed, he really hadn't been with a lot of girls."

I had to ask. "Where does that leave us, Dan? Is Matt a murderer?"

"I don't know. It could have been any of them."

"When you saw Bonnie, was she wearing the sapphire necklace?"

"How did you know… Well, it doesn't matter I guess. No, she wasn't wearing the necklace."

"John told me that he heard Matt and Bonnie arguing earlier that day about the baby."

Dan dismissed that with a wave of his hand. "Don't believe everything John tells you. It may or may not be true—I don't know—but, John never misses a chance to make Matt look bad."

"And you were the one who called the sheriff?"

He nodded. "I called from the guesthouse and then I got Matt out of there as quickly as I could. I didn't want the sheriff to find him there. When I got him back to the house, I told Ethan what happened and then I went to my office and stayed put. I didn't trust myself to talk to the sheriff and I didn't want to lie so I said nothing."

"And the payments to the Markowskis? Did Ethan tell you to do that?"

"Ethan doesn't even know. I just felt it was something I needed to do. Just like Eric and Ethan, I had the guilt of my own silence to deal with."

"Why have you been following me?"

"Ethan and I thought it would be a good idea. Believe it or not, I thought I could protect you, if the need arose."

"And Trisha? Had you been following her too?"

"What? No. Was someone following her?"

"That's what her mother told me."

He shook his head. "No. It wasn't me. The accident on the terrace that night really shook Ethan. That was one of the reasons he didn't want you left alone."

I looked at the table again and all the hardware spread out in front of me. "What are you doing?"

"It's an old CB radio of Matt's. I remembered it this afternoon. It hasn't been used in years, but I thought if I could get it working, maybe we could contact— someone."

"Do you know how to fix it?"

"Probably not. But it's worth a try don't you think?" He looked at me then back down at his work.

I watched for a few minutes as he unscrewed different parts and fiddled with colored wires. There was hardware all over the table, and I didn't hold out much hope for success.

I looked at Dan and realized something very significant about my life. "Ethan just admitted to me that he orchestrated all the players to be back in this house for one last hurrah."

Dan hesitated then nodded. "Yes, that's true."

"And I'm one of the players, aren't I?"

He looked at his hands and then back at me. "Yes, you are."

I had an overwhelming feeling of violation. "Why me?"

"I think because Eric trusted you. Ethan knew he would need outside help to pull this off. He was too emotionally involved to be objective and he was too much of a presence to ferret out the information he needed. You were an excellent candidate."

"A spur of the moment candidate?"

"Possibly. Trisha was here, but I don't think she knew what she was doing. Ethan had spoken of you once or twice, but as events transpired, he took the opportunity that presented itself. Had it not, he may have figured out another way to get you here."

It was bad enough what he'd done to the others, but knowing he'd manipulated me too made me angrier than I'd been in as long as I could remember. And the hell of it was, I'd fallen for it. I'd been deceived by Ethan, just like everyone else who'd traipsed through his life over the years.

Dan watched my face closely. "Don't be too hard on him."

"Are you kidding me? People are getting killed because of him."

"You have to understand what Eric's passing did to him—what the past twenty years have done to him. He started to go downhill immediately after Bonnie's death. I think it was the first time he realized he was human, that he couldn't make the world conform to his wishes. He was afraid for his sons—maybe even afraid *of* them—of what they might be capable of doing."

I folded my arms in front of me. "I'm not getting a whole lot of comfort out of this story right now, when there's a murderer loose on this estate."

"I know. Ethan can be self-centered and manipulative. And he's used to getting his own way. But, he's also generous to a fault and protective of those he loves."

"Where are you going with this?"

"He didn't think this through. That part's obvious now. But he honestly thought he was doing right by Eric and doing what needed to be done for Bonnie and Tommy."

"And Trisha Chatsworth paid the price for that."

It didn't help me much at that moment to know that Ethan Miller's heart was in the right place, but I knew that sitting there stewing in my anger wasn't going to get any of us off of that mountain. "Okay, so what do we do now?"

"I wish I knew."

"Is there another way out of here?"

"Back through the hills, there are trails, but it takes hours to hike out, and I don't think I could find my way in the dark."

We looked at each other for a minute.

"I'm going to keep working on this CB," he said. "What are you going to do?"

"Go back to the house and wait for morning."

"Please be careful, Jessica."

"I'll try."

The cabin door closed behind me, enveloping me in darkness. I was barely off the porch when the chill set in and I shoved my hands deep in the pockets of the yellow raincoat and started the long walk back up the hill. There was a lot to think about.

I sloshed along with my head down, trying to keep the rain out of my face, when I thought I heard a footstep behind me. I turned and peered into the blackness. "Dan?"

There was no sound except for the falling rain, and I called out again. When there was no answer the second time, I decided it must be Satan and turned back toward the house.

A sharp crack exploded behind me and something whizzed past my left ear. You'd think I'd be used to getting shot at by then, but that first shot really didn't register. I turned around again and called out for Dan.

The second shot caught me high in the right shoulder. I went down hard—hitting the ground flat on my back, knocking the wind out of me, and grazing my head on the side of a rock. I groaned. The searing pain burned and throbbed in my shoulder, and a sticky warmth ran down my chest. The throbbing started again in my head, reminding me I wasn't in the best shape to begin with. I was still physically vulnerable. I didn't know what to do.

I heard footsteps, moving around to my side, positioning themselves between me and the house. My heart pounded faster. Now what? The rain distorted all sound and it was difficult to tell how far apart we were. The footsteps moved closer—loud in the wet grass. I rolled to my left and struggled to my feet, and then I was running.

Another shot glanced off my left hand, and I cried out in pain. Every attempt I made to turn toward the house was being thwarted. Whoever it was seemed to anticipate my movements. When I switched direction to move back down the hill toward the cabin, so did my attacker.

I think I caught him off guard when I turned and ran in the opposite direction. Away from the house, away from the cabin, away from all safety.

Another shot rang out. He was behind me now, and I wondered how he could see me when I couldn't see him. The yellow raincoat must have stood out in the darkness like a neon sign. I slipped it off mid-stride, dropping it to the ground as I ran and slid on the wet grass.

I fell again and landed with my entire body weight on my knees. A new excruciating pain shot through me and I bit my lip to repress a scream. I was up again, limping and scrambling over the rugged terrain. There was some distance between us now, as the footsteps of my assailant dropped farther and farther behind.

Pain and fear reverberated throughout my body, and I was stumbling more than running. I couldn't keep going much longer and I couldn't stop. I needed a plan.

Then I remembered the caves. If I could just make it to the caves, I would have a place to hide.

It seemed like months had passed since the day I hiked there with Matt. Had it only been a few weeks? And would I even be able to find my way again?

Think. Find the trail. Reluctantly, I slowed my pace, hoping to see something recognizable. Feeling along with my feet, trying to gauge my surroundings. The meadow looked familiar, but then most meadows looked pretty much the same. Then I hit a spot that was harder than the rest, packed. The trail.

I followed with my feet. At least twenty minutes passed before I spotted the rocks jutting out of the earth—slick and shiny in the rain.

My hands felt along the cool surface until I found the opening of the cave. Inside, the darkness was disorienting—the enclosed space adding to the sense of unreality.

The walls were cool and dry and I moved slowly, my left hand feeling the way, my feet dragging like lead weights. When I reached the place where the chambers separated, I had to stop and think which way it was that Matt had led me. One fork led to the room where the bats lived, the other to the place where the boys had their secret fort—only I couldn't remember which was which. If only I had a flashlight, or the darkness hadn't been so unrelenting, I could have found my way. But I was entombed in darkness.

My shoulder was aching and it was difficult to concentrate. A chill had taken over my body, and I started to shake. There was no telling how much blood I'd already lost.

In desperation, I kept moving and turned down the corridor to the left, hoping it would lead me far enough into the cave to feel protected. To the little room with the stream that ran through it, where I could sit for a while and figure out what to do next.

It didn't take long until I reached an area where I sensed a change in my surroundings. I was no longer in the corridor of the cave, but in one of the inner chambers. And then I heard it. The sound of running water. I'd found the room—Matt's old fort.

My hand moved along the wall and I felt the familiar dampness of that room. Exhausted, I put my back against the wall and slid to the ground. The blood was still tricking down my chest. I had to do something. I kicked off my shoe and removed my sock. With my left hand, I wrapped the sock around my shoulder, pulling it tightly with my teeth then leaned my head back against the wall. That was the last thing I remembered for quite a while.

TWENTY

I AWOKE IN DARKNESS, with my face pressed against the floor and my body stiff and sore. When I tried to sit up, my shoulder reminded me why I was there.

There was a movement in the darkness and I froze. All I could think of was snakes. A killer had already put a bullet in my shoulder, I had a concussion, I was bleeding out alone in absolute darkness and my first thought was about snakes.

Something coarse and damp touched my cheek. I almost lost it then.

It touched me again and a faint movement of air wafted past my face. The wet object stroked my cheek again and again. Each time more enthusiastically.

"Satan?" I whispered.

His body moved up against mine. His fur was soaked from the rain and smelled like only a wet dog could. But he radiated heat and I snuggled up close to him. He wriggled around until he was on his back, waiting to have his tummy scratched.

"Sorry, old boy. I can't do it."

Every time I moved my upper body or tried to lift my right arm, pain and nausea swept through me. So, I lay still in the darkness, as close to Satan as I could get, hoping his body heat would take away some of the chill.

I lost consciousness again, but when I woke up, Satan was still there beside me. There was no telling how much time had passed as I drifted in and out of consciousness, but I couldn't stay there forever. Whoever was after me was determined enough to find me and, in my present state, I was utterly helpless. I was weak and lightheaded and had no weapon. The odds weren't in my favor.

Had anyone at the house missed me? Probably not. They would assume I was still in my room, unless someone asked and then John would tell them I'd gone to the cabin to see Dan.

Had Dan heard the shots and was looking for me? Or gone for help? Or was Dan even alive? If he'd happened upon my assailant, there was no reason not to kill him too.

I felt myself fading again and was determined to fight it. Satan put his face up next to mine when I stirred, his breath hot against my cheek.

"Good boy." I rolled onto my left side, sliding my hand up next to my shoulder. My left hand stung, but I still had enough strength with that arm to push myself up into a sitting position. Tears of pain filled my eyes and I was breathless even from that small effort. I scooted backward until my back touched the wall of the cave. Satan moved in closer and licked my cheek.

Minutes passed as I waited for the latest wave of pain to subside. When it finally did, I patted the ground to my left. "Come here, boy."

He moved obediently and sat with his back to the wall.

"Good dog. Now, let's see what we can do."

I braced my hand against his massive shoulders and pushed up with my feet, keeping my back supported against the cave wall, trying to stand. My bottom was barely a foot off the ground when I slid back down, exhausted. Satan seemed to understand his role and sat statue-like beside me, willing to be used in whatever way I needed him.

I tried unsuccessfully three more times, pausing in between each attempt to muster my strength and courage. But with each effort, my strength was diminishing, until I realized I couldn't do it. I would die in that cave and not be found for weeks. Or worse, I would be found before the night was through by the one person I hoped would never find me. Tears slid down my cheeks. I felt doomed and there was nothing I could do about it.

Satan seemed to sense my change of mood and nuzzled my neck.

"It's no use," I said.

He moved away from me and I could hear him pacing the small room then came back and barked in my face.

"I can't!" I said.

He sat down in front of me and licked the tears off my face.

"You wouldn't happen to know where Matt is?" I asked hopefully, when I'd finally calmed down.

Matt's name got his attention. He barked and thumped his tail on the ground. Then he stood and made another turn around the chamber, his feet padding across the packed earth as he moved. When he came to a stop in front of me, I could almost feel the tension in his body. He wanted me to move—to do something.

I reached out and found his head in the darkness. "I need help, Satan. Go find help."

His head cocked to one side. He knew I was giving a command, but he didn't understand the words.

I tried to force more enthusiasm into my voice. "Go

find help." When I realized he still didn't understand, I said, "Go find Matt. Where's Matt? Go find him."

Satan barked once and turned and ran. He'd understood the command that time, but it was futile. Matt was probably in Kansas by then and even if he found Matt, or anyone else, how could he possibly get them to return to the cave with him? Lassie he wasn't. He was just a big dumb friendly dog who spent most of his time playing. And he was my only hope.

I hated to see him go. He kept my mind focused on something other than the excruciating pain that radiated from my shoulder. He was also my only source of heat. My clothes were still wet and I was shaking uncontrollably.

Lying down could be fatal. I would stay awake as long as possible and wait for my strength to return or help to arrive. The time passed slowly, and I tried to keep my mind occupied, playing the same mental games I had those nights on the balcony. Only this time it was more difficult. Then it had been out of boredom; this time I was desperately fighting for my life as I tried to keep my hold on consciousness—and sanity.

I couldn't remember all the fifty states. I got lost somewhere in the M's. So I started over, mentally crossing the country region by region. Then I tried to remember all the ingredients that went into my grandmother's homemade chili. I tried composing emails in my head, to my family and friends, but that seemed too maudlin. "Hi Mom, How are you doing? I'm fine except for the fact someone is trying to kill me and I'm sitting in a cave freezing to death. Did I mention the bullet in my right shoulder? I've lost a lot of blood. Give my best to

Grandma. Love you, Jess." I ended up singing the alphabet song.

The unrelenting darkness was unnerving. There was no way of knowing how long Satan had been gone. I decided I would wait a little bit longer and then I would try on my own to make it out of the cave, even if I had to crawl.

I must have slipped into some kind of hypnotic state, because I didn't hear anyone coming until I realized I wasn't alone. Satan was almost in front of me before I even knew he was there. He licked my face and wagged his tail and shook water all over me as he tried to get the rain off his back. And there was no one on this earth I could have been happier to see at that moment. Pulling him close with my good arm, I buried my head in his wet fur and cried. I wasn't alone. He'd come back for me.

When I lifted my face, I noticed, for the first time, the wavering light shining on the walls of the cave—moving closer, growing brighter. There was barely time to figure out if I was elated or terrified before Matt stepped into the room, a battery-operated lantern in one hand, a gun in the other.

He looked at Satan and then at me.

"Good God!" He pushed back the hood of his rain poncho with his gun hand. "You look awful."

"If you've come to kill me," I said, "please do it quickly."

He moved across the room and set the lantern down then knelt in front of me. "Hey, I'm the Cavalry. Who did this?"

I shook my head. "It was too dark to see."

Blood had soaked the sock I'd tied around my shoulder and almost one whole side of my blouse. Matt unbuttoned my shirtfront, and I groaned as he slipped the blouse off my shoulder.

"You know, the last time a man undressed me, it was a whole lot more fun than this."

"Yeah? Tell me about it." He touched my shoulder and I screamed.

"Oh God! That hurts."

"Well, you've been shot. That's how it works." He stood up and slipped off his raincoat.

"Where have you been all day?"

"I tried to call the sheriff last night and discovered the phones were out, so I went into town to have a little talk with him about the shooting. I didn't want to drive back up here in the storm, so I headed over to Fred Connor's house."

"He's out of town."

"*Was*," Matt said. "I fell asleep in my truck, and he showed up about six this morning."

"What did the sheriff say?"

"Not much. He just listened. That's why I went over to Fred's. I thought if we could figure this thing out, maybe we could save you from…"

"Getting shot?"

"Well, that was the plan." Matt removed his blue plaid shirt and dropped it to the ground. Then he pulled his T-shirt over his head. Nice chest.

At any other time, that would have put me over the top. Now, I just wanted to get out of that cave and someplace warm.

He drew a pocketknife out of his jeans and went to work cutting and tearing the T-shirt into long wide strips.

"Did you and Fred figure anything out?"

"No."

"How did you get up here?"

"I hiked up the back way. It takes about two hours on a sunny day. It took me four in this rain. There are trees down everywhere."

"What time is it now?"

He looked at his watch. "About midnight."

"It seems later."

Matt slid his hand down behind my back and eased me away from the wall. Then he tried as gently as he could to remove what remained of my blouse. Every movement brought on new pain, along with loud groans and not a few tears. Nothing stopped him. He didn't quit until he had my shoulder tightly bandaged in the cotton strips from his T-shirt and then dressed me in the warmth of his flannel shirt. When he was done, he put the raincoat back on.

"Better?" he asked when I was leaning against the wall, breathing heavily from the exertion.

I nodded. "Hank's dead."

"What! How?"

"Someone shot him."

"When?"

"This morning—last night. I don't know."

He sat down in front of me, chewing on his lower lip.

"How did you find me?" I asked.

"What? Oh, I ran into Dan up by the house. He's been looking for you for hours. He thought he heard shots after you left the cabin. Anyway, I was out roaming around trying to figure out where you might be when I found Satan—or rather he found me. He led me here."

"Matt, what are we going to do now?"

"We need to get you to the hospital. I'll try to find Dan to come and sit with you. I'll get some blankets from the cabin so you can get warm and then I'm going to have to hike out again and get help."

I put my hand on his arm. "I don't want you to leave."

He must have thought I was afraid of being alone for he reassured me he'd be back with Dan in no time and that I'd be safe enough until morning. That wasn't my only concern. I didn't want him wandering around outside, not knowing who was roaming the hills with a gun, willing to kill the next person that got in their way. And... I was afraid of being alone.

The words weren't even out of my mouth when a voice said, over Matt's shoulder, "Well now, isn't this cozy?"

Jolene walked into the room, looking as out of place in a rain slicker as she did standing in the middle of a cave. Mascara had long since washed away, leaving her eyes looking pale and cold. And familiar. Blonde hair was matted to her smooth forehead. The light from her flashlight bounced off the shining barrel of the revolver she held.

And then, it all fell into place. Everything. Every clue. Every police report. Every last detail. Now. Now, of all times. When I was too weak to do anything about it.

Matt stood and turned toward her, his eyes glued to the gun she held in her hand. "What are you doing here?"

She waved toward me with the gun. "Looking for her. Ethan has everyone out looking. Is she okay?"

"She's hurt pretty badly. We need to get her to the hospital. Why the gun?"

"With all the weird stuff that's been going on around here, I wasn't about to leave the house without it."

"Well, you can put it away now. That was stupid of Ethan to send you out alone to look for Jess."

She lowered the gun to her side. "She doesn't look too good. I can stay here with her while you go for help."

Matt looked at me then at Jolene and back at me. He seemed hesitant. "Okay." He bent down to pick up his lantern.

"No." I struggled to get to my feet. "I think I can walk out with you."

With every ounce of determination I could muster, I made it to a standing position, took one step forward and fell against Matt.

He lowered me back to the ground. "Don't be stupid, Jess. You don't have the strength. Just sit tight. I'll be back as soon as I can."

I wrapped my fingers tightly around his arm. "Don't leave me," I whispered in his ear.

His gaze met mine, and he must have sensed what I was trying to tell him. But it was too late and he didn't know what to do.

"Maybe you should go back to the house and get Ethan," he said to Jolene, his back to her, his hand inching toward his gun on the ground.

"I can see we're going to have to do this the hard way." Jolene lifted the gun and pointed it at Matt's head. "Stand up and kick your gun in that stream."

Matt hesitated.

"Now!"

Matt stood up slowly and shoved the gun with his boot, just hard enough for it to slide across the ground and land, with a splash, in the middle of the underground stream.

Jolene leaned her back against a rock. "Okay. Now sit down next to her while I figure out what to do. You've made this more complicated than I'd planned. Getting rid of her wasn't going to be a problem."

"Jolene, what are you doing?" The tension in his voice echoed through the cave.

She narrowed her eyes at him. "Cleaning up a mess."

"I don't understand," Matt said.

She looked at me. "But she does."

Matt looked at me again then back at Jolene. "What the hell is going on here?"

"She's going to kill us," I said, with a surprising lack of emotion. "Just like she killed Trisha and Hank. Just like she killed Bonnie."

"Bonnie?" He looked me in the eyes, still not understanding. "What does she have to do with Bonnie? That was twenty years ago."

Jolene's vivid green eyes looked unblinkingly into mine. Without the tinted contacts, the resemblance to her mother was uncanny—even after all the cosmetic surgery.

"Matt," I said, "surely you remember Alena, Bonnie's sister."

He shook his head, then he slowly turned and looked at Jolene. "Alena? I don't understand."

"Why don't you tell him what happened, Alena," I said. "He deserves that much before you kill him. Why don't you start with why you murdered Trisha and Hank?"

She shrugged. I guess when you'd already killed three people, you developed a nonchalance about it.

"None of it matters anymore. Neither one of you will be leaving this cave alive. That Tina or Trixie or whoever started sticking her nose in where it didn't belong. I tried to scare her away, but it wasn't working. She seemed to think she was on to something, and I couldn't take any chances. And then Hank found the death certificate last night and went berserk."

Matt looked at me.

"All these years Hank thought he was the one who killed Bonnie. Somehow Jolene—Alena—had convinced him of that. But last night in my office, he finally saw the official cause of death and realized he hadn't killed Bonnie—Alena had." I looked at her. "What happened last night?"

"I found him in Ethan's office, drunk and ranting. He was going to find Ethan—tell him what happened. I tried to tell him Bonnie was dead by the time I got to the guesthouse, but he didn't believe me. It would only be a matter of time before Ethan put two and two together and figured everything out. I couldn't let that happen. Hank wasn't going to ruin the life I'd worked so hard for."

Alena really lived on a different plane than the rest of us. The life she'd worked so hard for entailed meeting Ethan at a cocktail party and going to bed with him. I was pretty sure she thought Ethan really was attracted to her. She obviously hadn't figured out that Ethan had planned the meeting, that he had tracked her halfway across the country and across two decades to pull her, like a pawn, into his elaborate game of chess. That he had positioned her right where he wanted her to be.

I looked at Jolene. "When did Hank figure out who you were?"

"The first time he came down here with Glenda. He came to my room one night. He wanted me to try to convince Ethan to buy his stupid paper or invest in it or something, and he saw me without any makeup or contacts." She shrugged. "No big deal, because he still thought he was responsible for Bonnie's death."

I looked at Matt and realized he was still struggling to gain some understanding of what was happening. I knew, too, he was stalling for time, as if there were some hope for our survival.

"That day in the guesthouse," I said, "Hank quarreled with Bonnie. He struck her and she fell and hit her head. It must have knocked her unconscious and Hank thought he'd killed her. He ran from the guesthouse and somehow got hooked up with Jolene, Alena. I'm a little hazy on the rest of it."

Jolene shook her head. "Bonnie was ruining everything. Everything. For both of us. I spent years taking care of her. Years trying to show her how to get a better life. And then she turned on me. She stabbed me in the back. It wasn't enough that she had Matt. It wasn't enough that she would be able to have a real life someday. She wanted it all. She wanted Ethan too—as if she was good enough for him."

"What made you come up here that day?" I asked.

"She came to the office that morning to see Dr. Fischer. She *told* me she was pregnant. She *told* me the baby was Ethan's and she was coming up here to tell him. I couldn't let her do that. I had to stop her before she ruined everything. She had Matt. Ethan was mine."

"Where did you run into Hank?" I asked.

Matt appeared to be thinking, calculating. I needed to keep her talking.

"My stupid car broke down on the way up here. I was headed up the driveway and Hank was running down the road like a madman. I stopped him and he blurted out what he'd done. It would have worked out perfectly if he had actually killed her, but Hank never could do anything right. I wanted to see for myself, so I made him go back with me to the guesthouse. I told him to wait outside, just in case she was still alive."

"And she was. So, you strangled your own sister."

"Don't you understand? She was ruining everything. She had to be stopped. She was spoiling all our plans."

"What plans?" I hoped with everything in me that with each passing second, Matt was figuring out a way to get us out alive.

"I wasn't going to live my mother's life—getting knocked up by every deadbeat who passed through town. Bonnie and me, we made a pact. We were going to have a better life. We were going to find men to take care of us. To give us all the things we deserved. She had Matt. I had Ethan. It was all going to work out—"

"But Bonnie didn't follow the plan. She slept with Ethan and got herself pregnant."

"What a tart she turned out to be," Jolene said, and I wondered if she had any sense of irony. "She seduced Ethan. Came up here one night while Matt was away at school and threw herself at him. When she found out she was pregnant, she thought Ethan would actually marry her, can you imagine that? Ethan marrying a kid like her? I told her it would never happen."

"What happened when you got to the guesthouse?" I asked.

"She'd finally come to by then. She told me about her fling with John. She thought it was real funny. Then she said Ethan had just been there and she told him about the baby. I knew she'd blown the whole thing. That she'd just ruined everything."

"And you were so angry that you killed her."

"It was so easy. It was just so easy."

I sensed Matt's body next to mine, every muscle tensed, waiting for an opportunity to make a move. I hoped that an opportunity would come. "And you thought you'd get away with it."

"I *did* get away with it. Eric and Ethan were falling all over themselves trying to keep their precious little boys out of jail. It was almost comical watching them."

"Did you cut the brake line on my car?"

"Bonnie's daddy taught me well. Too bad that one didn't work."

"And you shot at me in Millie's car."

"You can thank Bonnie's daddy for that too. I could shoot a gun by the time I was five. I probably could have taken you out right then, but I slipped on the wet grass."

"So, what are you going to do with us now?"

She lifted the gun and pointed it at my head. "What do you think?"

"Alena," Matt said, "you could get out of here tonight while we're all stranded up here on this mountain. You could tie us up and hike on out. My truck is parked at the bottom of the hill. You could be out of the state before anyone even knows you're gone."

"I can still be out of the state before anyone knows I'm gone, after I've taken care of you."

I could see Matt thinking, trying to gauge the distance between himself and Jolene's gun, wondering if he had enough time to grab for it before she killed one of us.

A voice came out of nowhere and it made me jump. Alena barely blinked her eyes as Fred Connor stepped into the chamber and told her to drop the gun.

He moved in along the far wall and stood with a gun aimed at Jolene's back. "I'll shoot if I have to."

"You wouldn't shoot me in the back, Fred."

"Don't bet on it, darlin'."

She hesitated a moment. "Okay." She brought her arms down in front of her, the gun still in her hands. Then she turned on her heel and just as quickly raised it again to aim at Fred.

The shot was deafening in the enclosed space and the echo reverberated throughout the cave.

When the sound died away, Matt walked over and turned over Jolene's body. There was a hole in her chest where her heart should have been and a look of utter surprise on her face as if no one had ever before gotten the better of her.

TWENTY-ONE

MATT WAS THE one chosen to go for help. He must have made good time. By dawn I was being wheeled into the operating room of the county hospital, a helicopter having arrived sometime during the early morning hours, carrying the sheriff and a team of paramedics.

The rest of that day was lost in a drug-induced haze that kept the pain at bay and my thoughts fuzzy. When I awoke the next morning, the sun was shining and Matt was asleep in a chair in the corner of my room.

I lay there watching a sunbeam slide across the floor, listening to Matt's gentle snores. A wave of melancholy overtook me, and a tear ran down my cheek. I wanted to believe it was a reaction to the physical stress my body had endured and the drugs that had rendered me all but comatose for the last twenty-four hours, but it was more than that. Something had changed inside of me and the sadness I felt was real.

I reached up to brush away the tear and let out a cry of pain as the white-hot fire in my shoulder reminded me why I was lying in a hospital bed.

Matt jumped out of his chair. "What's wrong?"

"I tried to move my hand and my shoulder—it hurts."

"Oh. I thought something was wrong."

"Well, it hurts."

"You got shot, remember? And then you had surgery. Did you think it *wouldn't* hurt?" His hand brushed my cheek.

"If you're going to be a bastard, just go away."

He raised his eyebrows. "I thought I was exuding the Miller charm."

"No. Honestly. You were just being a bastard."

He looked me in the eyes. "Have you been crying?"

"I just felt so incredibly sad. I don't know what's wrong."

His hand brushed my cheek again with small gentle strokes. "A lot has happened—to all of us."

"Matt, did you know about Bonnie and Ethan?"

"I figured it out. Bonnie told me she was pregnant. I did the math and knew it wasn't mine. When I confronted her, she admitted to sleeping with Ethan. He denied it, of course, but I could never be sure."

"How did that make you feel?"

"How do you think it made me feel? I've never experienced that kind of hatred before or since. It consumed me. All I could think about was the two of them together."

"How did you ever get past that?"

"Years of counseling."

"Seriously?"

"Seriously. It all took a very long time. But, I knew, at some point, I had to make a choice—accept Ethan for who he is—or not have him in my life."

"It was that easy?"

"Nothing easy about it. It took years to get to that place. I'll probably never trust him, but he is my father and I love him."

"And Bonnie?"

"If it hadn't been Ethan, it would have been someone

else. Or several someone else's. The marriage would have been a disaster. I couldn't have lived like that. What's the saying—*we marry our parents*? She and Ethan were two of a kind."

"I hate what he did to you."

He looked at me for a very long time. "I think when you get out of here, you're going to need some looking after for a while. Ever think about shacking up with a middle-aged, set-in-his-ways college professor?"

"The thought has never crossed my mind, but I'm always open to trying new things."

The door opened a crack and Dan poked his head in. "Are you up for visitors?"

"The second shift has arrived," Matt said. "I'm going to go home and sleep in a real bed for a couple of hours." He touched my cheek again and then he turned and walked past Dan and out the door.

"How are you feeling?" Dan asked.

"Weak and groggy."

He nodded then stood there looking at his shoes and fidgeting with the buttons on his shirt.

I couldn't take it any longer. "Why don't you sit down."

He pulled a chair up to the side of the bed and sat looking at the wall somewhere just above my forehead.

"What's going on now?" I asked.

"Fred Connor has been talking to the district attorney about getting the charges against Tommy dropped. With testimony from you and Matt, it shouldn't take too long. And the sheriff has contacted Trisha's parents to let them know what really happened to their daughter."

"And Ethan?"

He finally looked me in the eyes. "Tell me what you're feeling, Jessica."

I wanted to cry again. "I don't know what I'm feeling. Certainly disillusioned. Used. Betrayed. I'm sure there's more going on in there too."

"Because Ethan let you down?"

"He let us all down. He tried to play God and three people ended up dead. Four, if you count Bonnie. If he'd let the investigation run its course to begin with, maybe Alena would have been found out at the time and Tommy would be a free man today."

He looked at me for a very long time. "So, the great Ethan Miller has feet of clay."

"It's a bit more than that. He's a self-centered manipulator."

"That he is. But, whether you believe me or not, the truth is that even when he misuses his status, he truly believes he's doing the right thing. He just doesn't think things through to see how his orchestrations will affect other people's lives."

I wasn't ready yet to be as gracious as Dan—but then I didn't have the years of experience Dan had in excusing Ethan's actions. It was going to take time to work through my feelings.

He left a short time later and I dozed fitfully, dreaming of Trisha and Hank and Alena and the haunting images of death I'd seen on their faces. When I opened my eyes, Ethan was standing by my bed.

"Dan said we need to talk." There was a look of utter exhaustion on his face.

"It's a hell of a way to write a book, Ethan."

He nodded slowly. "I'm sorry, Jessie. I don't know

what else to say. I thought I knew what I was doing and then it just got out of my control."

"How did you find Alena?"

"I hired a private detective, shortly after Eric died. He tracked her down in Hollywood."

"How did you know you could get her back here?"

"I knew her pretty well from years ago. We'd been involved. I knew it wouldn't take much to persuade her. Money is about all it takes with Alena."

"Did she know you knew who she was?"

He shook his head. "She didn't have a clue."

"Did you know she was Bonnie's murderer?"

He shook his head again. "As far as I knew, it could have been—anyone," he said slowly, and I knew he was thinking about his sons.

"Why didn't you tell me who Jolene really was?"

"I guess I tried to play this one too close to the vest. I didn't think I could risk it. I was afraid you might slip up."

"Instead, I got shot."

He winced and rubbed his hand over his face. "I'm so sorry. I'm so sorry."

I lay in bed, thinking, long after Ethan left, saddened by the lives that had been ruined and lost.

When the thinking got to be more than I could bear, I sat up—moving stiffly. I swung my legs over the side and tried to stand. Holding onto the bed, I waited until I was sure my legs had the strength to support me then walked to the bathroom where I splashed cold water on my face.

The woman in the mirror was pale and her eyes looked years older than the eyes I remembered just two days ago.

I untied the back of my printed hospital gown and lowered it off my shoulder to expose the bandages that covered the wound. The scar that I would bear for the rest of my life would be a constant reminder to me of how very precarious life is—how our actions can tip the balance one way or the other and the decision is ours which direction we choose to go.

TWENTY-TWO

BOB ELLIOT, MY FORMER and currently-temporary boss at the *Trib*, sat behind the cluttered desk in his office. I often thought the external clutter was a snapshot of what was going on in his head at any given moment—bits and pieces of random information, that only he could pull together into a cohesive thought or story. "When are you leaving?" he asked.

"My mother wants a good-bye dinner Friday night. I'm heading back to Missouri Saturday morning."

"And she's okay with your decision?"

I shrugged. "Her daughter will be working full-time as an assistant and researcher for Ethan Miller. In her book, he's a rock star."

Bob raised a skeptical eyebrow. "A rock star?"

"Different generation."

"Ethan Miller got you shot."

I glanced out the window, then back at Bob. "Yeah well, she doesn't know that."

I could tell by the look in his eye, he understood. For many reasons, I hadn't told my mother the entire story. Something about my involvement with Ethan had drawn us together in a way we hadn't connected in years. It was still new and tenuous, and I'm not even sure I completely understood it, but I didn't want to do anything to jeopardize this new-found closeness.

The last two months—recuperating at her house in

Omaha—had given us the rare opportunity to get to know each other again.

Bob scratched his jaw. "You're sure this is what you want to do?"

I knew the question was coming. I'd needed the time in Omaha to heal physically and figure out where to go from here, but now I was itching to head back to Ethan's. "I'm sure."

"After your article about the murders and your interview with the elusive Ethan Miller, you're starting to make a name for yourself. You've already had two good job offers."

"It's a fickle business, Bob. My notoriety will fade as quickly as it came. It's not like I broke Watergate or anything. The job offer from Ethan is something I've wanted to do for a long time."

"How much of this has to do with Matt?"

I smiled, thinking of Matt's frequent trips to Omaha over the past two months. "Matt is—well, I need to find out if there's anything there."

I watched his face. "And what about you?" I asked.

"I'll be here for a while. I'll stay on through the summer until the merger is complete, then maybe for a few months into the fall. I hope to be officially retired before Christmas."

The paper had been sold. With new owners everything would be different. When I started my career at the *Trib*, when Eric was alive, it had been a wonderful place to work. After Eric's death, with son, Hank, at the helm, morale had gone downhill quickly. If I stayed on, I don't think I could ever feel the same way about the paper as I had under Eric's tutelage.

Bob got up and walked over to the window looking

out over Dodge Street, then turned to face me. "I'm not a fan of Ethan Miller's you know."

"I know."

"I can't talk you out of this?"

"No."

"And you trust him?"

I smiled. "Don't worry about me. All of Ethan's ghosts have been laid to rest. Seriously, how many skeletons could one man have?"

* * * * *

ABOUT THE AUTHOR

SUSAN RICHARDS WAS born in Omaha, Nebraska, and has spent most of her life in the Midwest. She has lived in Iowa, Colorado, Texas and Minnesota.

She has a BA in Elementary Education, a Master's in Education from the College of St. Scholastica and has completed graduate work in the field of Special Education from Seattle University and Learning Technology from the University of St. Thomas. She spent three years as a classroom teacher, but has also worked in a variety of businesses over the years. One of her favorite jobs was writing greeting cards.

After graduate school, she moved to the Pacific Northwest for a time, later returning to Northern Minnesota to be closer to her family. Every winter, she wonders what the hell she was thinking.

Write to Die, which takes place in southern Missouri, is the first in her Jessica Kallan series.